I0583990

Fragmented

THREE GENERATIONS, ONE FAMILY SECRET

KELLY WILSON

Fragmented © 2024 Kelly Wilson

Text and illustrations copyright: Kelly Wilson © 2024

All Rights Reserved.

No part of this publication may be reproduced or transmitted in any form or by any means. Including electronic or mechanical, photocopying, recording, storage, in an information retrieval system, or otherwise, without prior written permission form the publisher. Unless specifically permitted under the Australian Copyright Act 1968 as amended.

This book is a work of fiction. Names, characters, places, and incidents either are products of the author's imagination or are used fictitiously. Any resemblance to actual persons, living or dead, events, or locales is entirely coincidental.

Printed in Australia

Cover and internal design by Book Burrow

www.bookburrow.com.au

First printing: November 2024

Paperback ISBN 978-0-9756-4296-2

eBook ISBN 978-0-9756-4297-9

Publisher: Wings for Grace Publications

www.wingsforgrace.com

NATIONAL LIBRARY OF AUSTRALIA

A catalogue record for this work is available from the National Library of Australia

For my beautiful mum.

*One shattering moment of betrayal can turn you into a version of
yourself you never thought possible.
Discovering the truth and its dangers has left me
ruminating on the question:
Who should I fear more – them, or the monster within?*

Before

'Get the hell off me!'

Handcuffs snapped tightly around my wrists, instantly constricting the blood. The sting of hot tears began releasing my toxic rage. I remained defiant. Yanked to my feet, I was dragged backwards, away from the intensity of the fire. Yet I couldn't escape the heat within. It was near impossible to suck in a single breath; the acrid ash coating my tongue and burning my throat.

My balaclava was ripped aggressively from my head. I jammed my eyes shut, avoiding the blinding torchlight suddenly obscuring my vision. I lashed out instinctively at the bodies trapping me. Time slowed. A blackness closed in like the curtains signalling the end of a theatre performance.

I already knew my fate.

'Young lady, I am placing you under arrest. You have the right to remain silent. Anything you do or say may be used in court as evidence against you. Do you understand?'

Spitting in his face my scream became primal.

'Screw you, arsehole.'

So, it's come to this.

now

Squinting through the dusty window, the rocking movement of the old bus had lulled me into a light doze. For a while at least I'd had some respite from the relentless chaos in my mind.

Make it stop.

It was a prayer, a silent one, made many times before. If there was a God, he never listened to me. Maybe I wasn't good enough for him either. My breathing was shallow. I hated it when my body reacted like this, fighting its own silent battle. The heat travelled from my feet all the way up until I was sure my head would explode. Like I was hotwired from within.

You know this feeling, Grace, it will pass.

I picked at the old red vinyl seat in front of me, absentmindedly slashing at the fabric, my markings forming a row of crosses. My knife was a constant companion these days. I was good at hiding it and loved the fact it was my secret and mine alone.

Who needed to know anyway?

Who would care?

White foam, from underneath the seats vinyl began falling to the floor, making me think of snow in Christmas movies. I'd never seen real snow, in fact, there were lots of things I hadn't seen. Would I ever? Not where this bus was dumping me, that was for certain.

So much had happened.

Surely this could not be my life.

Could it?

As the bus rattled to a stop on the gravel road, I rubbed my stinging eyes, trying desperately to get my bearings.

Breathe, Grace.

Taking measured breaths, I willed my anxiety to calm. Slipping my knife into the side of my boot I stretched my arms above my head. I ran my fingers through my wild knotted hair, then turned down the music playing through my headphones, my disconnection and solace from this world. Once, I would have called it 'my' world. Now I travelled through it like an outsider. I didn't know how to fit in anymore, couldn't even decide if I wanted to.

Scanning my new surroundings, I crossed my arms tensely. I wanted to scream, to run. There it was. The junction on the dirt road, the red letterbox, landmarks my mother had told me to look for. My destination.

My prison.

I already despised it here; making that decision before I came. Chosen to hate it as this had been forced upon me. Against my will. Someone will pay for doing this to me. I'll make sure.

'Zarnish Estate' read the sign that hung above the red letterbox. What kind of a name is that for a country farm? And where the hell is the house anyway? I searched my immediate surroundings again. Maybe that was the house in the distance, beyond the tree line. It was hard to tell with the glare of the sun. If so, it had to be the longest driveway I'd ever seen.

Looks like I'll be walking. Perfect, just friggin' perfect.

Gathering my bag, I inhaled deeply, forcing my exhalation to be slow. I willed my inner body, just one more time, not to betray my well-practised tough exterior. Without a word, nodding thanks to the bus driver, I stepped off into the unknown.

The old bus rattled to life again, billowing large swirls of dust as it headed off along the isolated road. I suddenly felt very insignificant and alone. The deathly silence around me was unsettling, like nothing I'd ever known.

Where was the bustle of traffic?

The shrill of sirens?

The mishmash of smells from my city home?

Where the hell am I?

Born and raised in the city, I had little knowledge of anything else. This may well have been another planet. This Australian bush was completely foreign to me. Only in books or on the Internet had I seen such a vast, foreboding landscape. I'd have been more than happy to keep it that way.

The sky was a vivid blue and cloudless. The sun cast a long shadow, creating a silhouette that reminded me of Peter Pan. I stared at it for a long while. Peter Pan lost his shadow the same way he lost his mum.

Will this happen to me?

Through a glassy stare, I surveyed my new surroundings bit by bit, suddenly feeling weak in my legs, and needing to sit. Everything here felt wrong.

I don't belong.

'So, this is the country? Screw this shit.'

The instantaneous burn on my skin from the afternoon heat was oppressing, I welcomed the light breeze that swept momentarily across my face. And what was with the flies! I shook my head and waved my hands to escape the constant barrage swarming me.

'Bloody hell, rack off!'

My agitation grew as they tried to land on the sticky corners of my mouth. I couldn't decide what was worse, my thirst or the disgusting sweat under my jeans and jumper. What an idiot. I ripped the jumper off awkwardly and tied it around my waist. The T-shirt underneath was crinkled and worn, but I couldn't care less. There was no one to see me out here anyway.

I pulled the hair tie from my wrist and scooped my long mane into a careless bun, trying to tame the rambling curls. Limp and clammy, it was as disgusting as I felt.

I grabbed my duffle bag and backpack and began to walk towards the distant farmhouse that I could only assume was where I was supposed to be heading.

'Nice that someone bothered to come out to meet me.'

Jamming my eyes shut as I walked, I tried to ignore the incessant pests invading my space. Opening my eyes again, I stopped mid-stride. To my astonishment, there in the middle of this hell hole was one of the most beautiful things I'd ever seen. Despite my foul mood, exhaustion and absolute hatred for the world right now, I was mesmerised.

The flies had disappeared, and instead, fluttering around my head was a huge butterfly. I lowered my bag to the ground slowly, not wanting to scare it away. Reaching out in front of me, I willed it to rest on my open palm. As I stood in the middle of the dirt road, the sun beating down upon me, I remembered the butterfly song Mum used to sing to me as a child.

Butterfly butterfly, I really want to play,

So, butterfly butterfly, please don't fly away.

The tune danced through my mind, and for the briefest moment, I smiled, before the hollow feeling in my chest returned. This fleeting memory left me longing for home.

Mum loved me back then, but not anymore.

As the creature landed softly and elegantly on my hand, I could barely feel its light weight on my palm. Resting silently, right before my eyes, it reminded me of a fairy. It was a beautiful shape. Vivid blue and black, with golden tips on the top of its wings. After only a few moments, it was gone, fluttering off into the afternoon.

Like me, it was hard to imagine it belonged out here.

All I could see were trees, more trees and red dirt. The bush was dense and dry. Its only signs of vibrancy were brightly coloured wildflowers, like errant flecks of paint on a red canvas. Paddocks bordered by old rusty ring lock fencing lined the road I trudged along.

The smell of eucalyptus penetrated my nostrils, a minty pine scent mixed with the sweetness of honey. Luckily it dominated the other putrid stench wafting from the nearby paddock. I could only assume it was some sort of dead animal.

The bright crimson sun was beginning to lower in the sky, again causing my eyes to water. I kicked the dirt in frustration. Mistake, my white Converse runners were now tinted like the blush on my cheeks. Dust settled all over me.

'Why is this happening!'

I stood there, fists clenched, screaming into the vast unknown.

'Shit! Why?'

As the silence shattered, my body reacted swiftly. Crouching to the ground, instinctively, I covered my head. I'd never heard anything so intense as this piercing, explosive cry from above. More deafening squealing and screeching followed. Above me, literally hundreds of birds had taken to the air, all screaming a cacophony of protest. Highlighted by the blue-red hue of the horizon, a flock of brilliant white cockatoos, their wingspans broad and menacing, were swirling around the sky.

My brewing anger was momentarily replaced by awe. I soaked up the breathtaking sight until they settled in the surrounding gum trees. The collective screeching ceased as quickly as it had begun. The birds now expelled low cackling sounds amongst themselves, high in the branches above.

Were they telling me to go away? I would, given the chance.

Heat flushed through my body again. My anger was never far from the surface. Often it hit me without warning. One thing I knew for sure, this was penance. A sentence I had every intention of escaping as soon as possible.

Continuing the trek towards the house, the rumble of an engine in the distance caught my attention. I turned back to the junction to see an old white Holden Ute approaching. It looked beaten and rusty as dust plumed behind. Hay bales were piled high in the tray.

I edged cautiously to the side of the road, willing the vehicle to pass. No such luck, the Ute with its windows down, slowed to a stop beside me. Should I keep walking? Maybe then they would get the message and piss off. I wasn't in the mood for small talk with a stranger.

'G'day girl. I'm betting you'd be Grace, hey? Bit bloody hot to be goin' walkabout out here all on yer own, wouldn't ya say?'

I stared at the leathery skinned old man before me, grinning a smile almost bereft of teeth. I'd never quite seen anything like him. He was still laughing at his own joke.

There is nothing funny about this moment mate.

'Actually, it is way too hot, but as you can see, I had little choice. The bus dumped me all the way back there.'

He chuckled. I crossed my arms and felt my eyes harden.

'Yer lucky he made the stop. Silly bugger, that driver's been known to miss the mark a good mile down the road.'

I glared at him.

'Well, here I am, red carpet and all, Princess Grace… your chariot awaits my girl.'

He bowed, gesturing for me to get in.

'I'm not 'your girl'. You're a complete stranger! I'm not going anywhere with you!'

'Is that so girly? Well, Negeenah said you'd be arriving today. Asked me to pick you up on me way back from town if I saw ya. I'm doin' her a favour, see. So, either ya get in or enjoy the walk in the heat. Don't bother me none. I have jobs to do. So, what's it gunna be, Princess Grace?'

He smiled as he spoke, which only made me more pissed off.

'I'm no princess, for your information!'

'Ahh, relax, Grace. You're just like ya mum. She used to throw a good tantrum, too, from what I remember. You gotta be thirsty. C'mon, get in now; Zarnish Estate is still a way yet. And we don't want them dingos feeding on ya young bones. Getting near huntin' time, ya know.'

What the hell?

He pointed to the sun as he spoke, as if summoning the day's ending. I stood there, unable to decide whether he was joking with me or if there was some truth to his rambling. Could I really get eaten by dingos? My mind flashed to the Azaria Chamberlain case I had researched in Australian history at school.

And did this stranger actually know my mum? He was right, I was desperately thirsty and, as much as I wouldn't admit it, bloody tired. I couldn't remember ever being this hot and delirious. My clothing stuck to my skin with sweat. It was unbearable.

I'd never seen an Aboriginal in person. His skin was so dark, almost black. It was old and lined, like a well-worn leather couch. When he had laughed, the creases around his eyes showed his age. The eyes themselves were intense and knowing, seemingly full of mischief, defying his years, and his few teeth appeared so white against his skin. His nose was broad, matching his wide face. He wore an old black cowboy hat with a cockatoo feather stuck into its red strip. I could see his hair underneath. Once surely black, it was now almost white.

His old flannel shirt was faded navy blue, rolled at the sleeves. But it was his hands that drew my attention the most. They looked crippled as if riddled with arthritis from a life of manual toiling. There were many scars on them, some travelling up his forearms. I wondered about his story.

'I don't even know your name. I wasn't told anything about you. How do I know I can trust you?'

He walked over to the driver's side, disappearing inside the Ute.

'You're a smart girl. We both know that. The rest is up to you, hey? They call me Tracker. Me tribe gave me that name before they moved on. Been able to track just about anythin' that moved since I was a little fella. I work for Negeenah. Anyways, you gettin' in or not?'

I continued to eye him as I opened the door, slumping heavily on the seat beside him. Despite being unsure, it was good to be out of the heat.

'Let's get this over with then. Don't get used to me, though, Tracker. I won't be here for long. I don't belong here.'

Minutes of silence passed as we bumped along the road seemingly filled with endless potholes. Tracker looked across at me, his face more serious now.

'Mark me words, Princess Grace, you belong here more than any of us. You just don't know it yet.'

Her

Reliving the events leading up to my arrival caused my heart to physically hurt. My stomach churned, and eventually, I pushed the toxic memories down.

I messed it all up.

I hadn't meant for the fire to get so out of hand. The blaze had taken on a life of its own, engulfing the school library so quickly. I'd just wanted to be taken seriously, for someone to listen. If the teachers had just given me a chance to explain. I was the perfect target to accuse. Stealing… and arson. If they had only taken the time to hear me, things would have ended up so differently.

I wouldn't have been living this nightmare, that was for sure.

It all happened so quickly.

My arrest. Again.

Expulsion from school.

Now it was all just blurred and scattered in my mind. I had argued and pleaded with my mum not to send me here. Why didn't she listen? Fricken bitch!

'It's the only option now, Gracie… you've run out of chances.'

The memory filled me with rage all over again.

'Time away from here, girl, that's what you need… it might just be the thing that saves you, Gracie.'

The ultimatums kept repeating incessantly in my head.

I hate her.

This was not my plan at all. Not how I intended my future to be. I'm bright. I know I am. I always knew what I wanted, had my life all mapped out. I had plans and good ones, too. I'd easily won a scholarship. Always wanted to study History at university. Only last year, May of 2014, I proudly received the Victorian Community History Award. I was, in fact, the youngest recipient to be honoured with it. This had only served to fuel my desire to embark on a career, unearthing the mysteries of the past.

But that was before.

Before everything broke.

Shattered into a million tiny pieces… lost forever now.

Before all the things that made me desperate enough to become someone I never thought possible.

Before I was driven by anger and revenge.

Before I realised life wasn't fair.

Before I started wagging school and breaking the law.

Trying to hurt the people that had hurt me.

This was far from over.

So, Mum wants to play this card? She's going to regret it.

Finally, we came to a driveway lined with old post and rail fencing, greyed by the elements and rotting in parts. Big old trees lined the grand entrance, leading all the way to the homestead. They were different from the bush surrounding them. Thick trunks, full canopies lush with green leaves. Maybe oak trees? They were like giants guarding the property. I welcomed the shade they offered.

Hmm, not what I'd expected at all.

Clearly, this had been a prestigious dwelling in its time. The house and surrounding land had to be worth a small fortune. So, the question was, did all this belong to my grandma? The old lady whom I barely knew. The virtual stranger I'm supposed to trust with my well-being from today.

Negeenah.

Intrigue quashed my irritation briefly, as all I could do was stare and admire as the Ute rolled closer. The grand home was made of large bluestone blocks. It was huge, a double-story dwelling which dominated its surroundings. As we approached, I could see three chimneys, and the tin roof was worn and rusted. There were four large windows upstairs and below, French doors on either side of the huge double fronted entrance. So grand, my mind raced expectantly at what it would be like inside. I estimated it must have been built in the late 1800's. Fleetingly a memory of exploring historical homes with my mum surfaced, but I pushed it away.

That was another life.

I could see an old woman waiting in the distance. She was leaning casually against one of the brick pillars at the entrance of the homestead. Was she my grandmother? The woman was shaded under the long wide veranda that wrapped around the homestead. Wisteria curled its way around the roofline, displaying purple and white bursts of colour that softened the bluestone.

My mum had always been evasive about Negeenah. I knew she'd come to Australia early in her life from Central Asia. Had she come alone?

Here we go.

Tracker stopped the Ute near the entrance and hopped out to greet her. My eyes darted for an escape, and I could feel the colour rising in my cheeks, yet I stayed put. Weird. The car I was so reluctant to get into was now my haven. Awash with trepidation, my body was refusing to move anyway.

'Found this little firecracker along the road Miss Negeenah.'

I couldn't see his face but heard his irritating laugh as he gestured back toward his car.

'Thought ya might be able to put her to work. Save me a job or two around here, hey.'

The woman smiled at him, nodding her head. Her expression was guarded.

I could tell the dog was eager to come and check me out, but he stayed obediently beside his owner. As I reluctantly got out, he eyed me intently. Could he sense my dread? My body moved slowly and awkwardly, weighed down by some invisible force.

The dog had to be Rex. I'd heard my grandmother had rescued him when he was just a pup. He had apparently turned up a few years after she had made this place her home. Mum had told me how Rex had been left abandoned by the red letterbox. Whimpering softly in an old apple crate, tiny and all alone.

I know how you feel.

He was quite a big dog, with brown and black fur. Kelpie like, except for the large ears which seemed out of place on his head. I couldn't tell if he was friendly or not. Like his owner, he was giving little away. Not that I knew much about animals. I'd always thought them stupid, just something that needed looking after, a burden. Animals were just something else you gave your love to, then they just left or died.

Trying to summon fake confidence, I forced myself forward. I'd stalled long enough. Only briefly did I glance up, preferring to study the dirt as I walked. Truth be told, I was nervous, feeling intense anxiety. Those recurrent symptoms; stomach-churning, mind racing, palms sweaty. They were like second nature to me now. But I dared not let this weakness be seen. I'd learned to hide this well. I wore a painted mask of pride and self-worth. Showing emotion, in reality, got you nowhere. I'd learned the hard way to always appear in control, squash the self-doubt swirling inside at all costs.

While avoiding making eye contact with her, I noticed a horse loosely tethered in the front yard. It was saddled as if it had just been ridden. Its tail and mane were full and white, and sweat glistened on its golden coat. As I passed, the beast reared its head and neighed loudly, flaring its nostrils. Stepping back momentarily, I stared into its wild eyes. It was huge.

'Hush, Jinta, this is our guest. Behave yourself, old girl. Don't mind her, Gracie, she doesn't like strangers much, but will soon warm to you.'

Only my mum has the right to call me Gracie, old lady.

Stopping abruptly, when face to face, I dropped my bag onto the dirt by my side. I met Negeenah's gaze, determined not to look away. Tracker was already starting his Ute and driving off. I should have thanked him, I suppose. For the first time in as long as I could remember, I was close enough to spit on the mysterious woman called 'Negeenah'. My grandmother. She nodded.

'I know this must be hard for you. But it is for the best, lass. So, let's try to get along shall we.'

Fixedly staring, my voice was firm and low.

'How would you know what's best for me? You don't even know me!'

I crossed my arms, shielding my body.

'This is true. But maybe, just maybe, Gracie, your time here will prove to be a turning point in your life. It is my experience that times of great trial have revealed to me where my real strengths lie.'

'Don't call me Gracie. I'm not a child. And I'm not going to be here a minute longer than I have to be. I don't belong here.'

Negeenah raised her chin, Rex stood to attention eyeballing me closely.

'Is that right, lass? Well, where do you belong exactly, then? Doesn't sound to me like things have been going that great for you in the city, of late.'

'You know nothing about my life or what they did to me, so don't pretend you do. You don't want me here, in this shit hole, any more than I want to be here.'

Negeenah raised her hand, taking a step closer into my space. I held my ground.

'You will watch your tone when you speak to me, lass! That I insist on. I understand more than you know. It was at my insistence

14

you came here. Trust me, you will learn far more about yourself at Zarnish than any detention centre.'

Her voice was strong and demanded respect. The accent, I couldn't place. I took in the features of my grandmother's face as she spoke. Unmistakably, she had the same dark piercing eyes I saw in the mirror. She was so intense, hard to get a read on. I could see the likeness in her face to my own. Whether I liked it or not, our family connection was evident.

Her hair was like mine too, soft curls falling around her face, but with a light grey speckle through it, replacing the intense black of my own. Unusual, I thought, for an older woman to have hair that length. She wore a long rust-coloured skirt with a shirt draped casually on top. I stifled a laugh when I saw the leather boots under the elegant skirt.

Her skin was well worn, a rich brown colour which had an abundance of deep lines around her eyes and mouth. Aged but still beautiful, no question. And she had a sharp tongue to go with it. I hadn't expected that.

'How is Misha? All this business with you has been hard on her, you know. Your mum loves you more than life itself.'

I very much doubt that.

I could feel my rock exterior cracking and could do nothing more than stare at the flies buzzing around the bag. Without another word, she turned and headed inside the house, closely followed by Rex. I rolled my eyes and headed up the stairs after her. *I can see where Mum gets her bitch from. Negeenah has no idea who she is dealing with.*

Well lady, game face is on.

Another life

Time passed here desperately slowly. It had only been four days, yet the oppression made it feel like weeks. The nights seemed even longer. I wanted out, I needed to go home. Mum had said that my stay here was for as long as it took. Whatever that meant. I'd stopped arguing with her by then, deciding I'd win this battle another way.

And it was so bloody hot! This Godforsaken land could only be described as the end of the earth. I wondered how people actually survived in a place like this. What did they do for entertainment? Could there possibly be other teenagers living around here? From what I'd seen, we didn't even have close neighbours.

How could one person have so much land? Bloody different to our apartment, that's for sure. How did other girls meet a boy? Have a drink or a smoke? This whole outback living thing was mind-boggling.

I'll have a friggin' meltdown if there's no Internet. I hadn't asked Negeenah that yet, deliberately keeping to myself as much as possible. Even in juvenile detention, they would have Internet... It's a basic human right.

On the other hand, this historic place my grandmother called home was certainly grand. But, as much as my love of history was sparking my curiosity, I didn't want to appear keen in any way to be here; I refused to.

At least there were plenty of rooms to check out. My bet, it was built during the Victorian era with its steep gabled roofs and rounded towers. Exploring would simply help me to pass the time and keep out of my grandmother's way.

Despite her initial welcome, Negeenah it seemed, was a woman of few words. That is, after she'd handed me my daily chore inventory. It was so bloody long! Crumpled up on the floor in my room now, was where I intended the useless list to stay.

Make me!

She had instructed me to treat this as my home, but warned me to stay out of her room, the attic, and the stables. She didn't explain why, and I didn't care anyway. Reality was, if I wanted to snoop around, I would.

The grand staircase leading to the second floor was dark polished cedar. It felt magnificent to touch each time I climbed the stairs. There were Persian rugs and runners covering the polished wooden floors in every room. Upstairs comprised six opulent bedrooms, each with period glass windows.

The space I'd been given, I had to admit, was bright and airy and put my room back in the city to shame. High ceilings with an old brick fireplace taking centre stage. The four-poster bed, draped in white linen, was gorgeous. All just cosmetics, however. You can't win me over that way.

Today, I sighed heavily as I wandered without purpose. Had I been in Sydney, I would surely have treated myself with a small gift, just to lighten my mood. I stood contemplating the thin stairs leading to the attic, one of the 'no go' zones. They stood right at the end of the long corridor of bedrooms. The small attic door above had intrigued me from the start.

My grandmother had headed outside for the morning as she usually did, I was all alone. Taking one more precautionary glance behind me, I shrugged before lightly stepping onto the first step, then the second.

Making it to the top, I reached for the old brass door handle, expecting it to be locked. To my surprise, it wasn't. It turned easily and silently. Without hesitation I slipped into the vast room, closing the door quickly behind me. The space was dark, apart from a small window in the far corner providing light from dappled morning sun which danced across the room. The pitched roof with exposed rafters was covered in cobwebs. I fought to stifle a sneeze; it smelt stale and dusty up here. Still, my curiosity was high, especially considering I had been asked to stay out.

Stupid old bag, tell me not to do something, and that's exactly what I'll do first.

Sniggering, I moved quietly through the loft to check it out. There wasn't much in here; some wooden crates nailed shut, old suitcases and bits and pieces of antique furniture and framed paintings, and…

Holy shit.

I froze.

Oh mother of God…

Blinking rapidly, I felt the hairs rise on my arms. Two black figures were lurking in the shadows beside the far window. Had they seen me? Gulping down breaths to stay quiet, I began backing away.

Omg, maybe this place is haunted!

I waited, panicking, watching for the slightest movement. I kept my hand on the doorknob behind me, ready to bail, but the minutes passed.

Get a grip idiot.

Edgy, but convinced the shadowy figures were just that, I forced myself forward, scanning the room as I went. As I ventured closer, I could see the shapes near the window were, in fact, mannequins draped in black cloth.

I stood face to face with them, reaching out to touch the lifelike figures. Carefully placed on the mannequins were two dark burkas. I'd seen plenty of women in the city wearing head scarves for cultural or religious reasons. Even occasionally full burkas or chadarees. I respected their reasons absolutely, but why on earth would there be two of them here?

As I moved in closer, the head piece captured my attention. I tried to imagine being covered up with one. Reaching out to touch the mesh eye slits I couldn't help but notice how small the opening was. I needed to know. A slow smile was forming with my compulsion to try one on. It wasn't against the law, right? I wasn't intending any disrespect, just wanted to experience how they felt.

Lifting the weighted cloak-like dress over my head its fabric felt prickly on my skin, once on it draped to the floor. As I slipped the headpiece on, my curiosity turned and an overwhelming feeling of being trapped and constrained set in.

Heavy and itchy on my cheeks, I could barely see through those small eye slits. An old mirror in the opposite corner caught my reflection. Adrenaline shot through my system, as vertigo set in. I fell to my knees looking for stability.

This was wrong, I had to get this off. I began ripping at the headpiece, but it wouldn't budge. I moved to the dress. This, too, I was unable to get free from. I couldn't get it over my shoulders. Unable to breathe, a sudden onset of dread caused me to become disorientated.

Suddenly I stilled to the sound of crying from somewhere close, catching my attention.

Was I not alone up here after all? I was sweating and clammy under the burka. Why had I been so stupid? Now I've been caught snooping.

Idiot, Grace.

From my crouched position I searched the room for the voices. Something was different. It was much darker than before, and the air was noticeably colder. Suddenly a candle came to life only metres in front of me, giving enough light for me to see two bodies. They huddled closely together, sitting on a couch.

One woman I think, sobbed into her hands, the other consoled her. Both wore blue burkas.

What the hell was going on? Frozen in time under my veil, I could see I was no longer in the attic. My chest tightened as I searched for rational answers.

Somehow, I was in a smaller space, a lounge room perhaps? The home of these women? The windows looked as though they had been blacked out with paint and the room was sparsely furnished. A small dining table was strewn with books and papers. Plates of food, half-eaten, had been left to go cold. It was a dull and lifeless environment. Nothing like my home or Zarnish Estate.

Was I dreaming?

Despite my utter confusion, I remained still, attempting to listen, hoping for clarity. The woman stopped crying long enough to speak.

'How could this be happening? This is too much. I'm scared, Mum.'

Trying to breathe deeply to calm herself, her body shook as she grabbed for her mother's hands.

'We could have been killed today, no question, time will reveal the extent of this latest bombing. But we are safe for now. We must think carefully as to what to do next, my child.'

Unappeased, the woman shook her head.

'Where is Father?'

'I don't know child, but I spoke with him earlier. I'm sure he is safe and will return to us when he can.'

The women held each other close. Mother and daughter, I had to assume. But where was I? Who were they? And what had happened here?

As they huddled, I stayed down, still unsure what to do next.

'I just don't understand, Mum. How can the Taliban just storm in and override our government like they have? Look at what we must wear? Their laws are outrageous. They can't just lock us away like animals, take away all our rights. Now that they have overtaken Kabul, it's only going to get worse. What hope do we have? I'm terrified Mum.'

The older woman forced her daughter to look at her.

'Yes, we all are scared and confused. I don't know what lies ahead, my precious daughter. We need to be very careful of our movements from here. I will have to consider whether I continue teaching.'

This seemed to startle the daughter. She stood abruptly.

'Mother? You continuing to teach is out of the question. Women are being killed, tortured and jailed for far less. You know I was ousted from university. Schools have been shut down everywhere. Promise me you won't put yourself in harm's way.'

'My daughter. We must not give up. Listen to me now. It is women like us who need to fight these barbarians. We possess a strength others do not. But yes, we must be smart in our approach. If I can find a way to continue to empower women, protect them, then our people, our country, will rise again.'

I was struggling to keep up with their conversation. My mind raced looking for something rational to cling to. The rise of the Taliban in Afghanistan was horrendous, one of our world's darkest times in the late 1990's. Was this what they were referring to?

My legs were starting to cramp. I needed to move.

Did I dare?

Standing gingerly, I felt exposed. The room was silent, the woman remaining still, side by side on the couch.

Suddenly a piercing siren blasted beyond the walls. Without warning, my body was thrown sideways, and a deafening explosion smashed through the windows followed by a loud whooshing sound. Pain seared through my back and legs.

One of the walls crumbled around me in the darkness. Screaming I crawled away, trying to avoid the tumbling rubble. The air was thick with dust and what smelt like petrol. My eyes burned; I coughed and wheezed, tasting metal. Looking desperately through the haze, searching for the women, the couch was now covered in fallen roof beams and rubble.

Had they escaped?

Squeezing my eyes shut, I began to cry. Hyperventilating, as my full body tremored, I retreated into the fetal position, praying this would somehow go away.

I awoke with a fright. Still crouched on the ground, and wearing the burka. Openly staring, my thoughts scrambled to understand. I was back in the attic.

Panicked, I ripped the headpiece off. Standing despite my dizziness, I hastily removed the cloak, fumbling as I redressed the models before backing away.

What the hell? What's wrong with me? Was that a dream? Was I hallucinating?

Everything around me was exactly as it was before. I'd always had prolific dreams, since I could remember in fact. But this felt different, as it seemed so completely real. And now I was more than unnerved.

What possible relevance could this have to my life?

Why would I suddenly dream about two strange women living in Afghanistan, no less?

Maybe Negeenah knew something I didn't about this space, that's why she told me to stay away. Was Zarnish Estate possessed?

Another good reason to bail on this joint.

The horses

The following morning, my grandmother insisted I follow her out to the stables. Last thing I wanted to do after succumbing to my chore list. Chooks were disgusting I'd decided. Cleaning out their pen was gross, and collecting the eggs without getting attacked was an art in itself. And as for carting slops to the pigs… thank god my friends were not witnessing my existence here.

'I need to show you something, Grace. There are some very important family members at Zarnish I wish for you to meet.'

My grandmother, so it seemed, had an annoying habit of barking orders before turning and walking swiftly out of a room. This morning was no exception. She just always assumed I'd follow. I rolled my eyes and saluted slyly behind her back, leaving my much-needed coffee in the kitchen and stomping out after her. I kept my headphones in my ears, she wasn't going to take my music away from me.

Negeenah enjoyed setting a fast pace, so I'd also learned. She marched out through the old washroom adjoining the kitchen. Beyond the back entrance, a path led through established trees and gardens to bluestone stables.

Didn't you tell me to stay out of here?

The old building was amazing. Even in my disinterested state, I could admire its grandeur. Big wooden double doors adorned with black iron graced the entrance. Inside, high vaulted ceilings held up an expansive tin roof. Thick open cedar beams gave the barn a warm, inviting feeling. A wide pathway split the stables up the middle. The paved herringbone design was typical of the era Zarnish Estate would have been built. There were two identical stables on each side. They had solid wooden half panel doors in the middle. The black iron railing on each side of the door reached to just above head height. The barn was immaculate. Equipment was neatly stored in the end stalls, as was the feed.

I stood in awe; I'd never seen a set up like this before. Loud neighing and whining suddenly filled the morning air. Two huge horses appeared in the stalls, their heads reaching over the gates. They stamped and weaved, curious and impatient to see what was happening.

Did I dare move closer? I'd only had one pony ride in my whole life, and that was when I was seven.

'Grace, come to me, they won't hurt you. They'd like to meet you.'

Keen to stay behind Negeenah as I edged closer to the first stall, I recognised this horse. I had seen her on my first day here. D-day, I liked to call it.

'These horses are my pride and joy, Grace. This here is Jinta! She is mine.'

As she spoke, the horse nuzzled its huge nose into Negeenah's neck, biting at her hat.

'Jinta, settle down there now. You're making a bad impression girl.'

Negeenah shoved the horse's head away. She smiled but was firm in her action.

'They are always a little flighty in the mornings. They get anxious and frustrated at being kept in the stalls overnight. The paddocks are where they want to be.'

'The smell in here is full-on. I'd want to get out, too.'

I grabbed at my nose, a little overwhelmed at the odour of urine and manure.

Negeenah smirked at me, shaking her head slightly.

'You get used to it, Grace. Jinta is a palomino mare. She was a gift from my brother to mark my arrival in Australia. I had no idea how to ride or care for a horse, but I soon learned. New skills are good to acquire. Now I couldn't imagine my life without her.'

Negeenah's voice cracked as she spoke, and her eyes darted away. Rarely I'd noticed did she let her feelings be apparent. Interesting. I reached out my hand tentatively, offering a greeting to the inquisitive animal. Her white mane was soft, as was her golden coat. Her eyes were huge, cased in long cream, almost white lashes. They seemed to look straight into mine, and shifting uncomfortably on the spot, it was me who looked away first.

'And here we have Rahman. He is a bay gelding. This big boy is a little harder to handle than Jinta. He belonged to my brother. Horses never forget; he suffered terribly after my brother left us. Bluey, one of my farm hands, often rides him for me.'

Forget what?

I stared at this second giant towering before me. Again, I offered my hand for him to sniff but pulled away swiftly in fright at the sudden flick of his head and snorting of his nostrils. His black mane and tail swished around him.

'Don't mind him, Grace, his bark is worse than his bite, so to speak. I love these creatures. They are intelligent and intuitive. They have given me a reason to go on.'

I looked at her intently as she fixated on the horse. Funny, she appeared so strong, then in a flash, she appeared just as unsure and weighed down as I was. I wondered what had happened to her brother.

Was he still alive? And if so, where was he now? Obviously, he had been in Australia at some point.

I wanted to ask her, but did not dare.

Dream catcher

Luckily Zarnish Estate had Wi-Fi. This would prove to be my saviour. In fact, I'd been a little stunned, to be honest, when Negeenah revealed the latest Apple Mac in the study. Who'd have thought this strange old woman would be connected to the world. The study was lavish, like the front sitting room and back lounge room, with dark leather furniture and heavy velvet drapes. It almost gave the house a Middle Eastern feel, despite its Victorian design.

'As long as I am not working in here, you may use this whenever you want, Gracie. Please don't go into my personal files, but the rest you are welcome to use. I don't really know what teens do on the Internet these days, but I gather it will help you feel more at home. Do we understand each other?'

My stare was challenging. False bravado.

'Trust me, there's nothing of interest to me in your files. What are they, local garden club newsletters?'

My deployment of sarcasm was probably a little much, but so what. She frowned, clearly analysing me while waiting for my response.

'Yes, we understand each other. The same goes for you, my stuff is my stuff.'

Negeenah crossed her arms, curling her lip.

'Understood, lass. However, if I think you are up to no good under my roof, this privilege will be taken from you.'

'Got it. You stay out of my business, and I'll stay out of yours. I won't be in your way for too much longer out here anyway.'

I had to stay focused. This was a game, and one I intended to win. The old bag irritated me, acting all high and mighty, like she was so important. Clearly, she thought she was so much better than me. Wouldn't you think she'd be making more of an effort to get to know me, her only granddaughter!

I looked at old Rex lying beside me in the study. He was completely at peace. My longing for home was so intense, it was manifesting as pain in my stomach. Staring blankly at the computer screen I wondered why only one of my friends had responded to my messages. I wasn't talking to my mum much, either. The familiar rush of anxiety swept through my body.

'Have you ever seen the city, Rex? I promise you it is so much better than here. Heaps to do, people to see, places to go.'

Rex wagged his tail, opening one eye and giving a yawn. Great, the only one who would listen to me was a dumb, stupid dog.

Just do what I need to do, Grace, say what I need to say, and I'll get the hell out of here, back to reality.

Rex had been following me around more and more, despite me doing my best to ignore him. I even told him to get lost often, but he never seemed to tire of my company. So different to people. He was an old dog now. Occasionally, he appeared stiff but mostly moved around okay. Secretly it amused me that he never failed to greet me with an enthusiastic sniff and wag of his tail, like an old friend. Strange.

'He came to me at just the right time, Gracie. It was a desperately lonely period in my life. One I was not prepared for. Suddenly, I was very alone out here. Then Rex came along and, in a way, helped me to find purpose again.'

I hadn't noticed Negeenah in the doorway of the study watching us. She sighed before bustling away again. How could a person rely on animals to help them get by? I just don't get her, I think she likes her horses and Rex more than people. Come to think of it… maybe she was onto something.

'She is a strange one. You have done well to stick by her, Rex.'

Life had forced me quickly to dispel the belief I'd once held in this world. I now had a wariness about people.

Liars.

Yet there was something about Negeenah. Despite her air of softness, she was also cautious. To be fair, she was straight to the point, no question, but also maybe kind. I was yet to find out, I suppose. Her true self was veiled, but she seemed honest and willing to help. Still, I had no intention of letting my guard down just yet, if at all.

People often start out that way.

I just don't trust people anymore.

But despite trying to remain as distant and detached as I could from my grandmother, I often caught myself observing her with interest. She was intriguing, almost mysterious. Somehow watching her elegant yet purposeful movements connected me to my dreams. This bothered me because I couldn't work out why.

My dreams have always been vivid and explicit. For many years now, I have woken with them still very present in my mind. Dreams so realistic, I could recall the smells and sounds of being in another world or another time. Some had left me feeling tense and even distraught. Some returned, like they were on repeat, recurring again and again.

Groundhog Day.

From as young as five I'd dreamt of the little girl, wandering through the harsh Australian bush. She would look up, the trees surrounding her reaching way up into the sky. Stretching her arms up, she would jump and twirl like she was trying to catch a butterfly. I could smell the bush, feel the warm air, sense the stillness. I never saw her face, not once, ever.

This dream was peaceful when it began. It was always the same little girl. I sensed she wasn't scared. She played outside in the dirt and was always surrounded by bright flowers. Her dark curls were much like my own, a blue ribbon tying them back. Her dress was always identical, too, made of yellow cotton. It had tiny blue flowers sewn into the sleeves, neckline and hem. So many times, this little girl had been the focus of my subconscious mind.

Sometimes she'd play with a wooden music box covered in tiny intricate carvings. It contained little shiny lapis stones. The girl would wind up the miniature silver handle on the side of the box. Inside, a beautiful princess came to life, dancing in circles to soft, serene music each time the box was opened. She would lay beside the box, humming to the tune. Sometimes she would twirl beside the box in time to the music.

At times, another little girl, similar in age and appearance would join her. The second girl also had dark hair, but it was straight and wispy. She was smaller, very frail. She wore a white dress. For some reason, I could see her face and be able to look directly into her dark knowing eyes. She had a big smile and a raucous laugh. She always followed the little girl who dominated my dreams, reaching for her hand as they walked along. Sometimes they would sit on the red earth together, listening to the music box. Sometimes they stacked up the lapis stones, one on top of another, until they tumbled into the dust. Then they would giggle, falling into each other. Clearly, their bond was strong. It was peaceful to watch, even in the mind's eye.

I often willed something else to happen, attempting to understand why I dreamt like this. But till this day, who they were, and where this place was, remained a mystery. Often, I tried desperately to wake before the dream ended, as I knew what was coming. It left me feeling unhinged, shattering me every time afresh. I remember feeling like the loss was deeply personal.

A shadowy figure came, silently picking up the little girl with dark curly hair, never the other child. Each time she cried out.

She reached desperately behind her, over the shoulder of the adult figure. Her friend would always remain sitting on the ground. Her little hands were stretched out, too, pleading with them not to leave. Her music box was left in the dirt. The flowers around them would begin to fade.

Every time she was taken away, and always against her will. I'd see her blue ribbon fall from her hair, the wind blowing it into the surrounding bush. I could always hear the tune from the music box playing and the soft cry of the little girls as they faded into the distance, further and further away from each other.

War

Negeenah, a lean and strong woman could clearly take care of herself. She had a toughness about her, but despite her rural surroundings, she took pride in her appearance. Even in the sweltering heat of the day, digging up the soil in the vegetable garden or mucking out the stables, she managed to look poised.

How did she do that? I just feel filthy and sweaty all day every day here.

The only other people I'd seen since arriving were Tracker and the other farmhand, Bluey. They fronted up before breakfast and spent their days working around the property. The men mostly kept to themselves. They looked like old leathery cowboys, reminding me of a Clint Eastwood movie Mum and I watched once.

Even though there were two horses on Zarnish, the men used four-wheelers to move around the property. They worked out of the barn. I'd watched them from a distance so far, surprised at how much hard work a property like this took. No wonder my grandmother needed them. I pondered the point of it all. Why would you be tied to a property when you could sell up and live in a nice apartment, free to experience anything in life you wanted?

'Some good old fashioned hard work outside is just what you need, Gracie.'

Piss off, Negeenah.

My response was unwavering each time she asked me to join her, as she flitted around the farm, completing chores.

'I'm not interested, same as yesterday… and just so you know, tomorrow I will most likely not be interested either. The only thing I'm focused on is going home.'

That was my favourite. I threw it at her with as much sass as I could. Hoping I'd get a reaction. I liked it when she fired back at me; it broke the boredom. I relished knowing I could get under her skin.

Maybe she would send me back if I became too much of a handful. Unfortunately, I barely raised a reaction from her. Sometimes she would look at me darkly. Other times she would mutter to herself.

'Spoilt, privileged child!' She'd fired back once.

I gave her a tongue lashing that time.

'Spoilt? Me? What the hell would you know about anything?' I'd spat back.

She had no clue how tough things had been. Living her boring farm life, what a joke, so I continued to make a deliberate choice, to speak rarely and keep my thoughts private. It was safer that way. Easier to protect myself. I had lost enough already.

What would Negeenah know about life anyway? I would bet nothing bad or tragic had ever happened to her. It was pointless getting to know a person who knew nothing of my life, my pain, my ruined future. Why would I bother? I'm going to leave as soon as I earn my ticket out of here. And I won't be coming back, that's for certain…

I hate you, Mum.

I was, however, a little perplexed about the way my grandmother had spoken to me earlier that day. The conversation had come from nowhere, taking me by surprise. She had placed her hand on my shoulder as she spoke, making me jolt.

'Grace, you were given your beautiful name for a great purpose you know. To breathe grace into this world, to breathe beauty, kindness and mercy.'

Where the hell did that come from?

Both her touch and words had shocked me, thrown me completely off guard. I couldn't even summon a smart-arse response.

I felt exposed, like she could see to my core as she spoke.

'I used to tell you that all the time, Gracie, from the time you were...'

She suddenly cut herself off, shaking her head.

'Oh, silly old me, I mean, I used to think it all the time. When I did say it, I always hoped somehow the wind would carry my words to you.'

She smiled, and it seemed genuine. I felt the heat rise from my toes.

Not now. Hold it together, Grace. Breathe.

'I had no idea you'd thought of me.'

Why couldn't Mum have told me that?

I was more than a little dazed. Sometimes random kindness from people threw me. It's hard to explain, but I didn't know how to react.

'Maybe, I wish I had known you thought of me. I assumed you didn't care. Maybe then, all this, having to come out here, wouldn't be so hard.'

Negeenah nodded, avoiding my eyes.

'Truth be told, there is a lot we should have done differently child.'

I'd been helping her in the kitchen at the time. My grandmother had touched the stone around her neck, just like I saw her do the day I arrived, as she'd stood there, summing me up on the porch. I knew it so well, a lapis lazuli. Its beautiful vivid blue was unmistakable. The stone in my dreams. My mum had also worn one her whole life. Both necklaces were identical in size and setting.

Identical to the necklace I'd once worn.

Their delicate design was a silver cross, about as big as a coin. A deep blue lapis stone formed another cross on top of the silver. Tiny flecks of gold ran through the blue. When the sun caught the stone in the light, its glimmering appearance always made me think it was magical. Mum had often talked about the power in the stone. Many nights, growing up, I recalled curling up at bedtime with her.

The lapis lazuli, known throughout history as the wisdom keeper. Since the earliest of times, it has been associated with strength and courage, royalty and wisdom, intellect and truth.

I could hear her voice as clear as day. I'd loved the way Mum would talk about the stone's powers, its mystery. Each time was the same. We would wrap ourselves up in Mum's old quilt, its heavy and colourful squares of material smelling like lavender and vanilla. Cocooned happily, I'd wait eagerly for the enchantment to begin.

'One day, Gracie, this stone will allow you to awaken your true destiny, your divine purpose, but you must have faith.'

Why did everything have to change.

What a crock of shit believing in a stone.

I'm an idiot.

I just didn't think Mum would betray me.

She'd said we were invincible, unbreakable…

Now I understand.

In the end, I wasn't worth it, hey, Mum. Liar.

I closed my eyes, remembering the first time Mum had shown me a picture of Cleopatra. I was seven and wanted desperately to be a princess. I thought she was the most beautiful, captivating woman I'd ever seen.

'Cleopatra, Gracie, was once the Queen of Egypt. She was the most powerful and influential woman of her time. She was to be the last queen Egypt would ever have.'

'She was so beautiful, Mum.'

'That was deliberate. Cleopatra was often made up to look like the goddess Aphrodite. She would mesmerise men. But do you know what is very special about her beauty? She believed much of her wisdom and strength came from the lapis stone she wore and always adorned herself with large lapis jewels around her neck.'

I'd stared at the image for a long time that day, clutching my own necklace, wondering, could I have this effect on the world?

'But even better than that, Gracie, look at her eyes. On her upper eyelids, she wore a deep blue shadow. Those gold pyrite flecks were made from ground-up lapis stone.'

I can recall Mum making many references to the lapis stone in the Bible too.

'This is why I believe in God, Gracie; why I put my faith in Him. He knows the power of our precious lapis. In earlier translations of the Bible, the blue stone is referred to as a Sapphire. In later translations, however, research of history reveals they were, in fact, lapis lazuli.'

How quickly times can change. It didn't seem that long ago that I'd been deep in discussions with Mum about our pending trip to Cairo. This is where the famous death mask of Tutankhamen was on display. His mask was laced with lapis stones of vivid blue. The Egyptians held the stone in very high regard. We were planning the trip of a lifetime. On my return, I had been invited by my school to share my findings at an Information Night. This would have been added to my folio for university entry. It was an honour to have been asked.

They wouldn't ask me now I'm tipping… Maybe I could tell them what getting arrested is like. What it feels like to have your life shattered. Be fucked over by everyone.

Why hadn't I ever questioned Mum? Instead, I'd just gone along blindly believing, bedazzled by the lapis stories.

Never once had I asked why she believed the lapis stone and its mystery and power were 'hers'? Or why she believed she held such a strong connection to the stone? In fact, there were so many things I could have asked. Instead, I encouraged her to talk, as it was the only time the light would return to her eyes. The protective veil would lift, even just briefly.

Was I that self-absorbed? Brainwashed more likely.

The same heavy feeling I couldn't seem to shake washed over my body, like big waves pounding again and again as I was pulled and pushed, thrown around in an unpredictable swell.

I wondered how I wouldn't drown in this new version of my life.

Maybe it was best if I did.

Be the author of your own story, I was always told.

How could this possibly be mine?

Betrayed

Then, in that sliding door moment, everything changed.

I'd ripped my lapis necklace off and thrown it at my father's car as he drove off that day. A moment of rage that changed everything. I'd followed him out to the curb like the loser I was, fumbling with the clasp of my necklace before awkwardly hurling it at him.

Please come back. Please.

I'd screamed at him, crumpled on the curb as I watched his black sedan speed off. Did he even look back in the rearview mirror? To this day, when I see a car like his, my heart skips a beat. Wondering if he was home? Was he going to tell me it was all a mistake, beg me to forgive him?

Could I?

As much as I always tried to block the events of that horrible afternoon, they still played over and over in my mind, like a bad movie on repeat. I winced at the memory of him sitting me down, telling me he had to leave. Then just like a robot, he had stared right through me as all emotion seemed to leave his face.

'I'm sorry, Gracie, there is no easy way to say this. But I am not your real father. One day you will understand, I promise, I just need you to trust me now.'

How could I possibly believe him? How could I trust this person I'd always looked to as my father but was now telling me that was all a lie.

'One day, you will see this was all for you, for your freedom, to ensure your safety.'

I'd pleaded with him to tell me why. I'd begged him.

'Dad, Samir... I don't even know what to call you! I am not a kid. Whatever this is about, I can handle it.'

But he just kept saying the same thing, sadness obvious in his eyes.

'It's impossible, Grace, this is the only way from now on.'

Why?

What secrets was he keeping?

And my mum, what was her place in all of this?

Surely the truth could not be as bad as the stories my mind had since made up.

Despite hearing and believing the stories my whole life, suddenly, I couldn't believe in the lapis stone and its powers any longer. I lost faith because I didn't know what or who to have faith in. I didn't know where I belonged.

And most of all, just like that, I no longer trusted the people who were supposed to love me the most.

That's when the anxiety began silently invading my body.

Will it ever leave?

The cottage

Since arriving, I'd pretty well scoped out the entire property. As far as I could tell, disturbingly, it was slap bang in the middle of nowhere. Negeenah, I'd come to learn, often disappeared for hours on her horse, Jinta. Where did she go?

Be bloody hard to run away from here. But I guess my mum knew that.

Sitting on the edge of the veranda, I eyed my new boots, a gift from Negeenah.

Could they be any uglier!

I wrestled to get them on. She had strongly suggested I wear them, as the risk of snakebite was high. I wanted to throw them at her head, but the mention of a reptile was enough to make me pipe down. No one I cared about could see me anyway.

Movement in my peripheral vision caught my attention. I couldn't believe my eyes, as once again, the same blue butterfly casually fluttered around before me. It came so close it almost touched my hair.

'Hello, little lady. Nice to see you again.'

As I walked, I pondered on the grand farmhouse. The butterfly joined me for a while, fluttering about beside me, looping up and down in the breeze before disappearing into an old apple tree. It was beautiful, magical. A welcome distraction from the intense heat here that was already stinging my skin, despite the dappled shade from the fruit trees.

I couldn't deny my surroundings made me curious and keen to explore. It oozed history and significance. Surrounding the huge Victorian farmhouse were lush gardens, clearly planted many moons ago. I knew from my own research that properties like Zarnish were typically surrounded by prominent landscaping. Perhaps it made life out here feel more civilised as white settlers tried to tame the new frontier. Especially if you were new to Australia. It was hard not to admire the effort it must have taken to establish the vibrant flower beds, large ornamental trees, a pond dotted with lily pads, and a sitting area surrounded by roses of every colour.

A vegetable garden bordered by a white picket fence dominated a large area to one side of the home. I'd never seen a veggie patch like it. It seemed like such an effort when you could just go to the supermarket. Negeenah spent a lot of time out here tending to her vegetables. Nearby there was the large chicken pen. Speckled chooks fossicked around busily pecking at straw and pellets. The smell reminded me of a hobby farm Mum had taken me to once, a birthday treat when I'd turned six. Funny how smells can trigger distant memories and, without question, emotions.

On my first morning at Zarnish Estate, I'd woken startled by an intense crowing. It was around dawn when the hideous noise started. On and on it went, piercing the stillness of the morning. A friggin' rooster! Apparently, they have an internal clock that helps them anticipate the sunrise, so Negeenah pointed out.

'Stanley does that every morning. Reminds me I'm blessed to still have air in my lungs, Gracie. Been given another day to look forward to.'

Was she serious? What was she on?

I loathed that ugly creature from day one. Each morning the shock of the intrusion from sleep instantly set me off. It felt similar to waking in a panic attack, all disorientated and with a sense of impending doom.

Move on, Grace, it's just a bloody rooster.

Bluestone milking sheds and stables, matching the main house, were located to the left of the homestead. The stables housed Negeenah's precious horses. She sure spent a lot of time out there. I'd see her riding off most days, disappearing out through the paddocks. I'd never ridden a horse apart from that one pony ride. Maybe someone would offer to teach me while I was here.

The milking sheds seemed long out of use. Both were stunning pieces of history. If only the walls could talk. A huge barn stood alone on the right side of the main house. It looked older, with its faded wooden facade and rusted tin roof. The farmhands kept their machinery in there, and it was a constant hive of activity. Up 'til now, these were not areas I had explored, but my inquisitiveness was getting the better of me.

Behind the house, paddocks spanned as far as the eye could see. The pasture still had a tinge of green, which was surprising considering it was summer. Even I knew drought was an issue in the outback. I could see at least two tree-lined dams. I wondered if I could swim in them. A large windmill turned continuously in the light breeze. Heavy black cows grazed contently, munching away, rarely raising their heads, not a care in the world.

Like most mornings, I didn't really have a clue what to do with myself.

Today I headed in the general direction of the bush beyond the homestead again. I liked the solitude. There were so many different tracks. Once I would have been scared to venture into this type of environment on my own. I knew nothing about the Northern Territory and its terrain. But not anymore; I couldn't give a shit about what happened to me, almost like my subconscious enjoyed the risk of self-harm. I was good at self-sabotage these days.

What did it really matter?

Would anyone really notice or care if I never returned today?

I hate you, Mum. You haven't even called me.

At least I could be alone in the bush, without the prying eyes of my grandmother. Although I'm sure Negeenah meant no harm, I had often caught her staring at me. She was so hard to read.

Inscrutable human that one.

Time and time again, Negeenah's knuckles would turn white as she gripped the stone around her neck, often appearing lost, if not troubled by her thoughts. Sometimes she hummed quietly. It unnerved me. I'd actually prefer if she had something to say that she just come out and say it. Get the lecture over with.

Lost in my own thoughts as I walked along, I barely noticed the beauty of the land around me. I was becoming used to the oppressive heat and the flies, so disgusting and always swarming around my mouth and eyes.

Could they smell the rot in my heart?

Beads of perspiration laced my forehead. I was angry with Mum, there was no denying it. Angry that she had just stood there as my dad, or whoever he was, revealed the truth. Angry, she had refused to talk to me about it after he left.

How could she?

To this day, I can still feel the stabbing feeling in my heart. It was not going away but instead just intensifying. I was pissed off at myself too, reduced to begging, pleading with him not to leave. The same dizzy feeling washed over me, like a cold fog sweeping through my veins.

Maybe it was my fault?

Why had he told me now?

Where did Mum stand in all of this?

If they had hidden the truth for so long, why shatter my world at all?

He'd said it was impossible. What had he meant?

I am his daughter, or I thought I was.

Was I ever important to him?

Was I some sort of business deal?

Why had I not seen this coming?

I am such an idiot... I hate myself.

I stumbled, as tunnel vision set in, falling heavily into the scrub on the side of the track. Tears spilled into the dirt around me, causing the ants to scurry into their cleverly constructed holes and distracting me momentarily.

I didn't care how dirty and dusty I was. There was no one here to impress anyway. I stayed down for a long while, unable to move. My body trembled, all the while feeling like lead. An overwhelming sense of dread raged through me. So much had happened in such a short time. I literally had no clue how to fix all this from here.

Breathe, Grace. You know this feeling. It can't hurt you.

A loud bark snapped me out of my head.

Rex!

Bounding towards me he came to an abrupt stop. Face to face, we examined each other. He was breathing heavily. His thick brown and black coat was covered in bracken and specks of wattle. I met his eyes and strangely felt soothed, less alone. He had the biggest ears I had ever seen on a dog; they were always upright and moved at the slightest sound.

'What the hell are you doing here, Rex? Can't I get a moment to myself? Take a hint, rack off.'

Turning my body slightly away, Rex stayed put and cocked his head. My words sounded angrier than I really was, truthfully, I felt embarrassed to be found in this state, even by a dog.

'Go home Rex.'

To my surprise, he leaned in closer, whimpering softly he licked at my tears. For some reason this guy liked me.

As quickly as he appeared, Rex trotted off, nose to the ground, red dust rising in his wake. He was still very agile for an old dog. He darted off the main track, roaming further into the bush. I watched as he disappeared down a narrow, well-worn path I'd not noticed before.

I stood gingerly, dusting myself off and searching for another glimpse of Rex. Instead, I could just make out a structure, all but hidden by the bush. I began moving quickly, straining to hear the slightest sound. It looked to be an old building of some sort, barely visible from the road.

What the!

Curiosity took over, and I felt my pulse increase. What had I discovered? Was Rex leading me there?

Emerging through the thicket, I stilled, gazing with sudden focus. There stood a cottage, run down and overgrown. The little house instantly appealed to me. Its weatherboards had greyed over time. The tin roof was covered in rust and had a burgundy patina. Tiny windows on either side of the front door were still draped with lace curtains. The entrance was overgrown with plants and weeds. A thick mat of vines with bright flowers hung from the uneven, slightly drooped veranda, blanketing the home. They were striking but seemed oddly out of place in these bush surrounds.

Rex sniffed around ahead of me. His coat glistened in the sun, despite the remnants of the bush that had attached to him along the way. Clearly, he knew this dwelling and seemed excited to be here. As I drew nearer, I could feel the history of this cottage and felt a shiver down my spine. The hair on my arms stood on edge and somehow, I sensed sadness possessed this little house.

My earlier tears and anger were forgotten as new intrigue and adrenaline had my whole-body tingling. I closed my eyes and took in the smells and stillness of this little place as a strange feeling of déjà vu filled my soul. Somewhere beyond water trickled.

As I stepped onto the old veranda, my foot broke through the rotten floor. Luckily, I was wearing boots. My legs, however, were scratched in several places, already stinging from the cuts the sword grass and bush prickles had caused earlier. I didn't care, this was the most alive I had felt in months. My anxiety was forgotten.

I wondered if it was possible someone still lived here. It looked abandoned, but I didn't want to walk in on someone if it were their home. All the same, I had to check this place out. Knocking tentatively, I tried to open the front door, but it didn't budge. Seems it had been some time since the old lock had been opened.

Rex began barking and pushed his way in between me and the entrance. Standing firm he continued to bark, eyeballing me.

'What's the matter with you...? Move, you stupid dog.'

Pushing him aside, and trying again to turn the lock, I ignored his seemingly concerned and persistent whining. This time I used my whole body against the door.

The birds above began to screech at a deafening pitch. Looking up, I could see the bright red of rosellas, the shiny blackness of crows. Beside the cottage, a huge old gum tree housed some magpies. Their loud melodious carolling somehow had a menacing tone and strangely, for the first time since arriving at Zarnish, I felt a little intimidated.

I was curious, yes, but something cautioned me deep inside. I ran my hands through my hair and paced the small veranda. Rex continued to whine.

'Fine then, maybe another day, Rex.'

I sighed, losing my courage to explore.

For now...

Stepping off the entrance, I stood staring up at the cottage for a few more minutes. Consciously I forced my limbs to relax. My stomach quivered.

'It's a little eerie, Rex but I feel drawn to it, like I need to know its story, its history.'

Rex all but jumped up at me, pulling my shirt toward him and away from the cottage.

'Fine. Come on then. But I'm coming back here Rex. Let's go.'

I turned reluctantly and headed back toward the main house. Rex bounded ahead.

Negeenah will know. But will she tell me?

Torture

Each night, Negeenah had insisted we prepare a meal and eat together. On the first night I arrived, she'd been swift in laying down some rules.

'Gracie,' she'd said, looking me straight in the eye. 'I won't ask much of you, but I do ask that you join me at the dinner table each night, help with chores when I need you to and don't go disappearing on me.'

Dinner with her every night? Torture.

Back home, I preferred eating in the solitude of my bedroom, most often while on my iPad. Especially of late, as things had been so tense with Mum.

'We can work this out, Gracie. This is not the end of the world, but perhaps a way for you to begin again.'

Spare me the bullshit.

'I am not a child. If you knew me at all, you would know that.'

'Then don't act like one, Grace. Actions speak louder than words, remember.'

True.

Mum had told me to 'just do it' over the phone.

'I don't have to comply with anything, I'm here, isn't that enough!'

'You do, and you will, Grace. Or there will be further consequences. And you can cut the sass with me.'

I scoffed at that one.

'Really, what could be worse than this?'

'Don't push me, Grace. I mean it.'

Yet another conversation between us which had not gone well.

But tonight, for the first time, I actually looked forward to having dinner at the huge old table. I was thirsty for information about the cottage. It was now or never, time to be brave.

So, just keep on playing the game, I reminded myself. Smile sweetly. I'm out of here soon, and none of this will matter. And I'll never have to see this stupid woman again. I don't care if she is family, that means nothing to me anymore.

Do it, Grace, ask her.

I was shovelling in potato too fast. Building the courage to tell Negeenah about my day's adventure. I often ate and talked when nervous. Sometimes I don't even notice I'm doing it.

'So, this afternoon… I found the most extraordinary thing on my walk. I had fallen over on one of the bush tracks, you know. Then, out of nowhere, Rex just appeared, and guess what? He led me to this fascinating little cottage. I could tell he knew the place. In fact, strangely, I kind of felt the same way.'

I was so intent on picking up the last of the broccoli and carrot on my plate that I didn't initially see Negeenah had stopped mid-chew. She struggled to swallow the food that now seemed stuck in her throat. I stopped talking. I had thought this was a reasonably innocent conversation. I watched as her skin blanched and the sparkle in her eyes dulled. My own food felt like swallowing concrete. She stood.

What did I say that was so wrong?

Negeenah suddenly looked frail, her hands slightly trembling. When she finally spoke, she grasped the stone around her neck again as if willing it to give her strength. She looked at me, terrified. This was the biggest crack in her emotional armour I'd seen.

Interesting.

'Please, Grace,' she said in an earnest, raspy whisper. 'I beg you,

you must never go back there, ever. The cottage belongs to the past and needs to be left that way. No good can come of you returning.'

Ghosts

Over the coming days, I could not help but wonder about Negeenah's reaction.

She was frightened, but of what? Of whom?

What could this seemingly simple old woman have to hide? Questions swirled around my head. At least they gave me welcomed respite from my usual family predicament, normally all-consuming.

Growing up, there was very little ever spoken about my heritage or my family origins. I was now realising, in fact, how scant my knowledge was of Mum and Negeenah's early life. She had travelled from Central Asia to make her home in Australia.

But which country exactly had she left?

Why did Negeenah live all alone in this isolated, rural town?

How was I never curious before?

I was starting to sense there was more to this story, a lot more. My gut was telling me it was time I did some digging around. Too often, Mum had either been dismissive of family questions or simply changed the topic of conversation. I'd be heading back to the cottage on my first opportunity.

Later that night, in a moment of brilliance, I used the Internet to look up the meaning and origin of the name Negeenah. It was certainly not an Australian name. Come to think of it, neither was my mother's. Everyone called her Misha, but I knew her real name was Kamisha. I pulled my notebook out of my backpack, one of the few personal belongings I'd brought here. Sometimes I just liked to jot my feelings down. Perhaps it was the one good idea I'd taken from my stupid, pain in the arse, patronising psychologist.

Curiously, I learned both were traditional Afghan names.

'So, Rex, Negeenah means precious stone, and Kamisha- a happy soul. Interesting. And I know the lapis lazuli stone also has its origins in the mines in Afghanistan. More than a coincidence, I would say. Maybe the dream I had in the attic was in some way connected after all.'

Rex barely moved from his spot beside the desk, but wagged his tail encouragingly, making me smile.

'If no one thinks I'm important enough to tell me the truth, no problem. As always, I'll rely on myself. I can work this out on my own, hey boy.'

Out of nowhere the feeling came, that sudden and overwhelming sense of dread. Disorientated, I grabbed onto the chair my breathing quick and shallow. Spots appeared in my vision, and I crumbled onto the floor, hugging my tight chest. Rex crawled up beside me, tucking his body into mine.

I began to cry.

Breathe, Grace. This will pass, just give it some time. Breathe.

Over the last few months, more than once, I had questioned if something was really wrong inside my brain. No one I knew talked about it. Sometimes the feeling was like I had a split personality. I felt fine one minute, then angry the next. Other times it was different. I went from being calm and happy to jittery and dizzy, even panicky. When I had these episodes, I often found I was consumed with random, flitting thoughts, and my body felt wrong, like something really bad was about to happen. Anxiety, so I have been told. All I knew was it was a bitch of a thing. Right now, I was determined to push past it. I had things to sort out here.

That night, as I lay on my bed, my thoughts drifted back to Mum.

I wondered what she was doing right now. Rex had still not left my side and I think I was starting to like it.

Did Mum miss me?

Most likely, she was at work. Misha, being a lawyer, worked long hours. Her expertise was campaigning for and defending women's rights. I admired her so much for that. So often, I had become lost in the stories she, too, had shared, of many about women from other cultures.

A coincidence? Now I'm starting to think not.

I must have fallen asleep. It was a sound I could not place that woke me from a deep slumber. Voices. I struggled to open my eyes; they were foggy and non-compliant. My room was now dark. Funny, I thought, I had remembered leaving the lamp on.

I looked around. By my side, the pen and paper I had been using, were still on the bed. My phone was still charging on the bedside table. 9.15pm.

'In my old life, I would be heading out to meet friends right now.'

I mumbled sleepily into the darkness.

'Now look at me; I'm becoming like a grandma myself!'

A sharp cry pierced the stillness from somewhere in the house. I sat up, immediately wide awake, my thoughts of self-pity and irritation lost. More cries. Heartfelt cries. It was a woman. Negeenah?

I jumped up, grabbing my phone I rushed to help. As I entered the hallway, I tried to remember the exact address of Zarnish Estate. I didn't know it. What did you do in an emergency out here? Call 000? This was something I hadn't thought of until now. Idiot.

I flew out of my room and tripped on a hall rug. Since when exactly was there a rug in the hall? Certainly not when I had gone to bed each night. Heading down the long, wide passageway that led from the bedrooms to the main house, I stopped again. Why were there oil lanterns burning on the side tables? Normally a hall light was on. And above the hall table was a picture. I had never seen this hanging on the wall before. Inside the beautiful wooden frame was an old, enlarged sepia-tone photograph of a young couple. They were in a garden, perhaps the front garden of this property, it was hard to tell.

Am I going crazy?

Again, a high-pitched scream vaulted from the front sitting room. I hurried on, nervous about the scene that awaited. As I approached, I could see a figure leaning over a younger woman lying on the couch. A young man hovered in the room, clearly distressed by what was happening. They were all in their pyjamas. Why were they here?

I entered the room tentatively now. Strangely, it, too, looked different from what I remembered. I'd spent time here earlier in the day. But now, the furniture was not the same. It looked as though it was from an older period in history. Shaking off my confusion, I approached the strangers in the room.

'How can I help?'

I tried to sound confident.

'Do you want me to call someone? I have my phone. Should I call a doctor?'

I could see now, it was a middle-aged lady. She continued to tend to a younger woman, speaking to her in a gentle, low tone, in a foreign language. The sick woman was ghostly white, sweating and shaking profusely as if she were in the grip of hypothermia.

Had they not heard me?

Why aren't they responding?

I turned to the young man, now crouching beside the ill woman. He held her hand, gently stroking it and kissing her fingers.

'Please,' he whispered, 'Hang on, my love, please don't leave me.'

The woman mumbled faint words back to him, again in a foreign tongue.

'How can I help?' I demanded, louder this time. 'I can go and get my grandma. She will know what to do.'

But, again, it was like I wasn't there. I was close enough to touch him now, to touch them all. So close, I could smell the stench of sickness and feel the deep love and emotion between them.

How could they not see nor hear me?

I looked around again, this time noticing a teapot and small bowl of soup beside the woman. She moaned and cried out, grabbing her stomach, then her head. Her dark brown eyes looked frightened yet distant. Tears streamed from them. The middle-aged woman placed a cold sponge on her forehead.

What was happening?

Who were these strangers?

Where was Negeenah?

I tried one final time to talk to the people, to offer them my help. But as before, it was like I was merely an onlooker of a scene in a movie.

The fire crackled in the room. Why was the fire going? Since my arrival, the weather had been warm, day and night. A sombre tune softly danced through the air coming from the old record player. The music itself seemed oddly out of place, considering the urgency within the room. I had never noticed a record player here before.

Then, for the first time since entering the room, the realisation of how cold it was, hit me. Rain bashed harshly on the windowpanes, and the damp chill in the air was unmistakable.

But how?

It was the middle of summer.

Pulled from my thoughts again, I heard the man speak. He gently grabbed the arm of the middle-aged lady. For the first time, she looked up from the sick young woman into his stricken face.

'Please, Negeenah, please help her. She cannot die from this, I beg you to help me save her.'

I felt the oxygen had been stolen from my lungs. My body lurched back involuntarily.

Negeenah?

Why was he calling her that?

As I stared more intently at the woman, her skin was softer, younger, her cascading curls darker, but as impossible as it was, somehow it was her. Confusion reigned in my mind. I was trying to rationalise the implausible… Negeenah?

I looked both at the man and the poor young woman lying on the couch. I realised this was the same couple in the photo portrait in the hall. I moved my own hands to my face, trying to stifle a scream.

What the hell was going on?

It was my own scream that woke me. Again, I sat bolt upright in bed. Overheated, I was covered in sweat, just like the sick woman in the sitting room. Tugging at my ear I desperately tried to rationalize the memory of what I had just witnessed. It was all so clear. The dying woman, the man, Grandma, the house. So, was it all a dream or had I just witnessed a scene from the past?

Perhaps both? But how? Why?

Glancing at my phone, it was still plugged into the charger where I'd put it earlier. The time was 9.15pm, just like it had been when I heard the screams.

I stepped tentatively back into the hallway and repeated my journey, fumbling and feeling exposed. This time the dim light burned from the lamp I had come to know, the same lamp that had been there since my arrival. There was no hallway rug. The photo on the wall of the young couple in the garden was now gone.

See, Grace, just a vivid dream! This place was messing with me.

Still, as I entered the front sitting room, I felt really on edge. All was like it had been earlier in the day. No sign of a record player. Or a bowl of soup. I could feel the warm breeze flowing in from the open French doors.

I'm delusional.

The cicadas buzzed loudly in the garden beyond. Funny how quickly I'd become accustomed, even expectant, of this sound. The first night they were deafening and intrusive. Now, the sound lulled me to sleep. The house was quiet; the ticking of the old grandfather clock in the hallway seemed louder than ever before. Negeenah had gone to bed for the evening, no doubt. She always retired early and rose with the dawn.

Hot chocolate would calm my nerves. Taking a mug full back to my room, I grabbed my notebook. I laughed at myself, relishing the sense of relief as I jotted down some of the stuff I'd seen in the bizarre dream. For a minute there, I had actually believed I'd gone back in time.

The mind can play amazing tricks when it wants to. Yet somewhere, in my subconscious, something niggled at me, an unease. That nagging feeling I couldn't quite pinpoint, suggesting something deeper was going on with me. A slight chill swept through the air, making me turn and almost expect a figure in the shadows to appear.

Zarnish Estate held its secrets, and I think somehow, it was trying to expose them.

Deja vu

I took my chance one afternoon to return to the cottage. Of course, Rex decided to come with me, but I can't say I minded. The old bloke was certainly growing on me. Today was stifling, and there was not a breeze. The birds seeking shade in the gum trees were loud, too loud. It was like they were once again threatening me to turn back. For the first time in my life, I was beginning to take more notice of the world around me. I don't know why my senses were suddenly alert and awakened, but I needed my headphones less and less to escape.

I did know one thing, these surroundings, the bush, calmed my anxiety every time. Strange. I thought only the city could do that. I was in awe of the king parrots which today, stopped me in my tracks once again. Mostly travelling in pairs, the male was stunning with its bright orange chest. The colour almost seemed magnified against the green and brown gums. Their call was shrill and melodising, bell-like, as it rang out across the land.

As I approached the cottage, the bush itself smelt tantalizingly earthy. The fresh scent of the flowing creek water nearby reminded me of rain having just fallen in summer, only fresher out here, different to the city. Today for the first time, I walked over to the edge of the bank and watched the soft flow spilling over rocks and fallen bracken within the shallow creek bed. I wondered how it wasn't bone dry like everything else around here. Rex splashed in the water before sitting his entire body in the creek, gulping water as it flowed past. It felt good to laugh.

The parched timber facade of the cottage had weathered over many summers. From a different season, rust in the tin roof had long since rendered it ineffective for keeping out rain. It didn't look like it had ever been painted. Despite this, I still had the feeling it had once been cherished by its owner, whoever that was. Looking with fresh eyes this time, I could see the lace curtains in the front windows were tattered, and cobwebs had formed on the glass.

Again, I approached the front door cautiously, although I was super eager to get past it this time. Just like the first time I'd seen the cottage, I felt a deep sense I'd experienced this place before. It caught me off guard again, like I had two streams of thought colliding. I closed my eyes. Somehow, this place, its smell, the colours, the sounds, reminded me of my childhood. Exactly where in my lifetime, I couldn't place. The memory was dark and distorted.

A bird swooped me out of nowhere, its surprise attack causing me to stumble back. Looking up near the top of the door, I could see a small nest being protected by a sparrow. I could hear the excited tweets of tiny chicks inside the nest.

Would my parents fight to protect me like this little defenceless bird was for her babies? Clearly not. I'm not worth it.

Shaking off my overthinking, I jumped back into the moment. I'd come better prepared this time. In my backpack, I had water, some crackers and a pry bar. I had found the old tool lying next to the milking shed. I'd been careful to sneak it into my room and hide it in my bag, amusing myself by behaving like a devious little kid.

My mood darkened, as the lock on the door proved impossible to budge.

I was not proud remembering the last time I had used a pry bar. Breaking and entering, the bar itself was stolen from the maintenance room at school. I remembered that night so vividly. I had been scared, but my anger and determination had overridden everything. If only the police, Mum, anyone, had given me a chance to explain.

I had only wanted to find my dad's new address, or at least the man I thought was him. I knew the school administration office would have it. If I had his address, I could go and talk to him. Find out why he had told me we would never see each other again. If he was not my father, maybe he knew who was.

Stop it, Grace. Focus on the now. It's in the past.

Even a snippet of the memory returning still made me anxious and slightly nauseous and a little unsteady on my feet. I took a second to wipe the sweat from my brow, exhaling a slow breath.

Within a few minutes, I finally had the old door moving; it groaned under the force of change. It was as if the powers of the secrets behind the door were at play, resisting all the way.

Flakes of old blue paint fell around me, a lapis stone blue. I stood in the small entrance and took in the cottage interior in awe. Dust covered every surface, and I gagged at the intensified smell of must and mould that engulfed me. Despite this, the cottage instantaneously, made me feel at ease, as if we were somehow connected and the little dwelling had been awaiting my return like a loyal friend.

Placing the pry bar at the entrance, I stepped just inside. The room was warm. There was a bed and a baby cot in one corner, both made from white wrought iron and still laden with blankets and pillows, in soft colours of blue and purple. There was a small round wooden table and two chairs, a kitchen sink and a set of drawers. The only other furniture in the room was a rocking chair, which sat facing a potbelly stove and two old chests. A cream woollen blanket was folded on top of one. The smaller chest had a lock on it. Fascinated, I took in the stillness and silence of my surroundings. I could hear my own heartbeat, feel the sweat trickling down the middle of my back.

Edging closer into the small space, I felt a mixture of intrigue and fear. Still, curiosity soon got the better of me. This little cottage was clearly once loved. Wallpaper flaked off the walls with my touch. This was so much better than any historic home I had explored with Mum. I couldn't deny I wished her here now to share the experience. She would have loved it. In its day, the soft rose design of the wallpaper would have been very welcoming. It gave the cottage an Olde English feel. Was that the origin of its owners? As usual, my mind was swirling like a wild storm brewing.

The kitchen was basic, with a steel sink and wooden benchtop. A worn chopping board and glass water jug sat on the bench. Yellow cups hung from a rack under the small cupboards above the sink. I opened the cupboards below and fell back, startled as a mouse ran between my legs, scurrying out the open front door. Gathering myself, I counted a few odd plates, bowls and glasses neatly stacked inside. Above the sink was another small window, the same lace curtains covered its murky glass. I could see where once a garden had been.

I imagined many moons ago, a previous occupant gazing out, just as I was now. What was their life like? What brought them out here to this little cottage in the middle of nowhere? Were they happy? This place felt almost as if someone just walked out on it all that time ago.

As I turned to face the wooden set of drawers, I noticed something resting on top. I recognised it immediately. Sitting just behind an old photo in a frame was a large lapis lazuli stone.

'Why on earth would this be left here?'

My voice seemed to bounce off the walls and for a moment I felt like an unwelcome intruder.

Picking up the dusty frame, I looked at the man in the picture. He stood alone in what appeared to be a foreign land. Unlike the bush that surrounded me, or the city I was accustomed to, his world was desolate and lifeless. He was leaning against a small mudstone dwelling. Its simple structure had a low door and no windows.

'I wonder how old this photo is. And who are you, mister?'

Was this the person who had lived here?

Something told me it wasn't. However, it seemed plausible he was a person who related to those who had. He was wearing old loose clothing. He looked tired and dirty but at peace. A patterned scarf wound around his head, and a leather satchel bag was slung across his shoulder. It was hard to tell the man's age, but he was lean and strong. His eyes were piercing, dark in colour, much like my own.

'What secrets are you hiding behind those eyes? I wish you could tell me. No one else will tell me about my family.'

As I was about to put the frame down, I caught a glimpse of something blue in the picture. I quickly wiped more dust from the frame, straining to see. The man was wearing a necklace.

Squealing, I felt the blood rush to my ears. It was the same lapis cross not only my mum, and Negeenah had, but that I, too, had owned.

This feels big.

There was no denying it now. Somehow, this man had to be connected to me, my family, and our past. But how?

Adrenaline was causing hyper alertness. Lingering at the small cot next to the bed, I closed my eyes and pretended I could smell the scent of a baby. I imagined the tiny infant being rocked in the chair by the fire on a cold and clear winter's night. How many family members had lived here?

I opened the larger chest. It contained nothing other than two small books. Both were bound in black leather, soft to touch. In one, the text was in a foreign language that I didn't recognise. I took a photo with my phone, planning to search for its origin later on the computer. The other book was a bible, very old and clearly well-read. Whoever had lived here was bilingual.

The smaller chest's lock was jammed tight. Down on my hands and knees I wrestled to release it with the pry bar, but to no avail. Impatiently I scrunched up my face before sighing heavily.

Next time, there is always next time, Grace.

It was getting late, and I knew I needed to get back before Negeenah returned from town. She went there weekly for supplies. Where had Rex gone? He had followed me to the cottage on the last part of the journey but had not come inside. I was so transfixed that I had forgotten he had, in fact, accompanied me. There were so many things about this place that made me want to stay.

'I need to know your story,' I whispered as I left.

Secrets

Two weeks here. That's gone fast.

While researching the homestead's name, I had learned it was also of Afghan origin. It meant 'beautiful flowers.' I made an immediate link to the cottage, with its sweet scent and abundance of colour veiling its entrance. It seemed like a lifetime ago I was in the city. I closed my eyes, trying to recall the sights, sounds and smells, to remember the energy and fast pace of life in my beloved Melbourne.

I had arrived here so filled with anger and despair and battling the anxiety and confusion that raged within. Still, I managed to conceal the bubbling lava that lay just beneath the surface. I had a father somewhere whom I'd never met. Why hadn't he come for me? Did he even know I existed?

As much as I didn't want to admit it, things had begun to change. Intrigue, and maybe this location, had quelled some of my pain. This place was somehow beginning to grow on me. Maybe it was because I had a new direction, a distraction or dare I say it, a purpose. I was actively investigating the mysteries of Zarnish Estate, and I intended to do whatever it took to uncover more than those around me wanted me to.

I'd had very little contact with my mum since arriving. She called to chat every couple of days, but mostly I found myself too angry to talk. I always kept the conversation brief, telling her what she wanted to hear so she would hang up and leave me alone. I knew she was hurting, too. I could hear it in her voice. Part of me hated myself for tormenting her. But the other part knew she deserved it. She had ruined my life, with no explanation as to why. What hurt the most was the realisation my close relationship with my mum was not what I had thought it to be.

I believed we were invincible together, a power team.

No secrets. No lies.

She told me I was the number one thing in her life.

I believed her.

I was stupid.

The night after I'd visited the cottage, however, I decided to quiz her a little, without giving away any of what I'd been up to, of course.

'Mum, can you tell me more about Negeenah, please?' I had pleaded.

'I know you said to ask her, but she avoids talking about herself. She just starts banging on about one of her stories. I never know if they're real or fictional.'

There was an awkward silence on the other end of the phone line. Mum was thinking hard about how best to answer, was my bet.

'It's time you search for the clues, Grace. There are more than enough out there. If you are clever, which I know you are, you will find out what you need to know.'

So, I was right, there is something more going on out here.

I pushed for more.

'But Mum, that is so ridiculous. Surely you can hear yourself?'

I became more agitated as she went on, despite the pact I'd made with myself to stay calm.

'She is my family, too,' I protested. 'I have a right to know where she came from. Is this just a scheme both of you cooked up to keep me distracted? I'm not playing this game. All I want is to come home!'

Without realising, my tone was becoming louder and more aggressive. I was picking at my fingernails as I always do when I'm pissed off. Wincing from the self-inflicted pain, yet at the same time almost oblivious to the blood I was drawing from pulling the quicks out and scratching them bare.

'I know you do, Grace.'

Her tone had changed, she was attempting to pacify me.

'But first, you need to trust me, have some faith. That place and all its history is just what you need.'

I was furious as I ended the call. She had got to me again.

Why did she always win?

I took some deep breaths, closing my eyes. Sitting in the dark, bare feet dangling off the edge of the veranda, I felt very alone. Rex was there, of course, but tonight it made little difference. I felt the darkness inside me. The stars were so bright above, the deep yellow of the moon making it look magnified in the black sky. Stars always reminded me just how little I was in this big world. So small and insignificant, yet my pain felt so immense.

I could smell the scent of jasmine floating in the warm breeze. I forced the sweet night air into my lungs, willing it to replace some of my bitterness. The music of the cicadas filled my head, their song dulling my anger slowly.

'My family have taught me one thing, Rex, if you really want something, there's only one person you can count on... yourself.'

He wagged his tail, yawning and stretching out on the cool deck.

'Not a care in the world have you, old boy. That's because you already know all the secrets this place has to tell, I bet.'

It was time to search the big old barn. The next morning, I waited until Tracker and Bluey loaded up the tractor with hay before I made my move. Almost fondly, I smiled. I swear they always wore the same clothes. How many times had I agonised over what to wear in Melbourne? Image is important. People my age judge you harshly if you don't look right. Life here was different. It was simple for them. But how was it enough? I would go insane!

They headed out slowly in the tractor towards the vast patchwork of paddocks to feed the stock. I could see the cows were alert to them, and they began ambling toward the pair. Tracker's laugh echoed across the field. Bluey seemed to hang on every word he was saying. He, too, had a broad grin. I should introduce myself to him, I suppose, but not today. Waiting till the coast was clear, I stepped away from my hiding spot behind the wisteria surrounding the house. I willed the men not to look back as I made my way quickly to the barn.

Surprised as I entered at the enormity of the space, I scanned the high beamed ceilings and a loft floor. Perhaps I wasn't meant to be here, but I didn't care. After all, I hadn't been told to stay out. It was not on the list of rules Negeenah had insisted I follow.

I made a beeline for the back corner. Packed against the wall were a plethora of boxes and chests. There had to be something interesting here. Taking a quick minute to listen and ensure I was alone, I wasted no time in investigating. There were so many old books, clothes, paintings and household items. All covered in a thick coating of dust and an unnerving amount of cobwebs.

Why was all this stuff out here? Half of it looks like it should be in a museum somewhere, not shoved in the corner of a barn.

Bound with string, I found a bundle of old envelopes. Unopened mail, addressed to Zarnish Estate but to a married couple, dated around twenty years ago. The letters and documents had come from overseas.

Afghanistan.

'Azyan and Asadi Karzai. Now that's a mouthful. So, Negeenah didn't always live here alone then?'

I sat contently scanning the envelopes for some time, oblivious of the dirty concrete floor. Should I open one? Tilting my head to the side observing them, I scanned the barn for onlookers.

I liked it here. The smell was earthy, of straw and leather mixed with diesel. It was so quiet. Interestingly, that would normally cause me anxiety. But for the first time in a while, I noticed I was happy to just be surrounded by silence. Often a quiet space was a chance for my mind to get overactive, for my thoughts to create their own chaos. Then my body would react with its own physical symptoms from the inner panic. But not today.

My breath hitched as I spied the pile of photos jammed into one of the chests. There was no order to them, like they had been shoved in there without a care. Had someone been trying to hide them quickly? Or just pack them away so their memories could be forgotten maybe. My mind was in overdrive as I pulled them free.

In an instant, I recognised their faces. The same striking young couple in my dream, no mistaking it. The gravely ill woman. The desperate man, her husband. The couple in the framed picture on the hallway wall.

A knot formed in my stomach.

I had to presume now that they were the original owners here. Flicking through the handful of photos I'd grabbed, in many the couple were dressed quite formally. It was clearly the same farmhouse in the background, Zarnish Estate, for sure. Despite the photos being black and white, they still reflected the beauty of the gardens, and the house itself, bursting with life and charm.

But who were they? And where were they now? Had they died?

As I was about to pack the photos away and continue searching the rest of the barn, one photo fell to the floor from the pile I had in my hand. Staring, I became dizzy and needed to sit. My mind confused by the familiarity of the image. Deja vu maybe?

I feel like I've lived this.

The photo portrait was of a middle-aged lady and a younger woman, both standing in the vegetable garden. Sitting in the dirt were two small babies, happily playing in the flowers. These people were not Azyan and Asadi. My skin began to tingle, I shuddered to my core.

It can't be.

The brown leather hat the middle-aged woman was wearing looked like the same hat Negeenah had worn every day since I'd arrived. I was sure of it. But more unnerving, were the babies. One wore a yellow dress, the other white.

Exactly like the dream I'd lived a thousand times.

Naivety

What started as a bit of googling here and there, soon turned into something far bigger. I'll admit, I did try to hack into Negeenah's private files, but she certainly knew how to hide her stuff.

I began obsessing about Afghanistan, certain now that it was Negeenah's birthplace. That also meant Mum and I were connected too. The thought gave me goosebumps.

I'd spent hours so far, trolling the internet for anything I could get my eyes on. Afghanistan had a brutal history. Even today, the country was in much unrest, and in diverse contrast to my world. Why hadn't my private education enlightened me of the struggles, hardship and devastation these beautiful people had faced? Still, they remained threatened to this day.

The Taliban reign had been barbaric. Now I couldn't help but see the connection with my mum's advocacy for women's rights. For as long as I could remember, it had been a life driver, a passion close to her heart. The conditions the Afghan woman faced was more than I could comprehend. How did anyone really get over that kind of torture?

I still don't get why you wouldn't tell me, Mum.

I tried to imagine Negeenah in Afghanistan. Had she been there when forced change had happened so rapidly? Women went from being reasonably independent, educated and progressive before the mid-90s, to prisoners in their own world. Confined to their homes, their bodies were forcibly covered from head to toe. Women were stripped of their rights by the new Taliban rules when their strict Sharia Law was enforced.

Imagine their fear; I can't. I read an online article that flicked a switch deep inside me, leaving me breathless, tears streaming down my face. Overwhelming feelings of shame and guilt thrashed around my head.

I'm just a tiny dot in this world.

A young woman, not much older than me, was desperate to help her ill child. She was all alone, banished to inside her home, but her child needed medical assistance. It was illegal for her to walk through the streets alone without a male chaperone. This was seen as a moral crime of indecency. Taking the risk to save her precious child, she left the safety of her home but didn't get far. Despite pleading for leniency from the merciless Taliban soldiers, she was beaten within an inch of her life, all the while sheltering her precious baby as best she could. This occurred out on the street, in broad daylight, only metres from a doctor's clinic. No one came to her aid, despite her terrified screams. She was brutally thrown in jail for her crime. Her child died there, in appalling conditions, in her mother's arms. This was not a story from long ago; it was 1998. Only seventeen years ago.

How could this possibly be the same world I lived in?

Okay, I'd been self-absorbed lately. But I had the right to be, surely? I can't apologise for not knowing the same hardship. But perhaps it was time I became a little more aware. Maybe if I tried by walking in another's shoes.

Yet, I can't do it.

The war inside me raged. Thoughts of good versus evil swirled. I stepped back from the computer increasing the distance from my confusion. Maybe I did have two versions of my inner self. I began the familiar scroll through my head, scrutinising my flaws.

I mess everything up.

I'd done some stupid things. But so had they, Mum and Simar. If only I had been told the truth, maybe then I could accept it.

Attempting to calm my addled brain, I sat on the floor close to Rex, stroking his back and began to write. Negeenah's age: 54. I knew this because she had told me she was born in a foreign land in 1961. Tonight was the first time my gran had given up any personal information. She'd let her guard down, just a little.

So had I.

Standing side by side, washing the dinner dishes in the kitchen, I'd been talking a little more about my life in the city. Swirling the soapy water through my hands had somehow lowered my guard. Negeenah listened intently. I liked this about her. She didn't bombard my brain with a million questions or give me advice I sure as hell didn't need.

'I understand, Gracie, it's hard being young. I remember thinking no one really listened to me. I also remember the feeling of having my rights taken away.'

Negeenah's eyes had narrowed, and as if in confusion, she'd held up her hands in a defensive stance.

'How old were you when you had my mum? Were you married?'
I sound so cringe worthy.

Negeenah had taken a while to answer. I watched her silently grip the stone around her neck. Taking a step back from the sink she stared at the ground, the colour draining from her face. From the next room the grandfather clock ticked louder than my own heartbeat.

But then, her energy seemed to switch again. Negeenah had just as quickly regained herself; she was good at that. Clearing her throat to answer, she looked straight at me.

'I was only 15 when I was blessed with your mum, Grace. She was to be my only child, but one I am very grateful for, as I am you. Yes, I was married. It was a long time ago now, another lifetime, it seems. So much has happened.'

The soapy dish had slipped from my hand, smashing loudly onto the tiled kitchen floor. Negeenah barely seemed to notice. But for me, its shatter brought clarity, I suddenly *saw* her.

'But you were only 15?'

As quickly as I had felt a connection with Negeenah in that moment, it was gone. I stood staring, waiting for an answer, but I could see our conversation was clearly over. Her stoic and introverted defences returned, guarding her again like a personal army. She began bustling around, cleaning up the smashed china. I felt frozen, unable to budge, yet all the while, she moved around me like nothing had happened.

Her mask was restored.

I was still processing her words, hours later.

'I bet you know the answers, hey Rex.'

He looked sleepily back at me, whining for me to keep patting him. I knew now that both my mum and Negeenah gave birth very young. Mum herself was 24 when I was born. But Negeenah's new admission was mind-blowing. Suddenly I saw her bravery. I'm 15 and couldn't possibly imagine having a baby. For one thing, I was too selfish. I had so much to learn and discover in the world yet, and the thought of being responsible for another life was simply more than I could fathom. Had Negeenah had a choice?

'Life is very different for an Afghan woman. When I was reading up on their culture the other day, I learned that for a long time, parents could give consent for their daughters to marry very young. It was often a business or money transaction which the young woman had no say in at all. Can you imagine! Man, if my parents tried to do that to me, I would be gone. Negeenah had to have been devastated. How could she not be? I wonder if she saw her family after that?'

Rex looked up as I spoke, twisting his head to one side, eyeing me intently.

Turning away from his judgements, I bit at my lip.

I had grossly underestimated Negeenah. Life had delt her a harsh hand.

As I wrote, I began to realise the timeline didn't add up. Maths was not my strong point but as far as I could see, it appeared possible my own mother may not have been born in Australia. This was something I'd never considered. As a shot of adrenaline provided me with new focus, I scribbled over the page, willing my brain to keep up. Luckily my iPhone had a calculator.

'So, Mum is 39 years old; she had me at 24.'

I put a tick next to that information on the page. So far, so good.

'My grandmother was born in 1961 and is now 54; she gave birth to my mum at the age of 15, in 1976.'

I scrunched up my face once again at the thought of becoming a mum so young, placing another tick on the page.

'So, the question is, did my grandma travel to Australia before she gave birth to my mum, or after?'

I thought hard. My brain was starting to hurt.

'If she did give birth in Australia, where was my grandfather? Why have neither she nor Mum ever mentioned him? How could Negeenah possibly have coped on her own out here with a new baby?'

I thought back to the photos I'd seen earlier that week. Azyan and Asadi, could they have helped her? They would have been too young.

My headache was growing intense now. I gulped down the Coke sitting beside me while rubbing at my temples. Thank goodness I'd finally convinced Negeenah to get me some on her last visit to town. I was addicted to the stuff. Throwing my chewed pencil onto my notepad, I let my body fall back onto the bed. There was one fact I knew with certainty, I had heaps I needed to find out. The question was, how?

Misjudged

In the evenings, Negeenah had proposed the idea of providing for my education while I was in home detention. Initially, of course, I had laughed in her face.

'That's ridiculous. Why would I want to do that?'

She was clearly stung by my response. I suppose it was a little harsh.

'Grace, you are missing a great deal of school. I can offer you tuition. You don't want to fall behind. When you return, it will be hard enough, and your final years are the most important. It's time you started thinking smart, girl. Grow up a bit.'

Ouch, that stung right back.

It was hard to argue with that. Interestingly, a month ago, I would have fought venomously, without question. Perhaps it was the notion that Negeenah was supporting my return home.

'Well, maybe we could give it a go. But I don't want to be locked into it every night. I've got things to do.'

Negeenah smirked at my response and instinctively I crossed my arms defensively.

'What is more important than knowledge, Gracie? Knowledge is power, you know. And education is the most compelling weapon for change. Especially for women.'

My arms fell to my side. I couldn't debate that. Truth be told, I felt empowered just absorbing her words. And as the nights went on, it was becoming crystal clear. Negeenah had no doubt once been an engaging and successful teacher. Her ability to explain content, pose questions, debate answers and propose ideas for further study were those only an experienced educator could possess.

I'd misjudged her again.

'Were you a teacher? This all seems to come very easily to you. I mean, I've been taught at a private school my whole life, but honestly, I've never learned like this.'

I'd spoken with true admiration, surprising myself a little. And looking back, there had been a shift between us in that moment. Perhaps she recognised the attempt at genuine communication from me, and this had prompted Negeenah to answer truthfully.

Was a new trust developing between us?

Did I dare let this happen?

'Yes, my child, I was a teacher back in my homeland. I was very blessed to have been educated myself when I married my husband. His mother was a teacher, too. I moved into their home, and much like we are doing, many evenings were spent with her teaching me. She was very passionate about women being exposed to knowledge and world affairs. This was rare in a woman of her time, so I was very lucky. In my new life, suddenly a long way from home, I was lonely and unsure of what would come next. So, I'd welcomed the distraction it provided.'

Negeenah's voice became soft like a whisper again.

'I was terrified. Being forced to marry when I was barely a woman myself; I was just 14. But without question, still one of the few lucky ones. My own family were miners, sourcing Lapis Lazuli stones. We were very poor. I was married off in order for my family to eat and survive. They were tough times. My husband was very old, 56 when we married, but he was a kind person. He was a businessman from Pakistan. I was treated well and educated, even after I had your mother. Sadly, many women I knew had a very different fate.'

So that's her connection to the Lapis Stone. And mine. OMG and I threw mine away!

Tears were welling in her eyes, I blinked furiously to keep my own at bay. It was not right to probe any further now. She had opened her heart and shared something very private with me. I felt humbled. I was too stunned to offer a reply anyway.

Leaning slightly closer, I tentatively reached out to hold her hand. Her glistening eyes lit up instantly as she gripped me back, squeezing my hand tightly. Her touch was strong, and her hands felt powerful. Tears spilled freely now between us.

So, Mum had been born in Afghanistan, too.

Time travel

It felt like an eternity since I'd been able to escape to the cottage again. In reality, it had only been a few days. Rex wandered ahead, as usual, breaking the morning cobwebs laced across the overgrown track. I had been wrong about him; Rex was good company. As much as I fought it, I grew fonder of him each day. I think he liked me, too. I hope so. I'd never known the love of a pet. Perhaps that was why I'd been quick to judge, assuming animals were a waste of time.

Was I too hasty in assuming a lot of things?

Well, people have been quick to judge *me*.

'I stand corrected, Rexy boy, you're a bit of all right.'

Smiling, I watched as he doubled back to check I was still coming. As he approached, I crouched down, smoothing the hair around his face. I liked how calm he made me feel when I patted him. At this moment, I felt untroubled.

I thought about Negeenah. She had read me some quotes I quite liked last night.

'Angry people are not always wise.'

True, I suppose. So maybe I wasn't as stupid as I thought lately. Maybe my circumstances had just blinded me a little. Maybe I wasn't broken, just bent the wrong way.

I stood still, raising my face to the sky and taking in the sounds and smells.

'Allow nature's peace to flow into you, as sunshine flows into trees.' John Muir wrote that, Gracie. Think on it.'

Negeenah always had a quote to share, but the difference was, now I allowed my ears to listen and my mind to absorb.

Today the babbling creek beside the cottage drew me instantly. It was peaceful and mesmerising, blocking out everything else. That was until Rex leapt into the water, splashing me from head to toe. The chill of the water was surprising yet refreshing respite from the heat of the day. I couldn't help but laugh as he shook himself off.

The sun was piercing overhead now. Looking down at my wet skin as I sat on the dusty bank, I smiled. I was more tanned than I'd ever been, both my arms and legs a deep brown. I had gained muscle, too, with all the walking. Come to think of it, I had more energy also.

Scanning my surrounds I could see that this fresh water supply could easily provide a family with water to drink and bathe in. The perfect spot to hide away from the world in fact.

'Is this what the family in the cottage were doing, Rex? And if that were the case, what on earth could they be hiding from? Maybe it was Negeenah's old house? Had things gone so horribly wrong in her homeland, she had to relocate?'

It was pretty obvious now that would easily have been a reality for Negeenah. It wouldn't have been hard to piss off the wrong people during the Taliban reign. Rex gave an excited bark as I tousled his wet fur.

When I had dared ask about the cottage again, Negeenah had become tight-lipped. Something about it clearly haunted her. We all had our demons I suppose. Plenty of times since arriving, I had engaged in my own pity party. But was her past as bad as mine? After all, I was the one who had been forced to leave Melbourne, expelled from school, lost the man I had thought to be my dad, and realised my mum had lied to me my whole life. And now it seems most of my friends have ditched me. Stuck up traitors.

No matter how hard I tried, I was not enough for them.
Stop it, Grace.

That same disjointed feeling began to sweep through me.

Breathe. I am here, I am now. The past is gone.

Samir's image flashed through my mind. I felt my stomach harden as I swallowed hard.

Who the hell is he really? If I was being honest, the reality was that I knew him very little. Growing up, he had been absent much of the time. Most of my memories were just Mum and me.

'Away on business,' Misha had always said.

'What business? What was it that he even did?'

I knew he travelled to many countries, once seeing his passport had confirmed this. I was told he was a businessman who worked for a global stock company. Now a little more fell into place. His name. Another name common in Afghanistan. So where exactly had Mum met my real dad?

Memories of Samir returning home when I was about five swirled. Another long business trip had seen him absent from home for weeks. I remember launching myself into his arms as he swooped me up, spinning me around until I was dizzy. I wore my best party dress that day, put the prettiest blue ribbons in my hair. My dress was red with yellow spots. It always made me feel like Cleopatra. So dumb. I remember that day vividly because I had been shocked at how different he looked. He had a long dark beard. It felt like wire, so prickly. He had shaved it off that night.

The reality was, I thought now, in the last five or six years, he hadn't been around much at all. But he was still the only Dad I had ever known, and I loved him. At least, I thought I did. Did he ever love me? I racked my brain, trying to remember details of my parents being together, spending time as a family. When together, they were always pleasant to each other, like business partners themselves, really. Never had I seen them share affection nor been subjected to them fighting. That was my normal.

Come on Grace, flick this mood off.

As if reading my thoughts Rex licked at my face, softening my heart in an instant.

Be present.

Sitting in the shade, the coolness of the creek bank was magical. I stretched back, lifting my face toward the dappled sky. Sensing movement nearby, I was momentarily startled. She was back. I instantly recognised her vivid blue. Today the gold flecks on the wingtips sparkled brightly. Was this butterfly following me? I stayed very still as the tiny dancer twirled around my neck and shoulders. Once again, she drew me in completely with her beauty.

Negeenah had told me butterflies were not uncommon in the Northern Territory. However, it was rare to see one this far inland. She recalled the story of when she first arrived here. A blue butterfly had followed her around, too, for weeks, always appearing when she least expected it, often when she felt unbalanced or disturbed. She said it gave her the courage to press on. I didn't tell her the same thing had happened to me.

'Butterflies are very spiritual, Gracie,' she had said. 'They symbolise change, a representation of resurrection and hope. They are said to encourage us to embrace the transformation we need, live a better life.'

Of course, I had thought her to be full of shit, but what if she was right?

Today, no sooner had she come than my butterfly was gone.

My thoughts returned to Mum. Misha had always been very independent. I loved this about her. I admired it. I had always wanted to be the same as her in every way possible. So many times, I would dress up in her clothes, put her makeup on, and jewellery. I would pretend I was at work, prancing around. I had always looked up to her as a goddess. My very own Cleopatra.

Pathetic.

Mum's features were striking. She was naturally tall and slim and always wore the most beautiful dresses that flowed, accentuating her frame. She had dark, almost black eyes with long lashes. Her thick black hair shone, and her ruby lips were so captivating when she smiled. I was always so proud walking into a room with her. Despite her presence, she rarely noticed when people stopped and stared. I did.

Misha was a natural-born lawyer, I'd watched her in action many times. Her intelligence and approach were something to behold. Mum always made me believe I could make a difference in the world, just like her. I was not so sure anymore.

Who was she really?

Did she, too, wear a mask like mine?

Mum was fiercely private, and I grew up never really having many close friends around. Come to think of it, she acted very similarly to Negeenah. No question they looked alike, but now I was seeing how closely linked their personalities were.

Was this related to their past?

They were seemingly always looking over their shoulder, suspicious. Always ready to pack up and run, but from what? Growing up, we always had a bag packed in the entrance hall cupboard. It contained clothes, toiletries, money, our passports and documentation.

'In case of an emergency, Gracie, you just never know what life may bring.'

I had always just accepted this as normal. It was not.

I'd seen the same set-up here at Zarnish. I shouldn't have snooped, but Negeenah's bag caught my eye in the broom closet one day. I didn't get the chance to go through it, but I could see what it was for sure.

Surely, it's all a bit over the top ladies, don't you think?

'If I can't find out while I am here, once I get home, I am going to make Mum tell me what the hell is going on. Then we can sort it out and get on with our lives. Seriously, it can't be that complicated.'

Before I knew it, I was opening the door to the cottage. A little more accustomed to moving now, the effort required was far less. Rex ambled around outside before resting in what shade the little veranda offered. I was determined to search for more clues as I sat my red backpack down on the table and got out my notebook and pen. A bit nerdy but hey, I might as well use the brains I got my scholarship with.

The large lapis lazuli stone caught my eye once again, glistening on top of the old drawers. I tried to imagine the caves from which it was mined and what it looked like in a natural state. I made a note to check this out on the computer when I returned. I hadn't picked the stone up when I was last here. This time I couldn't resist.

Surprising me with its weight, the stone was smooth and cold, with flecks of gold, darker blue and white running from top to bottom. Pressing it into my cheek and then my chest, my eyes pricked with tears, as my breath slowed. Strange memories began to take hold. Overcome by sudden deep heaviness, I stumbled back with slow languid movements, sitting heavily on the small bed.

Was it the heat? I felt as though my awareness had dulled. Tunnel vision set in. I gripped the stone tightly.

Shivering, I could feel the intense cold, sense the dampness, even before my eyes adjusted to the new darkness. Squinting to focus, I searched to find the cause of the dim light glowing in the distance. And that smell! Jamming my hands over my mouth and nose I held my breath as long as possible.

What the hell?

The earth around me was hard and uneven. Whatever I was leaning against was wet. Rock maybe? I sat hugging my legs around my chest, shivering, both from cold and confusion.

Something told me I was not alone, not that any of this made one bit of sense. I was in some sort of mineshaft. I dared not make a sound, fearing even my rampant heartbeat was too loud. My breath, expelling hot air, would it be seen?

It had happened again.

But where was I this time?

Quietly, I got up and looked around. As my eyes became accustomed to the surroundings, I could see the cave was quite large. Lanterns barely lit up the corridors, which were joined by more narrow dark passages. The freezing air hurt my chest; I felt a little breathless despite barely moving. My eyes stung, and I needed to cough as the air was damp and thick with dust. I could smell smoke.

Abruptly, I jolted back, as yelling broke through my thoughts. Crouching again, I willed myself to blend in with the cave wall, terrified they would see me.

Who were they?

I watched as three men neared, animated in speech and pointing to a part of the cave further down. Their dialect sounded very similar to that spoken by the young woman in my first dream. The men's eyes were hollow and red from mine dust, their hands calloused, and arms covered in cuts and bruises. They wore ragged, dirty, long loose clothing. The men appeared middle-aged, with beards and dark hair. They had scarves covering their heads, leather satchels on their backs and carried lanterns and sticks. Clearly agitated, the men looked worn out and as frozen as I was.

Relief swept through me as the men began heading toward a fire burning further down in the cave. Once there, they crouched and huddled around it, continuing to talk in low voices. I got to my feet, aware of the rocky, uneven ground and how easily I could fall. I touched the walls of the cave for balance, its surface was freezing and rough.

The men had started to move again and were getting further away from me. Soon I'd lose sight of them if I didn't follow. Was it better to stay or go? Deciding to follow, I picked up my pace but without warning I was met head-on by another two men of similar appearance.

I froze. Should I run or try to explain to the men I had no idea how I got here? Or should I fight?

With my heart feeling like it would explode through my chest, I stared them straight in the eyes. I had no choice now but to stand firm.

I braced.

But they simply kept walking past, like I was not there at all. Invisible… just like before.

'Hey!' I yelled out to them. 'Please, can you help me?'

Clearly, they were unaware of my presence, were oblivious to my calling. Confused, I turned and headed further into the cave where I had seen the first group of men. I followed the lanterns toward their voices. Approaching tentatively, I tried to appear confident as I once again spoke.

'Please, hey there, please, can you help me?'

I was less than a metre away from them now. It made no sense, but I knew they could not see nor hear me. They simply carried on like I did not exist. One man caught my eye. For a moment, I thought we'd connected. I was sure our eyes had locked. Like a mirror, his eyes were the same colour and shape as mine, strangely familiar.

It was the man from the photo in the cottage, no question.

What the hell was happening?

In my haste to follow the men, I hit my head on a sharp rock lining the low roof of the mine shaft. Crying out in pain, I stumbled and collapsed to the ground. I could feel the rough ground cut through my bare legs, gashing my knee. I grabbed at the side of my forehead with one hand, my knee with the other, willing the pain to subside. I could feel the blood already trickling down the side of my brow. This was not good.

'Help me, please. Somebody… please!'

The pain was making me nauseous and disoriented, my body began shaking and time skewed.

Certain I could feel warm blood on the side of my head, I lay curled up on the ground wincing in pain and too scared to move. Becoming aware something or someone was close, I flinched at their touch. A gentle nudge from behind was trying to get me to move. Opening my eyes, I was confused by a bright light.

Rex?

Just moments ago, everything had been so dark. Coughing, I attempted to sit up as my lungs searched for oxygen. The respite of clean, dry air was a welcome change from the damp and dust in the mine.

Rex was by my side.

But how?

Licking my face, he pressed his body into mine. He whined, staring at me, pawing me out of concern as I sat, still disoriented. I was no longer in the mine, instead back on the little bed in the cottage. The large lapis stone I had lifted off the drawers earlier was still in my lap. Confused, I forced some deep breaths.

Suddenly I remembered my injuries. My body had hurt all over, and my head had throbbed from the gash. How would I get out of here if I was injured? Nobody knew I was here. I had gone from being freezing cold to clammy with sweat. I reached my forehead and gently prodded around for the wound, but there was nothing there. No cut, no blood at all. I looked down at where I was sure I had cut my legs again, nothing. Everything was just like it had been before. No dust from the mines, no dampness from the ground, no injuries.

'I don't understand, Rex.'

He tilted his head beside me on the bed and gave a friendly bark. I reached for him, needing a hug. I'd never embraced an animal before and it felt good. Rex pushed his body into mine, like he knew.

'It was so real, Rex, I was there. I don't even know where 'there' is. I was in a mine, and not in Australia, I'm sure of that.'

Swinging my legs off the bed and onto the floor, I stood, instantly becoming lightheaded. Walking gingerly over to the chest of drawers. I replaced the lapis stone carefully and picked up the photo frame to inspect it more closely.

'And *you* were there.' I whispered to the man staring back at me.

'We connected, I'm sure of it. Who are you?'

I sat on the front steps of the cottage for a long while, furiously writing down everything I could remember. I had no idea how this could be happening to me right now, but I had to trust myself, believe it was for a reason. Did everyone experience episodes like this? I hadn't really ever asked, so maybe people did.

Or maybe I was just bat crazy.

Since dreams had been a big part of my life, I didn't feel scared or threatened by them anymore. Mum had taught me to see them as a blessing. Despite this, the emotion and drama they inflicted were exhausting and these latest episodes seemed very real.

'Dreams have been an important part of history in many cultures and in many religions, Gracie.'

I remembered my mum holding me close one night, having woken from a deep sleep startled and confused. She had whispered words I had never forgotten.

'They are not to be feared. We can learn from them. Maybe they don't always make sense at the time, but one day they will. Look at them like pieces of a puzzle. Not everyone gets to dream like you, Gracie; it's a gift. Perhaps because you are so intelligent, your subconscious mind can see things others cannot. Perhaps they are even trying to reveal things to you.'

I'd only been about twelve at the time. I didn't want the burden of dreams, being twelve was hard enough.

'I just want to be me, Mum; I just want to be normal.'

My mum had thrown back her head in laughter, hugging me tightly, kissing my forehead.

'You are so much more, my dear girl. And thank goodness for that. The world doesn't need more 'normal'. It needs you. Soon you will see.'

Mum doesn't think that anymore.

Before returning to the homestead, I visited the creek again.

Kneeling beside the cool water, I splashed it over my body, refreshing and soothing on my skin. As I pushed my hands down beneath the moving water, they became blurry under the bubbles. I swirled them around, causing the dirt on the bottom to stir. My life was like this, really. All stirred up and blurry. At least the water had a clear direction. It knew where it was heading, surging forward with great purpose.

Would I ever know?

I thought I did once.

Stupid girl.

I knew nothing.

Bashir

The lapis stone had to be connected to my dream. Was Afghanistan the only place in the world where they were mined? I remembered how many times I had played the game Minecraft with friends. The lapis lazuli stone was a big asset to find in the game. I wish this mystery was as easy as being a little Lego man in a Minecraft world.

I knew it was time and carefully approached the conversation at dinner the following evening, bracing for it to go pear-shaped.

'I used to have a necklace just like yours, Gran.'

My voice was a little high pitched and I cleared my throat. Like clockwork, Negeenah moved her hand protectively over the deep blue stone around her neck.

'I decided it wasn't for me.'

'Why ever not, child?'

She spoke in a calm tone, her eyes soft, giving me the confidence to continue.

'I suspect the necklace was of great importance to the person who gave it to you.'

I thought on this for a minute, head bowed.

'Maybe, but, well, that was before. Mum always told me my family had it made for me. I don't even know who my family is anymore.'

I looked directly into Negeenah's eyes, which narrowed, as if in confusion. Picking at my nails again under the table, the air between us was suddenly thick.

'Yes, you do, Gracie, we are your family, your mum and me. And there were many before us, too, who loved you very much.'

Negeenah reached out and grasped my hand. Would she feel the heat surging through my body?

'Then tell me about them, Gran, please! Or at least tell me why this necklace is so important.'

I could hear the begging in my tone, but I didn't care, I was desperate for answers. I'd been kidding myself to think it didn't matter. For months, I had been telling myself I could make it on my own. Convinced myself I didn't need anybody. But right now, at this moment, I knew that was a lie. I desperately wanted to know who I was, who my family were. I needed direction on just how I could possibly fit into this world any longer.

The homestead was so quiet. The old clock ticking on the wall was the only sound breaking the silence. I waited for Negeenah to respond. Taking a long, slow breath, she sighed wearily.

'Secrets are a burden, lass; they wear you down. Misha and I, we never wanted that for you.'

Releasing my hand, she rose and began to clear away the evening meal. I stared at her intently, tensing I gripped the table as the events of the last few months swirled and crushed me within. Another internal storm was brewing.

She is not going to fob me off again.

I'd done everything in my power up until now to try to understand, but truth be told, I understood very little. I'd listened as Samir had told me his truth. Despite arguing with my mum one too many times, Misha remained silent on the topic. I had been moved out against my will, sent here, to this place.

I'd submitted, living the way Negeenah had asked me to. But, right now, I'd had enough. I stood abruptly, knocking my cup over and spilling hot tea over the table. Negeenah turned and froze as she looked me up and down.

Enough.

'I'm leaving tonight, Negeenah; I mean it. Unless you start giving me some answers. I know you want to, I can feel it. I have the right to know. If you really are my family, then I deserve to be told what the hell is going on! Why all the secrets? What could possibly be so bad?'

I was yelling now, standing with my fists clenched, tears streaming down my face. I no longer cared if she saw my weakness. I was weary, too.

'Are you even my family? Well… are you, Negeenah?'

She slumped down into the nearest chair, her shaking hands cupping her face. Rex pulled at my jumper as though telling me to sit. I did, slowly, never taking my eyes off Negeenah. I didn't even attempt to wipe the tears away. I waited silently for her to talk.

'For many generations, my family have been miners in Afghanistan. My father and grandfather worked their entire lives mining and selling lapis lazuli stones. We lived in a small town in the Badakhshan province, not far from the Kocha Valley. This is such a beautiful place in the world. I remember it all like it was yesterday; I miss it every day. The land was lush and green. Rivers flowed, and the air was clean. It was a sight to behold, I tell you, Grace, to look up at the mystical blue mountains that surrounded our village. Their peaks were covered in snow most of the year. When I was a girl, I pretended I had x-ray vision and could see the precious stones inside those mountains.'

Negeenah paused to have a drink of water, still shaking, her voice was wavering.

'I was born into poverty, like so many Afghan families. These were hard times. But we made our own fun, and I was happy. My family were loving, and I cared for them very much. Year after year, my father would go to the mines. My grandfather and uncles would go, too. They were often gone for many months, as it took a long time to get enough stones to sell. Conditions were very tough for the men. For the women left behind, it was hard also. But for them, it was much worse. The men went to live in what was called village housing. Only the miners lived there. We could not visit, and no women ever went there. They lived in a community of anywhere up to two thousand men for sometimes six months of the year. They lived in little stone huts, all closely built together.'

I listened intently, fascination quickly dissolving my anger. I had thirsted for this information, taking it all in, even the fact that Negeenah's description of the huts matched the photo in the cottage.

'The lapis stone was our livelihood. Just like I know your mum shared with you, we were always told of its magical wonders and powers. The lapis stone was as important as religion to us. When I was 14, I was forced to leave and marry. As devastated as I was, I knew it was something I must do to help with my family's debt. As I have told you, it was not unusual for a family to sell a daughter. I will never forget the look in my mother's eyes as she hugged me that final time. I tried to be brave for her. It was better I was naive to what was to come. My lapis stone connection kept me going. It is what I have always believed in when I've had nowhere else to turn. It helped me stay strong, have faith and get through as best I could. Especially when your mum came along, Gracie, I was just a babe myself.'

Tears welled up in Negeenah's eyes and her pained look caused a sharpness in my chest.

'I was just a babe… my body was barely that of a woman, and suddenly, I was a mother.'

Her voice trailed off and became but a whisper. I sat in stunned silence, crying for her. That was enough for tonight, my other questions could wait. I reached out and held Negeenah's hand again, moving closer, closing the distance between us.

Completely spent as I crawled into bed, too tired to even change into my PJs. It was a warm evening anyway. I welcomed the light breeze coming in through the French doors, flopping on top of the doona, sighing. Yes, undoubtedly, I had greatly underestimated how tough Negeenah's life had been.

'Why did she end up here, though, Rex?'

I shoved him, suggesting he get off the bed, as his warm body just increased the heat too much. He stretched a little but refused to get off, pretending he was oblivious to my prodding.

Sleep would prove hard tonight. I tried to relax my tense body beside him, to still my mind.

Eventually, in the early hours of the morning, I felt myself finally drifting from my ramped thoughts.

A loud explosion shook my body awake. Sitting upright and swallowing rapidly I tried desperately to adjust to the darkness. The air surrounding me had changed, and the coolness of night had set in.

Sliding across my bed to get up and shut the open French doors I froze mid movement; this rough surface was not my bed.

My eyes adjusted quickly, and I could see I was in the corner of a small room, one I hadn't seen before. The makeshift bed I had been lying on was nothing more than a few rough blankets made up on the hard dirt floor below.

I caught my breath, comprehending suddenly wherever I was, I was not alone.

A man was here, too.

Why did this keep happening?

The air was so bitterly cold, the kind of chill that made your nose hurt and your fingers numb. I wrapped my arms around my bare skin, feeling the goosebumps along my shoulders. Returning was the same tightness and restriction in my breathing I'd experienced in the mineshaft. But the smell in the air was different. A slightly smoky aroma, mixed with earth and damp rock, was the best I could describe it.

Silently I scanned my surrounds. The dwelling had another crumpled bed made up of similar old blankets in the opposite corner. The roof was low, and there were no windows. A bulky wooden door was the only way in or out. Hanging from a bolt in the wall was a large canvas backpack. Beside the door was a long stick, reminding me of the hiking poles I had used on school camps. The door was open slightly, revealing darkness with only a slither of the moon and a few stars.

From what I could make out, the walls around me were made of hard mud, as was the uneven floor. The only other items in this small space were in the middle of the room: two wooden stools and an old crate used as a makeshift table. On the table were a few bits and pieces, but it was hard to make them out from the corner I cowered in.

A bowl and tin cup, maybe some bread. I could see a burning oil lantern, identical to those I had seen in the mineshaft. A man was sitting with his back to me. He wore loose dark clothing and no shoes. His beard covered much of his face. He wore a scarf around his neck and an old hat, dark curls escaped the edge of the headpiece. Even in the dim light, I could see he was covered in dust and dirt.

The man looked middle-aged and appeared to be carving something in wood. He held a small box in one hand and a long slender knife in the other. I could hear the scraping on the wood, slow and precise as if he was well versed in his craft. There were no other sounds in the room, but I could hear muffled voices somewhere close by.

I was startled again by another loud explosion, close enough that it rattled the spoon resting in the bowl. The man looked up at this sudden intrusion, resting the box and knife on the table. He rose and stretched, then he knelt on the dirty floor of the hut as if praying silently. He remained there for some time. I couldn't see his face nor make out his whispered prayers.

I contemplated what to do next as I battled the strange mixture of fear and curiosity. The man seemed calm, and from what I could see, apart from the knife, there were no other weapons or evidence he would harm me. I breathed in, building the confidence to speak as I stood silently.

Suddenly the heavy wooden door was thrust open. A large older man stood in the doorway. He had a similar canvas bag on his back and carried his own long wooden stick and lantern. He spoke quickly and *with urgency to the man who was still on his knees, his prayers now interrupted.*

'Hello?' I had blurted it out before really thinking through my actions.

'Excuse me, I am sorry to intrude, but I need…'

Stopping mid-sentence, I could see it was just like my other dreams. Tentatively I took some steps toward the pair, but they remained oblivious to me, deep in conversation.

'Hello?'

Nothing. I stepped in between the two men, needing to be certain.

'My name is Grace. Can you hear me? Can you see me?'

The older man, grinning from ear to ear, was urgently beckoning the younger man to come with him, the pair seeming excited now. Had they had encouraging news? The man put on some sandals and took his green metal water bottle from beside his bed. From the hook at the front door, he grabbed his backpack and stick and proceeded to leave, walking closely out behind the older man.

Whatever was going on, I intended to follow.

Dawn was approaching over the roofline of the houses beyond, and a thin layer of ice covered the ground. The men stood huddled outside the open door trying to warm themselves by the small pit fire in the alley way. Others began to arrive and were greeted warmly.

Standing in the doorway I cast my eye back over the hut. Getting my phone out, I took snaps of each angle of the house. I zoomed in on the old crate with the belongings on top. Would these images still be on my phone when I woke? Did it work like that? I admired the wooden box that had been so delicately carved. Overwhelmingly, I felt like I had seen this before.

It was then I saw the photo. Just a single picture.

Quickly I moved toward the crate, dropping to my knees in the dirt. My mouth went dry, and I blinked rapidly trying to process what I was seeing.

'How could this possibly be?'

I stared for a long time, my body stinging with discomfort. I dared not touch the photo of the young couple. The picture was only centimetres away from my face now, but I feared it would disappear. They were hugging, clearly happy, smiling widely for the camera. There was no mistaking it. The lady in the photo was none other than Misha. A younger version of Mum, but it was her.

Time slowed.

Who was this man? Then, with the force of a powerful wave knocking me under a swirling sea, the realization hit.

'It's you!' I whispered, my voice disbelieving. 'Your photo is in the cottage. And I saw you in my last dream.'

Grabbing the photo, I hugged it to my chest. Desperate to comprehend, I searched the photo straining to see the man outside who had been in this very room only moments before.

How could I have not recognised him?

It was unmissable now. Keeping the photo close, I headed back to the door, staring intently at the man just metres from me, who at one point had also known my mum.

So how does he fit into this story?

Pulled abruptly from my rapid thoughts, I became aware the men had begun moving away from the hut. Keen to discover more about my surroundings, I had to follow. The smell of smoke was strong, and the light hazy.

The cramped street was mostly dirt and rubble. On each side small houses lined the narrow gateway. They were all identical, low-lined mud brick, none had windows. All had just one wooden door to enter and provide light. Lanterns were glowing along the street, becoming less intense as the daylight grew stronger. A number of small fires were burning, some had billies or pans on them. Reused bits of rope strung up the men's washing.

Another loud explosion pierced the air. My eyes followed the gazes of the men as they stared toward the surrounding mountains. They didn't look alarmed, more so as if it was something they expected.

Smiling triumphantly, I knew instantly where I was. From my

research on the Internet and the beautiful descriptions Negeenah had shared, this had to be the mining village out from the Kocha Valley.

Somehow, I was witness to life as a miner, lapis stone miners no less. I was in Afghanistan. I knew this humbling moment would replay many times in my head.

I followed the men as they moved away from the housing. They began a steep climb up a narrow, rocky path. I could only assume this climb would lead us to a mine. The cool air made my lungs sting, which had to be due to the high altitude. Despite all this, I couldn't deny I was intrigued, and dare I say excited.

My bright mood was short-lived, however. A mist began settling over the mountain. The rising sun disappeared, and the air was becoming increasingly thick and deathly cold. I felt the sharp pain in my chest worsen as I tried to keep up with the men. It was difficult to draw a breath deep enough to fill my lungs. The path was slippery, as it was carpeted in small rocks that moved under each step. I fell forward many times, landing on my knees and cutting them repeatedly. My hands, too, were soon grazed as I tried to stabilise myself. I was happy to sit on the rough ground, relieved when the men finally stopped.

More men gathered at the entrance of the cave which was just ahead now. A rocky opening led into the mine. The sheath of rock surrounding it was vast. A thin path was all that separated the mine and the rocky mountain edge. The men I had arrived with greeted the miners with genuine smiles and fast talk. I wished I understood what they were saying.

'How can you possibly be cheery living like this?'

Exhausted and still struggling to breathe, I was quickly becoming less enthusiastic. I remembered Negeenah telling me about these mines. Their men would live like this for six months of the year. This was more than I could handle for a day at most. I felt overwhelmingly grateful for my life suddenly and again, a little ashamed for being so absorbed in my self-pity over the last few months.

The sunlight was slowly returning as the mist thinned. Shining intermittently through the grey clouds, it still provided little warmth. I kept my eyes fixed on the man they called Bashir. He was somehow the key to all this. He was the man from the photos, and the man from my dream, and now, here I was again, mixed up in his life.

The men huddled over a large drum at the left of the entrance to the mine. It was filled with rocks of all sizes. The sun's thin rays revealed many had blue veins running through their dusty brown exteriors.

The men began piling the stones into their backpacks. Others were already on their way down the narrow, steep track with full bags. It looked treacherous, descending with such heavy loads.

'So, this is how the lapis stone is mined. They used explosives. All this for the precious stone. The keeper of strength and wisdom, so you say. I hope it's worth it.'

Even talking softly caused the sharp pain in my lungs to worsen.

Frantic yelling from within the mine suddenly halted my thoughts. The men began crouching down and covering their faces as if the yelling had warned them of impending danger. Then, within seconds, somewhere deep in the mine, an explosion erupted. Its force penetrated out through the entrance of where I stood. It was deafening and my reaction to take cover was too late.

My body was thrown back through the air. Tiny stones mixed with thick dust hit my skin from every direction. I tried to cover my face yet at the same time protect my body from the inevitable fall. The toxic smell of smoke made it impossible to breathe. Someone caught my hand. Shocked at the unexpected connection, I gripped back.

Confused and terrified I searched through the haze for my saviour, willing him not to let go.

Then the intense eyes of Bashir met mine.

We stayed connected, for just a moment.

'Remember, I will always love you, Gracie. We did it all for you.'

Had I heard that right?

How could he see me?

How did he know my name?

Then he was gone, disappearing into the dusty smoke. His grip on my hand was no longer. I was again hurled through the air, falling down the side of the steep mountain, unable to stop. I could hear my own screams as the rocks cut through my flesh again and again, as I slammed into the rough surface. I attempted to grab for anything I could, claw my way onto something stable.

I was going to die.

'Gracie, Gracie, wake up. Lass, you are dreaming. You are okay. I'm here.'

Yelling out and rolling onto my side, I opened my eyes in confusion. I felt frozen, my breathing was loud and heavy. Still grasping my shoulders from shaking me awake, Negeenah held me tight. Her own eyes were wild with fright.

Looking around, I could see I was back in my bedroom at Zarnish. The air was warm once again, the slight breeze soothed my heightened senses as it flowed through the open French doors. Just like before, Rex was on the bed, intensely he looked at me, head tilted to the side, whining quietly out of concern. I reached for him.

Sitting up beside Negeenah, I scanned my body, expecting and bracing for a range of injuries. Shaking my head and closing my eyes for a moment, it registered that once again my body showed no sign of the trauma from the events at the mine. Tasting the saltiness, I realised I was crying and tried to wipe the tears away with my trembling hands.

'Sorry, Gran, I must have been having a bad dream.'

I couldn't tell her this.

I needed time to understand it myself, if that was even possible. How do you even process something like that?

'My child, I could hear you screaming from the other end of the house. You gave Rex and me quite a fright. You were calling out a name but I couldn't quite make out what it was. I am just glad you are okay. Dreams can haunt us, this I understand.'

This was more than a bad dream.

Without words, Negeenah reached out to me. I was more than willing at that moment to fold myself into her warm embrace, letting myself sag into her, it felt soothing, like I belonged.

Later that evening, I returned to my notebook. I knew without question the name I was screaming out before Negeenah had woken me. I wrote it over and over in my book, in capital letters. I could still feel his rough hands in mine as he had tried desperately to hang on. The terror in his black eyes as they locked onto mine, I'd never forget.

BASHIR - who are you?

I thought about some plausible answers. A family friend? A brother to my mum? A cousin? The reality was he could have been anyone. But one thing he was not: a stranger. He was intertwined in my family's history... somehow.

As I stripped off my shorts for a shower, something fell to the floor. Crouching down to retrieve it, I caught my breath doing a double take. There before me was a small piece of rock. The bathroom light reflected an unmistakable speckle of blue underneath its dirty exterior.

My world had just collided with his.

Bitterness

I slumped down into the wicker chair outside my bedroom. As much as I was trying to be in the peace of the moment, truth was, I was pissed off. Fresh from a phone conversation with Mum, she had a way of doing that to me.

Will I ever be strong enough not to let other opinions bother me?

I had purposely relayed all the things I knew about our family to her, hoping my mum open up a little and shed some light.

'Sounds like you have been doing some digging, Gracie.' She'd laughed.

'But I am glad to hear you're getting along with your Gran a little better. She's not so bad after all, right! Sounds like everything is working out.'

Here we go. Working out for who Mum? You, right, because I'm out of the way.

Breathe, Grace… keep it together.

'Just because I'm getting along with her doesn't mean I don't want to get out of here. I miss my life. I miss my friends… I miss how we used to be, Mum.'

There was a short silence on the other end of the line.

Why had I just admitted that? Cringe.

I was on a rant now, nothing would stop me. I was like a steam train, at full speed, unsure of its destination.

'And I still don't get why all the secrets when I was growing up.

Why couldn't you just tell me about our Afghan family? Did you ever think just maybe I would have been fascinated and proud to be associated with it all? Why can't you trust me?'

I heard her sigh. I could visualise her twisting her hair through her fingers, as she always did when we argued.

'There is far more to the story, Grace. It was your Gran's wish that it remained confidential. And she has very good reasons for that. I know what you're like, don't go sticking your nose in where it doesn't belong. You need to respect her. She has provided a home for you. She didn't have to do that, remember.'

What the hell, bitch!

I exploded, my whole-body quivering with rage.

'No, you remember Mum, I didn't ask to come here. And what are you talking about? It *is* very much my business. You're the one who told me to search for the clues. You said I would find out what I needed to. Well, mother, that's exactly what I've been doing, so you had better brace yourselves. You still treat me like I'm a child. Well, here's a news flash for you. That day, I'm sure you recall the one, well, you and my so-called Dad made sure I grew up fast. You ripped my entire world apart!'

With that, I'd disconnected her call, throwing my phone across the room onto my bed. I thought ripping into her would feel better than this. But the same emptiness returned. Now it was mixed with a clenched jaw and nasty headache. Where did I go from here?

Why do I always mess everything up.

As I'd stormed down the hall, heading to this very spot where I could hide in the darkness of the night, I'd realised Negeenah had been within ear shot the entire time. She looked tense, giving me a sad smile as she stood, walking away, leaving me to cool down.

The graves

I decided another trip to the cottage was in order. Yesterday I'd found an old set of keys in the study and despite knowing I shouldn't, I slipped them into the pocket of my jean shorts. They were just way too intriguing to leave behind. I had every intention of returning them of course, and Negeenah wouldn't be any the wiser. For some reason I had a strong feeling one of the keys might just unlock the smaller chest in the cottage that had so far eluded me.

The perfect opportunity to duck away presented itself when Negeenah went into town for household supplies. She headed off with Tracker in his old Ute. As soon as I could no longer see the plume of dust trailing behind, I headed to my room, quickly packed my backpack and took off. The heat was scorching outside, but it wouldn't diminish my excitement. There was something intrinsically magnetic about the cottage.

I smiled at Rex, he, too, had a skip in his step this morning. As we meandered together through the bush I could feel a stronger breeze in the air. The season was changing. I wondered what autumn would be like in the top end. Would I be here long enough to find out?

Did I want to be?

I was becoming accustomed to the screeching of the cockatoos, the wildlife, and even the spiders hovering in their webs across the tracks. The red dirt and dust mixed with the flies sticking to my sweat. It all bothered me much less. I found myself stopping to appreciate a small wildflower popping through the dirt and a new bird I'd not seen before.

What would my friends think of me now?

Would they even care? More to the point, did I care what they thought?

Today I had new hope. For the first time since arriving, my mum called to say she was coming to visit in the next few days. Hopefully, she would agree it was time to take me home. Strangely however, I seemed to be battling my emotions on this.

I should be happy at the chance to get out of here, so why was I feeling this heaviness.

Could it be that I had found comfort and solace?

But I'm an imposter here, right? Or had I been an imposter in Melbourne all along?

Maybe it's just because I still have much to find out about my family, and this is the only place to do it. OMG Grace… shut up with the brain dump.

Shaking off the loudness in my brain I stopped walking for a minute to grab some water. Somewhere along the way, Rex had disappeared. How long had he been gone? Oh well, he knew this place better than me, he'd be fine. I think it was me that needed his company more.

'Rex, where are you, boy?'

I listened to the bush sounds for a few minutes, calling again. Out of nowhere Rex came bounding at great speed toward me. For a moment, I thought he was going to knock me over. His sudden dramatic stop threw dust in my face. I coughed and spluttered.

'There you are. What have you been up to, hey?'

Rex stood firm, blocking my path and barking. As I tried to move around him, he bounced on the spot, blocking me.

'Move, you crazy old dog!'

He continued to bark incessantly.

'What the hell are you doing?'

Then, just as suddenly Rex turned and trotted out front again. Shaking my head, I followed.

'Finally!'

Again, he stopped abruptly, this time, heading down a track we hadn't used before. Normally we walked over the slight ridge ahead to the cottage. But this track took a sharp left turn into dense bush.

'Okay, but this better be good, Rex.'

I picked up the pace to keep up with him. The track was narrow, but I could see it had been well used. In fact, the wear appeared quite fresh. A tingling sensation began at the base of my neck as I paused to examine.

Minutes later, we stopped. The track had opened up to a clearing in the bush.

What the hell was this? Should I be here?

On one side of the grassy area, the creek bubbled away peacefully. It was the same creek that ran alongside the cottage. Thick bush hemmed in the rest of the clearing. In the middle stood two graves, one much bigger than the other. I rested my hand onto Rex's head for reassurance, he remained like a statue standing beside me. I couldn't move.

'Whose graves are these, Rex?'

I felt like I was intruding, speaking in barely a whisper.

Rex looked up at me whining before moving toward the graves. He looked back as if willing me to do the same. I took a few small steps.

There's nothing to be worried about. I'm not doing anything wrong by respectfully looking.

It felt eerie and heavy with sadness, I could somehow feel the presence of those long gone. The headstones were clearly old. One was shaped like a cross, it was detailed with small flowers in each corner. The other simply took my breath away. Much taller than the cross, stood a divine angel in the figure of a woman. The entire structure was lovingly intricate. Her hair, her flowing dress, bare hands and feet were so elaborate and lifelike. She had huge wings behind her frame. Her face was beautiful, gazing down at the treasure cradled in her arms: a small baby swaddled in cloth.

At the base of both graves were bright, fresh flowers. Someone had been here very recently. A slight chill passed through me, I listened intently for any sound around me suggesting I was not alone. The flowers were the same as those growing on vines on the cottage veranda. No mistaking it.

Then came the sudden realisation. They were also the same flowers that were in my dreams. I felt dizzy and fell to my knees, trying desperately to steady my body. Rex whined. As I looked up, I focused on the names on the graves before jamming my eyes shut, trying to process. I just needed a moment for the dizziness to subside. The light seemed too bright, I was breathless and tight in my chest.

Breathe, Grace, breathe. This will pass.

I don't know how long I stayed at the base of the graves. Time had skewed, and somehow day had turned to night. Eventually, feeling clearer in my head, I stood. There was a distinct chill in the night air and the half-moon was almost entirely hidden by mist like clouds. Hadn't it been only mid-morning when we'd headed to the cottage?

'Rex, where are you, boy?'

I gulped down breaths to stay quiet, wanting to bail yet feeling rooted to the spot.

'Rex, come on, buddy, where are you?'

Flinching at the snapping bracken to my left, barking alerted me that Rex was coming out of the bush. He seemed so full of energy. I reached down for my backpack, keen to get out of here but stopped. Was that music? There was no mistaking it; it was the familiar tune from the music box.

But this time, the same soothing melody I had heard so many times in my dreams made my limbs start shaking. Things were moving too fast to process. The music echoed through the night; its sound carried on the breeze.

I strained to see further into the bush, listening intently to discover its origin. Moving closer, I heard voices. A man and a woman? Had Negeenah returned early from her weekly trip into town? Maybe it was Bluey and Tracker? I shivered both from the crisp night air and confusion.

Would whoever it was be annoyed I was here?

Trying to move quietly through the bush, I stumbled, falling hard onto a spiky tree and did everything I could to stop myself crying out in pain. Idiot Grace. The dim light ahead was getting brighter as the bush cleared. At least four lanterns were hanging from trees around the grassed space.

A man and woman stood closely together, their backs to me, like blackened figures, almost shadows. All the while, Rex continued to return to me, then disappeared up ahead again.

'Rex.' I tried to whisper for his return fearing he would give us away.

I was back at the graveyard. Not that I remembered leaving. Was this another one of my dreams? That would make sense as to how the day had suddenly become night from day. And if so, was it present time or once again a glimpse back at the past.

Abruptly, the man fell to his knees, sobbing loudly, uncontrollably. Punching the ground with his fist. The woman stood beside him, but it wasn't long before she too knelt and began to weep. The lady had one hand on the man's back, the other absentmindedly stroking Rex. He had crept close and joined them.

But how could she see Rex if this was a dream? Could he see us both? Stepping into the clearing I knew there was only one way to find out.

'Hello,' I called softly.

'I'm so sorry to interrupt, but I was wondering… can you see me? Can you hear me?'

The couple didn't respond. I moved forward again, kneeling close enough to see their breath expel in the cold air. It was Negeenah.

'I am so sorry for your loss.'

But just like in my previous dreams, to them I was invisible.

Negeenah appeared of similar age to what she had in my previous dream, the awful night I'd witnessed her trying to help the ill woman. The man crouching beside Gran now was also the same man. Azyan and Asadi Karzai had been the young owners of Zarnish Estate, according to the records I'd found in the barn. A sickening feeling flushed over me as the realization came as to what I was looking at right now.

I stared up at the beautiful woman's headstone again.

'Asadi Karzai.' I read from the headstone in a whisper. 'Beloved wife and mother. Always loyal and full of beauty. Rest In Peace. 1982-2002. You were only 20, Asadi, how did you die so young?'

I moved my focus to the smaller grave. Swallowing hard, I took a slow breath. I could guess what was to come.

'Kinaaz Karzai. Beautiful daughter, our precious baby. May you Rest in Peace in the flowers of heaven. 2000-2002.'

Crossing my arms, holding my shoulders, I wanted to escape the sadness as I looked over at the devastated man. Asadi, father and husband of the deceased, buried in front of them now. He looked broken and frail. Negeenah and Asadi were quietly crying, their bodies huddled closely and trembling as one. Hot tears spilled from my own eyes. Rex remained between us.

'Kinaaz would have been 15 now, just like me. She hardly got to live. What had happened out here?'

Rex nuzzled me.

'I can't stay here. My heart is broken, I will die if I remain.'

Azyan stared up at the freshly dug graves as he spoke. His voice was weak, hoarse. Negeenah looked at him for a long while before responding, her hand still resting protectively on his back.

'Please, don't leave me here; I can't do this on my own. It is simply too much. I don't know enough about farming for one.'

Kneeling beside the couple I could feel their pain and grief as I listened to their heartfelt exchange.

Should I even be here? Was I intruding?

'I can do no good here anymore, Negeenah. I will return to Kabul, resume my business trading there. I will send you money and make sure you still have the farmhands required. But I need you to stay here, to watch over my family for now.'

Negeenah got up slowly. She looked unsure on her feet, weak and defeated.

'We have all been through so much, my dear brother. I wanted things to be better for us, for this new life in Australia to be safe, to be our salvation. If this is what you need, I will do it. You have sacrificed so much for me.'

Azyan stood too, holding her hand.

'We are family, Negeenah. Together, we are unbreakable. Our father would have been proud of the life we have made, despite it all. I will contact Bashir on my return. He can come to Australia sooner than we had planned. He will look after you all.'

Silently Negeenah continued to stare at the headstones as she stroked Rex on the head. The chill of the night air was now almost unbearable. It was misty. Dense rain began to fall, soaking the bush around them.

'Did I just hear that right?'

Rex turned his attention to me, the sound of my voice breaking through the silence.

'Rex, Negeenah just said Azyan was her brother! Did I hear that right?'

How had I never thought of this as a possible connection? Now, I could see it would make sense. They had helped her leave Afghanistan and travel to Australia, but why? I took a moment to try to process what this all meant. Heavy rain continued to soak through my clothes, and the increasing wind whipped at my face. Still, I didn't move.

That means he was my great uncle, and Kinzaar was my second cousin. Had they not died, they would be here right now. I could have met them, met my real family. I stood as my teeth began to chatter and looked across at the couple, still staring absentmindedly at their loved ones buried beneath the ground. Tonight, much had been revealed. But what did Bashir have to do with all this?

This was a lot to take in. I needed to sit. My body felt the weight of sadness and the bitter cold. I needed to rest. Close my eyes for just a moment. Laying back on the wet earth, I was too deep in thought to care about the dampness or chill.

It took a while to register the warmth suddenly penetrating my skin, infusing my body, almost making me feel weightless. Blinking feverishly as I opened my eyes, I was not quite ready for the brightness of the sun high in the blue sky.

Still in the clearing of the gravesite, I had to assume I was back. Returned to the morning I had ventured off to the cottage with Rex. Back to the 'before' Rex had led me down the little track revealing the graves of my family. Exhaling deeply, I rose, no longer soaked through.

'Rex, where are you, boy? Please, buddy, I need you.'

Rex wandered up beside me. I studied every detail of the headstones again, all the while hugging him tightly. Whatever was going on with me sure was strange. It was such a weird feeling coming to and from alternate time, past and present.

No one would believe me even if I tried to explain.

But I was not frightened. My dreams or visions, or whatever they were, helped. I felt strangely grateful, despite it being emotional in its revelations. Rex settled beside me as I retrieved my notebook from my backpack scribbling down as much as I could.

'I need to get into the barn again, Rex. Go through more of the boxes and chests. I bet I missed something important. And today, we were supposed to go to the cottage, remember? I found a key to try to get the little chest open. You kind of distracted me, my friend.'

Looking around, I realised I was talking to myself. Rex was again nowhere to be seen.

I'm pouring my heart out, and you've disappeared.

It was good to lighten the mood and laugh a little, I thought. As I stretched my arms above my head in an attempt to freshen my energy, Rex re appeared from behind, suddenly dropping his newfound treasure into my lap.

'Gran's hat! Where did you find that, boy?'

Negeenah must have left it there while tending to the graves. I wonder what she will have to say when I return this to her, hey. Do I dare tell her I was here?

Blue ribbon

Looking at my phone, I saw that once again, no time had passed during my dream. It was like time stood still when I was in a subconscious place. This meant I would still be able to execute my original plan.

As I got close to the cottage, I could smell the sweetness of the flowers mixing with the scents of the bush. Taking a deep breath in, the smell made me feel peaceful. The sky was filled with black cockatoos today, dancing from tree to tree with not a care in the world it seemed.

It was just as I had left it. Perfect. I felt a familiar nostalgic pull at my heart. The tiny cottage looked alone and forgotten in time. All except for the colourful flowers which seemed to breathe new life into the dwelling.

Carefully turning the door handle, Rex stayed close by following me in. He sat in front of the fireplace like it was something he had done many times before. Panting heavily, he rested his head on the wooden boards. I decided to sit as well, choosing the old rocking chair. So much had happened today and I was feeling quite weary.

'I love it here, Rex. I can't even explain why. In this cottage, I feel… well, I'm not sure… I feel somehow like I belong.'

The sun shone through the little kitchen window, and the sweet breeze wafted in through the open front door. The lapis stone on top of the chest of drawers shone brightly, the sun highlighting its gold flecks.

As I rocked gently, I tried to imagine what it would have been like living here. It would have been simple but peaceful. But with all the modern appliances I'm accustomed to, the reality is, I'd struggle. No power for one, and no Uber eats out here!

'I'll ask Mum about it when she arrives this week. Surely, she knows something.'

Searching my backpack, I grabbed the old set of keys I had discreetly borrowed from the study.

'Let's hope these are the right ones, Rex. And don't look at me that way, obviously I have every intention of putting them back.'

Was I talking to him too much?

I knelt on the floor in front of the smaller chest, catching a splinter in my knee. But despite many attempts, none of the three keys would turn the lock. One seemed to fit perfectly, but turning it was impossible. Frustrated, I admitted defeat for now. Eventually I'd win.

'I need the pry bar again, Rex, but I've left it back at the house. That was bloody dumb.'

We ventured outside, back into the heat of the late summer, deciding to do some more exploring around the cottage before leaving. I'd just have to take my chances and escape back here as soon as I could. This time armed with the right tools. Sitting on a fallen log, I scrolled through the photos and footage taken over the last few weeks. Every photo I took while in my dreams simply failed to exist, but the images were vivid enough in my mind anyhow.

Missing was the gravesite, I couldn't quite bring myself to photograph it. Somehow it felt disrespectful. But I knew I could visit whenever I needed. When it was all put together, along with my notes, I could see quite an incredible story unravelling.

Staring up to the sky, I made a mental list of what I knew to date.

I knew Negeenah was born and raised in Afghanistan. Her family were lapis stone miners. Hence her obsession with the stone. She was forced to marry very young to a much older man. She gave birth to my mum at just 15.

Incomprehensible.

I also knew she gave birth to my mum in Afghanistan. What I needed to find out was how and why did they end up here in the middle of the Australian outback? Zarnish Estate had belonged to Negeenah's brother. He had a wife and baby, but not for long. That was another thing I needed to find out: how did they die? Azyan left to return to Kabul at some point in 2002, shortly after their death.

I thought about this for a long while, my silence obviously perplexing Rex by the way he twisted his head from side to side, willing my attention. Vacantly staring into the bush, I wondered how I would feel if my own Mum died.

Stop it, Grace.

A flush of anxiety rose from my feet, burning all the way to my ears. Man, I'd been such a bitch to her lately. So consumed with my own anger and confusion in the last few months, had I even factored her in?

Out here in the isolation of the bush, I was starting to see just how many mistakes I'd made. Was it too late to get my life back on track? Would Mum give me a second chance? Did I want to give her one?

I sighed, my brain was at capacity, and I needed to switch off for a bit.

'Let's go home, Rex. We can look around another day.'

As I walked down the side of the cottage, I sighted a wooden swing. How had I not noticed this before? It was hanging from a big old gum tree and swinging ever so slightly in the gentle breeze. Slowing, my steps almost became uncertain as the king parrots above suddenly seemed so much louder. Overwhelmingly I felt like I was walking toward something I'd seen before.

More flowers were planted in the small rock garden beside the swing. I lowered myself down carefully on the old wooden seat. Gripping the thick ropes holding up the swing, I tilted my head skywards, closing my eyes. The gentle movement gave me feeling of being carried away, such a freedom for my mind, if only for a short time.

Rex's bark crashed me back into the present. Blinking rapidly, my eyes rested on a small branch to the side of the swing.

What the hell?

My ribs tightened as I bent forward to get a closer look before stiffening back up.

There it was, right in front of me. A small piece of blue hair ribbon. It danced and twirled silently in the wind. I touched the soft silk material. The same ribbon I had seen so many times before.

Closing my eyes I saw her clearly. The beautiful little girl in the blue dress. She wore a blue ribbon in every dream. It tied back some of her dark curls.

This was starting to get a little creepy.

The missing piece

Negeenah was busying herself preparing for the pending arrival of my mum. I was still grappling with the whole thing, unsure how I felt about her coming here. On the one hand, I hoped my mum would agree it was time to pack up and go home. But on the other, my desire to keep exploring the cottage and my family's history was gaining momentum.

I had a growing feeling I was close to discovering something big.

Negeenah was sure going to a lot of trouble, I thought, as I wandered through the living area of the house. Fresh flowers in each room, a spring clean, fresh linen and towels in the guest bedroom. Cooking up a storm.

Did she do all this before I arrived?

What if I mess everything up when Mum comes?

Maybe she is coming to tell me I'm staying here for good.

I headed silently toward the study, wanting to replace the keys before their absence was noticed. Pausing, I pondered on my reflection in the hall mirror. My face was definitely softer than before, tanned and healthier. The hardness had dissipated.

The hostility was less.

Did I still hate myself?

Do I hate her?

The dark circles that had rimmed my eyes for months were gone. Perhaps this time away had done me good. The sun-kissed glow made me feel more radiant.

Was I pretty like Mum?

I hadn't had my hair this long for a while. My dark curls cascaded around my face and spilled down over my shoulders.

'I definitely look a little more grown-up, I think. Now I just need to work out how the bloody hell I fit into this world.'

'That will come, lass. You are getting closer, I believe.'

I spun around, startled. Negeenah stood in the doorway, beaming at me, hands on hips.

'I love that old mirror. It was my brother's. He travelled a long way with it so that it could take pride of place here.'

Azyan.

'Is there anything missing, Gracie, when you look at yourself?'

Omg where do I start!

I turned back to the mirror, shaking my head. What was she talking about?

'Close your eyes for a minute, lass.'

I looked at her puzzled, shrugged my shoulders and, without protest, closed them tightly. Negeenah moved up behind me and carefully placed a chain around my neck. I could feel her secure the clasp.

'Now, open those wise eyes, my child.'

Drawing a sharp breath, I saw the unmistakable blue and gold lapis stone immediately. My finger traced the shape of the cross as I'd done so many times before. And right now, I was incredibly grateful to have it back.

Negeenah did this for me?

'But how? Where did you get this, Gran?'

I turned to her, grasping it protectively and reaching for her hand. Negeenah smiled broadly.

'Well let's just say I'm returning it to its rightful owner. It belongs to you, I believe. You deserve it. You must keep it close from now on. Use its strength to go forward in your life.'

The familiar sting of hot tears spilled down my cheeks. I think

I had cried more here in the last month than I had since Samir left me. I didn't try to hide them anymore. What was the point.

'Thank you, Gran. I realise now how important this is, I should never have thrown it away. I was just so angry and confused.'

Negeenah pulled me into a hug. Whispering in my ear.

'Be proud of who you are, Grace. As I have always said, you are destined for a great purpose. You are so close now.'

She pulled back, still gripping my hands tightly, her eyes locked with mine. They reflected such sorrow all of a sudden.

'I'm so sorry for it all, Gracie.'

'Gran I'm proud to discover I have Afghani heritage, to know I come from a lapis mining family. But please, I need to know more. I need to understand it all... I'm begging you.'

Negeenah smiled, her eyes becoming noticeably dull and her stare empty.

'You have the same spirit we do Gracie. You never give up. I promise you will understand it all very soon. But first, you need to tell me something. Tell me about that night, and how it came to pass that you ended up here.'

I can't. She will hate me.

I did nothing to resist as Negeenah led me down the passage to the front sitting room.

Yes, I can. I'm so tired of hiding behind my mask. Secrets are too big a burden.

I sat down, dropping heavily into the pillows on the soft sofa. My body ached. I was exhausted, another side effect of anxiety and living in a hyper-vigilant state. It always bubbled under the surface. I wanted to be free of it. My burdens, carrying them, had taken their toll.

Rex, sensing my mood as always, jumped up protectively by my side. He flopped down close to me and rested his head on my lap. I couldn't help but smile at him. Rex looked up and licked my face. He had become such a loyal companion, even when I'd been a bitch. Without question, he would be hard to leave. I loved him.

Was I beginning to feel the same about Negeenah?

Truth

The afternoon breeze flowing through the open French doors was welcoming on my skin as it danced quietly through the room. The scent of the wildflowers in the vase next to me made me feel comforted like I belonged. I knew these could only have been picked from the cottage.

'Well, you know the story, probably better than I do, Gran. But yes, you deserve to hear my side. I'm sure it hasn't been ideal to have me land on your doorstep like I did. I am sorry for the trouble I've caused, really. I hate myself for it.'

Negeenah shot me a steely look.

'Gracie, never speak like that about yourself. Words have more power than you know. What you speak, your mind believes. There is nothing you can say or do that will make me love you less. We all have a past, child. But this does not define who we are, or what our future can hold. That depends on your courage. For what it matters, I am glad you came here. I have waited a long time. It was a mistake to let fear keep you from me. Finally, we can be a family.'

I needed to hear that every day, to undo the self-hate.

And she said she loved me?

I didn't quite know where to start.

So much of it, I didn't understand myself.

'When I found out Samir was not my real dad, understandably, I was confused. Then I got angry, really angry.'

Absentmindedly, I was twisting my own lapis in my hand. The memory of that day seemed to burn a fresh wound in my heart each time.

'I was devastated by him and furious at Mum. But mostly, I was angry at myself.'

Negeenah forced me to look up, cupping my face with her hands.

'Why would you be angry at yourself, child?'

'How could I not be? I'm so dumb. So stupid… I knew something was wrong, but stupidly I trusted them. I loathe myself, there was so much I didn't know about my family, but I never questioned Mum growing up. Why didn't I?'

I stood, feeling the tingle of agitation running through my body. Anger welled up once again, and I begged for it not to drown me.

'I'm meant to be this bright girl. A history buff, no less. I actually believed that once. I was so self-absorbed. I never even asked about the important stuff. I'm such an idiot.'

I paced the room, Negeenah remained silent. Rex watched me move around but made no attempt to get up.

'I always believed they loved me. Especially my mum. But how can she say she loves me and then lie…? My whole life is a lie… and I let it happen.'

'Grace, listen to me, none of this is your fault. I know it doesn't feel like the truth, but please just hear me out… What if it was all done to protect you, to keep you safe?'

'From what? I am so sick of hearing that!'

'I know, Gracie. I know. We will get to that. But please, keep going, tell me what happened next.'

I sat back down, my face in my hands. I had a throbbing headache. I just wanted it all to go away. But I knew better. Over the last few months, I had learned that it didn't matter where I went, what I did, who I turned to, or what I dabbled with to forget the pain. You can't run from a mind in turmoil.

'The truth is, I was so lost, still am. I just didn't care anymore.

Why should I? They don't care about me... So I started skipping school. My grades went down. I got caught cheating on tests. Then I got done for defacing the school and the subway with graffiti. I was stealing without caring who saw me, almost daring the shop owners to catch me. You have to understand, that it's not who I ever thought I would be. I got caught a couple of times stealing alcohol and cigarettes. I'd never dreamt of doing those things before. But eventually, I honestly didn't care. It was almost like I wanted to get caught. Self-sabotage, the psychologist called it. I wanted to make them pay. Make my mum hurt. I was numb to everything, and I only felt alive when I was doing something I knew was bad. It got a reaction.'

Negeenah smiled at me as if encouraging me to keep going. It felt good to tell her and I felt safe sharing what I had done and not being judged.

'I understand that, Gracie, I really do. Trauma can make us different to who we thought we were.'

That's for sure.

'Then I started hanging out with the wrong crowd. I didn't even really like them. I tried different drugs; it made me forget. All the while, I was arguing with my mum. I was so mean to her, Gran. I still feel angry, I don't want to, but I do. The bottom line is that I don't understand why she hasn't opened up to me. Surely, she could have told me why. But she says nothing. That tells me all I need to know.'

I picked at my nails, my internal void returning.

'Grace, I take responsibility for much of your Mum's silence. I had asked her to keep you away from the truth, fearing for your wellbeing. Perhaps I was wrong. I have made some choices in my past that still haunt me. My greatest fear was that I had put my family in danger.'

Okay, so this was new...

'Tell me why, Gran?'

She nodded.

'You need to get your story out first, Gracie. You will feel better, I promise. When the time is right, you have my word, you will know my story, all of it.'

I breathed deeply, and for the first time, chose to trust her. That was big for me.

Please don't prove my judgement wrong Negeenah. It wouldn't be the first time.

'My real friends started to disown me. My school was constantly on my back, warning me I would lose my scholarship. They tried to hook me up with counselling. I told them to shove it. My mum was desperate. I could see that. That only made me rebel more. To punish her. The longer she stayed quiet, the more I wanted to make her pay.'

Needing a minute, I got up again and walked through the open doors onto the veranda. Moving around helped me think and gave me courage. I looked intently at the land around without really taking anything in. My mind was buzzing with the memories of the last few months, filled with random flitting thoughts.

'Then I had the bright idea that my school must have a record of Samir's whereabouts. He was one of my next of kin. I assumed in case of emergency they'd have his details. Well, I figured this situation qualified as an emergency. I needed to talk to him. I planned it so carefully. Even down to leaving the office window slightly open the day before. I had made an appointment with the guidance counsellor. It was easy to make them believe I'd had a change of heart, realised the error of my ways, you know? I was just scoping out the office, preparing for my entry later that night.'

Negeenah raised her eyebrows, smiling.

'You are so very clever, Grace.'

'After Mum went to work, I grabbed the bag I needed, pry bar and all, and headed off. It was all supposed to be quick and simple. Obviously, it didn't turn out anything like I'd hoped. I spent half that night in jail. My prior offences didn't help.'

'So, you got caught in the act? Did you, in fact, find his details? You must have been so frightened, child.'

'Nope, that's the shitty part. I never got the information I needed. Maybe there was a silent alarm. I'm not sure. As I climbed through the window, I was smoking a cigarette. I was so hyped up it gave me head spins, so I flicked it away. I was not thinking straight and never noticed it landed inside the building and straight onto a pile of papers. I'm such a loser! The fire must have taken hold really quickly. But I had moved further down into the office, to where I knew the filing cabinets were located. I was so focused on finding my personal details that I just didn't see the fire. It got big, fast. It was just too late.'

My legs were so restless, I was unable to stand still.

'Then you got out of there, right?'

My smile was hard.

'No. I wanted the information I had come for. In a way, the fire just made me more determined. As I said, I was stupid. The smoke was getting so thick that it was becoming harder to see and breathe. I could hardly see the filing cabinet in front of me, but I kept looking. Then, just like that, I was grabbed from behind and arrested. I honestly didn't care if I died right there and then. I still feel like that sometimes.'

Negeenah stood now, facing me head on.

'But you didn't, and there is a reason for that, many reasons, Grace. Child, your great purpose is coming, I wish you could see that.'

I don't deserve it Gran… can't you see.

'I was charged and ordered to do a stint in juvenile detention. But somehow, Mum got them to agree to a deal. Home detention, but not at home… out here, with you obviously. And here I am.'

Negeenah's hand cupped my chin, lifting my head until I met her gaze.

'Yes, here you are. And I am here to help you, child. *You* have been given another chance, Grace. My question is, what are you doing about it? Are you going to help yourself?'

Bluey

The sun streaming into my room woke me the following day. Rex was still on the bed beside me. Sensing my movement, he stretched out on the crumpled sheets.

'You will have to sleep with Gran after I leave, boy. That might even be this week, you know.'

As soon as I'd said it, the same pot of mixed emotions began rising in me as before.

'Well, it might be a little longer. I still have things I need to sort out here. No rush, hey?'

Rex wagged his tail, his paw reaching onto my chest. He always knew how to make me feel important. Like he needed me right back. I liked that.

Negeenah had gone riding with Tracker beyond the paddocks. I headed back to the barn and its treasures. It was like the memory of Azyan, and his family had been all bundled up, put out of sight and jammed into boxes. Perhaps it had. I wondered why Gran would have done this. After all, they were family. Surely, Azyan might still return, his wife and child are buried on this land.

Maybe all this stuff was too hard for Negeenah, a painful reminder of what could have been?

Or were they being hidden on purpose?

Heading through the large open barn doors, I spied Bluey stacking hay in the far corner. I hesitated.

Maybe I'll come back later. I don't know what to say to him.

In all my time here, I hadn't seen him up close. I really should have introduced myself earlier. Now, it was a bit awkward. An older man, his skin had clearly seen many summers, brown and worn. His red checkered flannel shirt was dusty, as were his jeans. He wore a brown leather hat and farm boots that appeared older than him.

As I stood there, summing him up and debating whether I should leave, I was oblivious to the fact he had already seen me. He turned suddenly, nodding and dusting himself off.

'G'day, lassie.'

His greeting was warm and kind, like that of an old friend, instantly putting me at ease.

'I was hoping we would meet again. My girly, you certainly have grown since I last saw you.'

Huh?

I walked directly up to him, a little confused.

'Hi, I'm Grace. I'm sorry I haven't introduced myself sooner. Nice to meet you.'

He smiled broadly.

'You should know me, lass. It's Bluey, remember?'

I don't know you.

He took off his hat and pointed to his red hair.

'Me mates gave me the nickname a long time ago, all because of me flaming locks. Though the grey's taken over a bit now.'

He chuckled to himself.

'Well, I suppose you were just a wee thing when you last saw me. I was the one who used to make you laugh, pretending I was a scarecrow in the veggie patch, you and Kinaaz. A couple of real little cuties, you two. Inseparable, as I remember.'

He let out a roar of laughter as if captured by the fond memory.

But just as suddenly, his face darkened, and he looked at the ground. Appearing miles away, he rubbed his forehead.

'I think you have me mixed up with someone else, Bluey. This is my first visit here, ever.'

The old man looked at me for a long while, clearly his turn to feel confused now.

'I don't think so, girly. I'd remember that hair anywhere, ya pretty little blue ribbon, and those eyes of yours. Yep, no doubt about it. I'm glad you've finally returned to claim what's yours.'

Paralysed, I felt my body heat rising.

Blue ribbon? Like my dream?

He gave me a heartfelt smile and picked up a bale of hay, loading it easily on his shoulder. Winking as he walked past me, he didn't look back.

What the hell was all that?

What did he mean, claim what's mine?

Was he bat crazy?

Frowning, I stood there, in the middle of the barn, and watched Bluey walk down to the paddock fence. The cows were beginning to meander toward the old gate to greet him. What a strange character. I willed myself to remember anything from my past that could link his story. Nothing came to my mind. It never did. Why would it?

I wandered over to the corner where all the old furniture and chests of belongings were stored. Once again, I sifted through photos. Asadi, so young, was a beautiful woman. Even in the old photos, I could see her radiant energy. I held the photo up to the light. It was Asadi, holding Kinaaz high above her head. The baby had a look of delight on her little face. To one side was Azyan, smiling contently at them.

I wonder who took this?

More photos showed the happy couple around their property. Someone certainly liked capturing these moments. But who? There were pictures of the stables, the barn, the glorious gardens. Then

I found pictures of places I'd never seen around here. Where were these taken? If I could find the lagoon or water hole in this photo, I would love to explore it. A picnic had been set up at the spot. I bet Bluey or Tracker would know. Maybe they would even take me there. And another couple of photos showed fields of vibrant, red flowers. I hadn't seen anything like that around here. Maybe it was somewhere else.

What did Bluey mean with my blue ribbon?

Finding a fresh stack of baby photos, I moved through them quickly, willing my mind to keep up. Then it dawned on me, and I was so confident I was right, I felt my chest expand. It was so completely obvious.

How had I not seen this before. Idiot Grace!

I was holding in my hand the exact image I'd seen so many times in my dreams. Blinking to make sure it was real, I refocused.

'How is this possible?'

There she was, baby Kinaaz, playing on the ground in her white dress. Soft, wispy hair and dark eyes. Flowers all around. Next to her was another little girl. Black curls, yellow dress, little blue flowers on the hem and neckline. And a blue ribbon in her hair. Between them in the dirt was the music box. Instantly the soft tune began playing in my head.

'Is that me?'

I traced the image of the child carefully with my finger.

'I must have come here when I was little.'

So why has my mum never mentioned it?

Why can't I remember?

Leaping to my feet, I felt an urgency to find Bluey again. He had so casually mentioned he knew me when I was young. Like it wasn't a secret, neither of us realising the impact his bombshell would have. With this photo, he could tell me for sure. Leaving behind the open boxes and chests, I headed out toward the paddock. I didn't feel weary or anxious but had a high sense of purpose and an unmatched curiosity.

Bluey was spreading the hay for the cattle. The gate was swinging open in the breeze. Photo in hand, I made a direct line for him, almost jogging. Rex bounded beside me, excited to be on another hunt, nose to the ground.

'Bluey?'

The old man turned, waving to me as I approached.

'Hey, can I ask you something?'

He walked toward me nodding, dusting himself off. The cows were munching contentedly on the feed he had spread.

'Is this me? Is this Kinaaz?'

I thrust the photo close to his face, urging him for an answer. He took a step back, raising his hands defensively.

'Hey, steady up, girly, give me a minute to get my bearings. The old eyes aren't what they used to be.'

I forced a smile but watched impatiently as he took his hat off and wiped the sweat from his brow. Replacing the hat, he finally took the photo.

Staring at the image, he seemingly became lost in time again, like the photo itself.

'Ahh, girly, I always loved watching you two play. She adored you, you know, worshipped the ground you walked on. I'm sure your mum has told you the stories. I used to pick the flowers from the cottage and sprinkle them over your heads. Just to hear you both laugh… it filled me old ticker with joy every time. Diamonds in the rough, you two were. As precious as the lapis stones themselves.'

I swallowed hard, stunned by such simple honesty. How could I be such a fool?

Always the last to know.

I stifled a cry of frustration.

'Are you sure, Bluey? Is there any way you could be mistaken?'

He looked at me, perplexed himself now, seemingly confused I had no knowledge of my past.

'Don't be fooled by this old body, lass. My mind is still as sharp as a pin. You don't forget a tragedy like that.'

He looked at the ground, releasing a slow whistle and shaking his head.

'Little Gracie, you were so lost without her, too young to understand. It broke my heart watching you search for her after she was gone. Everyone was fragmented after that.'

Nausea rose up through my body as a deep chill caused an involuntary shiver. Bluey seemed unsteady on his feet. He was shaking as I took the photo from his outstretched hand. Tears flowed freely down his dusty, craggy face.

'Sorry girl. Best we leave the past where it is now. No good can come from diggin' around. But it's good to see you back here, lass. Zarnish needs ya energy.'

He turned away and walked back into the paddock, heading toward the windmill, which turned quietly in the wind.

'So, I was here Rex. At some point in my early years, I was here.'

Enigma

Lost in a million thoughts, I continued to sift through the forgotten belongings in the barn, all the while hoping Bluey would return.

Why would my mum keep that from me? Liar!

Gran has never mentioned it, either. How convenient.

All my dreams… bloody hell, they were real?

I didn't know what to think or feel at this point. Letting out a long slow sigh, that overwhelming desire to flee returned… Instead I slumped down beside one of the old chests. I was too tired to bother going anywhere right now.

Dragging myself up, determined to keep searching for anything that might help, my gaze shifted, instantly drawing my attention. There, underneath layers of paperwork and books, right at the bottom of a chest, I spied what looked like an old satchel.

Within seconds I had the bag in my hands admiring its dark, well-worn leather. It smelt rich and earthy. Thin straps wound around it many times, binding up its contents. On the front were the initials N.K.

This had to belong to Negeenah.

If Gran or Bluey or even Tracker turned up, my snooping would be hard to explain. But I just had to check this out. Yep, it was wrong to pry, but what choice did I have if no one would tell me anything? Jumping to my feet, I strained to hear movement, but everything around me was quiet. Spying a thin ladder leading up to a mezzanine floor at the back of the barn, I smiled.

'At least up here, I can see someone come in before they see me, Rex. Keep guard down here, boy.'

Rex looked at me, then trotted off outside into the sunshine.

'Fine, no worries, you go do what you need to then, hey.'

I laughed, shaking my head. Tentatively, I climbed the fragile ladder, avoiding the rotten and broken steps as best I could. The leather folder was tucked safely into my backpack.

Popping up through the small square opening, I saw that the compact loft was covered in straw. The smell reminded me of visiting my friend Molly's house when I was little. Molly owned a rabbit. Together we spent many hours in the tiny hutch, feeding the little brown furball carrots and celery. That was the closest I ever came to interacting with a pet.

Until Rex, that is.

What a cool space this was. Private. I'm coming back here for sure.

A small window was cut into the peaked tin roof above. The shards of light mixing with the dust in the air, gave a mesmerising ambience. It was so still, so quiet up here. Sitting in the middle of the floor, legs crossed, I lifted my head to the window. Closing my eyes, I let the sun dance on my face.

Without warning, the feeling changed dramatically. Something rough and prickly covered my head and entire body. Struggling to draw breath, my body temperature was rising fast.

Grappling to stand, I blinked rapidly, desperate to remove whatever was covering my head. Only through a small gap in the material could I see out at all. I was shrouded in black material.

Confused, I fought to calm myself and get my bearings.

My surrounds had changed, too. There were voices nearby, lots of voices.

Clearly, I was no longer in the barn loft.

But where exactly was I this time?

Still sitting in my cross-legged position on the floor, this room was dimly lit, with only two dangling lightbulbs as its light source. Many other people were in the room. Some were sitting on thin pillows, others standing. Huddled in groups and talking in hushed voices, all wore Burkas.

The air felt thick and oppressive, yet chilly. The walls and flooring were grey concrete, and the two small windows were covered with black material. A single wooden door connected the room to the outside world. It was heavily bolted from the inside. In one corner was a large free-standing backboard, with books piled beneath it.

Was I in Afghanistan?

Looking more closely around me, I could see I was surrounded by women. My guess was that I had somehow found myself back in the mid-1990s. Harsh changes were implemented after the Taliban came into power at that time, and one of those was the dress code. Women were no longer allowed to show any bare skin. Many small children were also in the room, some resting in their mother's laps, others playing together quietly.

Strange, I thought, another law imposed during that time stated women were not allowed to leave their homes without a male chaperone. Yet this room was full of unaccompanied women.

I stood, nearly tripping over the long black shroud around me as I stepped forward. The burka was uncomfortable and heavy. Moving further into the room, I felt pretty sure, much like my other dreams, I was unable to be seen nor heard.

'Hello? I decided to test this theory. 'Ladies, can you hear me, can you see me?'

Nothing.

No one spoke above a whisper.

The calmness was interrupted by a quiet knock on the door. Instant panic swept across the room. I shuffled a few steps back toward the wall. The women grabbed their children, covering them protectively with their burkas. Each woman dropped to the ground, shielding themselves and their children as best they could. They were clearly terrified. But of what?

Who did they think was behind the door?

What would happen if they were found?

Not a sound. Then the soft knock came again. Six quick taps.

One woman got up. Putting her head against the back of the door, she listened for sounds from the other side. Then she used a small peephole to view beyond it. I walked up to her, somehow, her movements seemed familiar, but it was impossible to identify her under her burka. The woman proceeded to unlock the bolts and let the person in. Not one sound came from within.

What was going on?

Silently, another woman entered, also dressed in a dark burka. Instantly the door was locked securely behind her. The silence was broken as the visitor addressed the room, her voice confident and commanding. I wish I understood.

The women began to sit up quietly. Two women at the back of the room went to check the windows. Curious, I followed. I was just tall enough to see through the thin crack in the black window covering. Bars also covered the dirty glass. We were high up in a building. My guess was that it was a block of flats or similar.

The busy street below bustled with people and cars, carts and motorbikes. Shopfronts spilled out onto the streets, selling all manner of produce and merchandise. The street was heavily populated, all the women were draped in burkas.

My eyes were drawn to a green jeep moving conspicuously through the street.

I was struck by a horrific realisation; the occupants looked exactly like the Taliban.

Could this be happening?

Could I possibly be this close?

The men in the vehicle wore army clothes and headscarves covering their faces. Even from a distance, I could see their menacing appearance.

They cruised the street at a slow speed, eyeballing the civilians, gesturing menacingly as they passed. High-powered weapons rested in their laps. The throng around them seemed alarmed at their presence, many turning their backs or facing the ground to avoid eye contact, if possible. Children were shielded. No one spoke back to them.

It was hard to tell which city this was. Maybe Kabul? It was like I read about online, but now it was real. These people were terrified. Grasping the stone around my neck from under my burka, I turned away from the window.

The women began taking off their headpieces. It was a magical, uplifting sight. Whatever the lady had said gave them the confidence to do so. I had recently read that the consequence for doing this in a public place was jail. A moral crime.

As I scanned the room, I could see some of the women were old, but many were very young. They were so beautiful. Lovingly, they grasped each other's hands, appearing grateful to be together. Smiling broadly, they were clearly enjoying this moment of freedom. I thought back to images of Afghanistan I'd researched. How naive I have been to think these humans were any different to me. We all shared the same emotions and need for interaction and love.

I glanced back at the woman standing at the front of the room, her burka had been removed too. I caught my breath, not expecting to see the familiar face.

'Grandma! It's you!'

I laughed openly, both shocked and filled with admiration at the same time.

Negeenah herself was smiling and nodding at the women and children as they hung on her every word. She opened her arms to embrace many who came to her, whispering what could only be words of encouragement.

'What on earth are you up to here, Gran?'

Negeenah began handing out books to the women, then writing the alphabet on the blackboard at the side of the room. What an absolute legend. Despite the imminent dangers, she was here to teach them! This had to be what was called a 'safe house' for women. I'd read about them; they still existed today. Gran was risking her life every minute she was here.

Another younger woman moved forward from the back of the room. She weaved in between the others, crouching beside each one momentarily before moving to the next. It looked like she, too, was helping them with their learning. She stood and headed to the front of the room towards Negeenah… Her long dark robes covered her entire body. But now, her beautiful face was free. Dark wavy hair tumbled down her back.

'Mum, do we have any more books? I think we should let the children look at them.'

Wait, what! Mum?

Negeenah smiled and spoke back softly to her.

'Good idea, Misha, hand them out for me, would you, lass? I need to work with this group.'

I stood in stunned silence. Looking from one woman to the next, my eyes tried to help my addled brain process. That was the thing about my dreams, they were different to other people's. Mine were not just the subconscious mixing up events and people. I knew they were real, a window to actual past events.

Studying both women now, I could see they were much younger. It was difficult to tell, but I thought perhaps my mum was around 20. That would make Gran in her late 30's.

Why had they risked their lives like this?

Without question, this was a secret gathering. These inspiring women, despite wanting to be educated, would've known the dangers. I had never thought of education as such a privilege. How carelessly I'd thrown mine away.

Idiot Grace.

I tried to imagine the ramifications of having no opportunity to legally be educated. Negeenah had said that even now, in 2015, nearly half of the children in Afghanistan did not attend school because of widespread poverty, cultural factors or war. She also had read me an article stating that in 2011, Afghanistan was declared one of the most dangerous places in the world for women.

How could this be my world?

How could the western world stand by and allow this?

My thoughts were interrupted by a loud, aggressive knocking on the door. I watched as the room instantly transformed and one dared move. Again, there was knocking, more like banging now. Many of the mothers desperately gestured for their children to come to them. Each woman, including Misha and Negeenah, rushed to put their burkas on, covering themselves.

There was pure, unmistakable fear in their eyes. Like earlier, the women crouched, face down, on the floor. I could hear them whispering faint prayers. Negeenah reached out for Misha's hand. I instinctively moved toward them, scared for their safety, despite not really understanding what was happening.

The banging on the door got louder. I could hear the muffled voices of men outside. Crouching beside my mum I could hear her crying. I knew these women and children were all so vulnerable right now, and there was nothing I could do. Who exactly was on the other side of the door?

Then the loudest bang of all came, followed with the door bursting open. Bright light filled the room. I buried my own face in the ground, terrified at what was to come.

I'm not sure how long we'd been down on the ground. I squinted, reaching out blindly for the comforting hand of my mum.

Where had she gone?

Where was Negeenah?

Sitting up from my crouching position, as my eyes adjusted, I realised I was alone. My body resisted any effort to move, stiff and sore from the anxious tension swimming through my veins. Gone were the women and children. The dimly lit room and the dangers it presented were no longer. I was back in the loft of the barn.

The warmth of the day and the sun steaming in through the little window above surrounded me once more. I was alone but wasn't at peace. My previous dreams had not frightened me as this one had. My very own flesh and blood had been in danger.

Vivid images and sounds from the scene raced through my mind. Retrieving my notebook from the backpack, I began to write. Closing my eyes and taking another deep breath, I tried unsuccessfully to erase the image of terror in the eyes of both my mum and Negeenah.

My only solace was the knowledge that obviously they had somehow survived that day, but still, what had happened to them after?

Confession

Misha was due to arrive tomorrow.

'It will be late in the day,' she had said as we chatted earlier on the phone. The trip itself out to the farm takes hours, I clearly remembered the torture of it all. And that was after a four-hour flight. Mum had flown into Darwin with me and made sure I got on the right bus out to Zarnish Estate. Tennant Creek, the bus was charted. We were somewhere in between, hours from life itself, so it seemed. Tension had been high between us the entire trip. I hated her that day more than I ever thought possible. Looking back, the reality was, I was terrified, but I wasn't about to let my mum see that.

I found Negeenah baking furiously in the kitchen. I loved the smell in there, a mix of coffee, spice and the garden outside. When she baked bread, the aroma was simply irresistible. So homely. I'd never had that before, never knew I craved it.

'Looks like you have let off a flour bomb, Gran.'

I laughed. Rex trotted in behind me and soon had the white powder on his paws and nose.

'Yes, in my haste, I was clumsy and dropped it, as you can see.'

She seemed somewhat rattled, flustered even. That was unusual.

'Is something wrong, Gran? Can I help?'

She stopped, sighing and smiled fleetingly.

'That would be wonderful, my child. Very perceptive of you. I am a little out of sorts today.'

Negeenah continued to gather supplies from the open pantry, lining up spices and ingredients that I'd never seen. I set about sweeping up the flour on the floor, ushering Rex outside as I did. He was only adding to the mess. It felt good to be helping Gran.

My feelings had changed so much. I wanted to let myself love her, wanted to be brave and believe she could love me. Negeenah was incredible, and I bet I only knew a snippet of who she really was.

'What's bothering you, Gran? You yourself told me that sharing something that is troubling you can help ease the burden in one's mind.'

Negeenah threw her head back and laughed, raising her eyebrows with a questioning gaze.

'Oh, did I just?'

Clearing her throat, she smoothed her clothing.

'I suppose it's just been a long time since your mum was here. Lots of memories, you know, both good and bad. I just want her to feel at peace while she is here. I need everything to go well.'

I had not seen this side of Negeenah before.

'Gran, it will. Don't put so much pressure on yourself. Look at it this way, lots of her time will be taken up with me. I intend to badger her about going home. I've got a million questions about my real dad and well, so many things really… so in fact, you can sit back and relax and enjoy the show.'

Negeenah beamed at me, shaking her head fondly.

'I would expect nothing less of you, lass.'

We both laughed this time. It felt nice, I thought, to at least be at the point where I could put a little humour into my situation. Was I actually healing? Or just growing up a bit? Maybe both. As Gran always said, knowledge is power. I'd certainly had my fair share lately.

My recent dreams had highlighted my privileged life. Many women around the world have not had the opportunities I've been given. Had I ever really appreciated them? Australia was very much the lucky country for most, that was for sure.

'I know there is so much you need to know, child. We will get there. Go easy on my daughter, if you can. The tongue is a double-edged sword, remember. So very powerful.'

Negeenah continued to add ingredients to her bowl at lightning speed.

'It will be nice to have three generations here again... and safe together. That's half the reason I am so flustered, I think. I'm trying to bake two of Misha's favourite Afghan desserts. It's been a long while since we have eaten these. I hope you like them. My own Mum used to make these on special occasions. I followed on with her tradition long after we parted. She would bake these always when my father was due home from the mines. I remember playing outside, and the glorious smell would drift through the air. My brother and I would get so excited, for we knew what it meant. Our world would once again be complete.'

Tears glistened in her eyes. Even after all this time, it was evident her memories were crystal clear.

'Let me help then.'

I was rolling up my sleeves, already washing my hands in the trough before Negeenah had a chance to respond. I suddenly wanted to carry on this family tradition.

'So, what exactly are we cooking?'

The sparkle returned to Negeenah's eyes.

'I love you, Gracie. I hope you know that.'

I swallowed hard. Did I dare respond the way I really wanted too?

'I love you, too, Gran. Thank you for helping me through all this... I know I've been... well, difficult.'

She was worth the risk to my heart. I knew I had to start to trust someone.

'Right then, well, we are now going to attempt two traditional Afghani desserts. After I moved in with my husband, as well as educating me, my mother-in-law also taught me how to cook many things. As I said, she was a kind woman. I think I understand now that it was simply so I could please her son. Nonetheless, I was grateful for the skills and knowledge. We all need to build upon ourselves and have a growth mindset every opportunity we get. Always remember that, Gracie, okay?'

I nodded silently.

I want to belong here.

'So, Gracie, we are making Firnee, which is like a spicy rice pudding, and Malida, a sweet bread pudding.'

'Sounds good, Gran. I've never done much cooking, but I'm a quick learner. Lead the way. Maybe I can cook these for my children one day. Keep our Afghan traditions alive.'

Negeenah shifted on the spot, and drawing a sharp breath, tears appeared in her eyes again.

'I couldn't imagine anything better, my child. And I can see you doing just that.'

The hours in the kitchen today had so far provided the most fun I could remember in a long while. Spending time together, I could see again just how similar Negeenah was to my mum. Her movements, her facial expressions, her laugh. I wondered if that was because Misha was born when Negeenah was barely a woman herself. In a way, they were almost like sisters, even working together as educators. I suddenly longed for the closeness to return with my own mum.

Could I ever get it back?

Had I caused irreparable damage?

'I have many strange dreams, you know, Gran, and not just the type that come in the night.'

I needed to get the secret off my chest. I hoped now that Negeenah could help me understand why. Help me to see I was not crazy.

'Yes, child, I believe it is a special gifting you have. You are very blessed. Now can you pass me the nutmeg, please?'

I was a little perplexed at this calm and almost dismissive reply.

It came too quickly. Almost like she was fobbing off what was such a personal disclosure. For some reason, it agitated me to think she was playing them down as if they were normal, nothing of any great consequence. That twitchy feeling returned to my hands as I crossed my arms.

'I saw you in my dreams, Gran, with your brother... twice, actually.'

I'd adopted a challenging tone, blurted it out before I really thought about what I was saying. Why did I always use my mouth to try to hurt people?

I was so stupid sometimes.

The last thing I wanted to do was upset her further today, but she'd pushed me into a corner.

Had she, or was I just being irrational?

Negeenah stared out the kitchen window. I held my breath waiting for a response. The tension had returned to her face, and her knuckles tightened over the chair she was leaning on.

'He was a very kind and brave man. I miss him very much... every day.'

Her focus remained fixed outside. I was deep in it now, might as well continue.

'I know this was his farm, and he relocated from Afghanistan earlier than you. He had a young wife and a small baby. I also know they died here. When they did, he returned to Afghanistan broken-hearted.'

When would I learn? Talk about poking the bear! My tone was still harsher than intended. But as aware of my behaviour pattern as I was, it seemed I was unable to stop it. Fact was, whenever I felt insignificant or rejected by someone I trusted, I fought back and lashed out. My words had stung.

Just shut the hell up, Grace.

Negeenah slumped into a chair, her eyes vacant. My invisible bullets had wounded her. Surprisingly she didn't question how I knew. Silence thickened the air around us. So, did that mean she really was aware of this gift I possessed? Finally, I sat, too, reaching for Gran's hand. I had to fix this.

'I'm so sorry… I'm an idiot… It must have been a terrible time. I didn't mean to upset you. Once again, I let my big mouth ruin a good thing. I'm so sorry, Gran.'

Negeenah composed herself somewhat.

'It's alright, Gracie. I know you need to feel heard. Truth be told, I guess it's time we discussed it. I, too, have the gifting you do. So, tell me everything… what exactly did your dreams show you?'

I explained my first dream about Asadi being very ill. As I spoke of the dream at the gravesite, Gran held her hands to her head and cried.

'They were so young. It was a harsh winter that year. Too harsh. Asadi became ill. We tried everything but couldn't help her. Our beautiful girl was so full of life and love. She died of pneumonia. Then, when little Kinaaz also became ill, we were distraught, desperate. We called for a doctor, but it was too late. They died within hours of each other, lying huddled together. It was not supposed to be like that. They had come here to escape the torment of a country we all once loved as our home. They were the ones who helped your mother and I leave. It was meant to be a fresh start. A second chance. We had no choice.'

Negeenah was becoming short of breath as she sobbed. I moved my chair closer to hers, hugging her protectively. She remained slumped over the table. I had no idea what to say, but I knew I'd stay by her side in that moment for as long as she needed. It was the least I could do.

'It's all my fault. Everything, every secret, every lie, everything. No wonder your mum wanted to leave me out here. She left for the city with you soon after they died. I am so sorry, Grace. Please, forgive me.'

I was processing as quickly as I could, but still, I couldn't comprehend. I drew the courage I needed with a deep breath.

'I knew her, didn't I? I knew her.'
Negeenah stared at me through defeated tears.
I knew for sure.
Her silence said it all.

Forgiveness

Biding time, absentmindedly my boot moved the red dirt on the road. Earlier, I'd wanted to mark an SOS sign on this spot. Only weeks later, however, I found myself creating the outline of a flower. It's funny how I'd grown to love these boots; they made me feel like I belonged to this land. Even more confronting was the fact I wanted to.

Rex and I waited at the front gate for Mum to arrive, I wondered if Rex still remembered being dumped by the red letterbox. I sure did.

'Was I really that self-absorbed when I first came, Rex?'

He looked up at me before continuing to sniff out a cavernous hole nearby.

'I guess this place has helped me after all. I feel so different now. Still, I have reservations, I'm unsure about what's next. What if my friends don't want to know me anymore? What if I no longer belong in the city? Rex, are you listening? I was going to tell you something important... I think part of me wants to stay here, you know? Is that weird?'

I could only see his rear end sticking out the hole on the other side of the road. I imagined a wombat rushing out at him any second, annoyed at being disturbed. Rex always made me laugh. Crazy old dog.

The afternoon was similar to the one when I'd first stepped off the bus. The birds screeched in the sky relentlessly, but they no longer scared me. The air was a little more humid than it had been that day, and the wind was stronger. The sky held more fluffy white clouds. The eucalyptus had that now-familiar scent, calming me.

The red dirt underfoot felt natural, and I barely noticed the flies that taunted me not so long ago. The old Akubra hat Gran had given me helped ease the heat. It had been Asadi's hat. I was unsure whether I should take it. But Negeenah had assured me Asadi would be honoured for me to wear it. It felt like a privilege, and I wanted to be connected to her, to them, in any way I could.

'She always wanted to watch you grow up, you know.' Negeenah had said.

'It brought her much joy watching you and Kinaaz together. She had lost her own family tragically, and we all meant everything to her.'

Her voice had been but a whisper, the memories clearly still raw. I'd tried to pursue the topic further, find out how many times I had, in fact, visited the farm as a little girl. But to no avail.

'When Gran wants to shut down a conversation, Rex, she sure is good at it. It cracks me up when she hurries off like she never really heard you at all.'

Rex was still preoccupied, I might as well be talking to the dirt, but I was okay with that. I wondered why I had zero memories of Zarnish Estate. I'd thought Bluey crazy when he said I'd been here. Clearly, again, I was wrong. Gran did say we had gone to the city after Asadi and Kinaaz died. But where were we before?

Secrets are a burden, Gran had said. She was right about that, and they pissed me off, too.

Dust began rising up along the road ahead. Mum had arrived. Pacing, I rubbed my suddenly clammy hands on my shorts. I began picking at my fingernails.

Stop it, Grace. It's happening again… who keeps turning the dial up to 11.

Suddenly, my butterfly appeared, fluttering beside me as I paced, stopping me still.

Freaky!

As Mum's car turned up the driveway, I plastered a smile and tried to look like I wasn't about to explode. I couldn't see Mum's face with the sun's reflection to get a read on her mood, but she was waving at least.

Rex bounded beside my mum's rental car as if ushering her to the house. He had a surprising amount of energy considering the heat. He barked excitedly.

Interesting, he never left Negeenah's side that first day and never barked. Rex remembers Mum without question.

I felt a little sick as I walked up behind her car. I'd pushed Mum to the limit in the past few months, relentless in my quest to really make her pay. Now that my eyes had been opened to a very different reality, I knew I'd undoubtedly hurt her deeply and embarrassed her, too.

Mum got out of the car and stretched. Despite her long trip, she looked as beautiful and alive as always. Her boho pink dress flowed around her, almost touching the ground. Her hair was swept up, tied in a bun. I could see the lapis stone necklace was around her neck, just as I knew it would be.

'Rex, hello, my old mate, I was hoping you would still be here.'

She bent down and embraced him with a warm hug and pat. Rex wiggled with delight from head to toe. I felt a little jealous. I hoped he still noticed me now Mum was here.

'Been a while, hey, old boy. Have you been looking after my precious little girl?'

I was standing just behind her car now.

Did she mean me?

As if hearing my anxious thoughts, Mum began walking toward me, arms outstretched. Her smile was radiant, her dark eyes sparkled. I couldn't move.

'Hello beautiful, I see Gran has reunited you with your lapis. That's a very good thing.'

Without saying another word, Mum embraced me. We stayed like that for a long while as I melted into her arms. I didn't care that tears were streaming down my hot cheeks.

'Everything is okay, Gracie. I love you.'

My voice was croaky as I replied. But I managed to look her in the eye.

'I am sorry, Mum, for everything.'

Words

Watching Mum and Negeenah together over the coming days was fascinating, yet at times still confusing. They had such a strong bond and now I partially understood why. I took heaps of photos of them together, trying to capture moments that I could always remember. I figured I'd try to replace some bad memories with good, perhaps. No matter what happened from here, these moments of us all together again at Zarnish Estate were worth capturing.

As yet, I'd dared not ask either of them about our family, nor all the details I knew.

But I would.

I had to.

If Mum and Gran didn't like it, well, that was simply bad luck. The secrets between us needed to end here and now. If we were all trying to be a family again, we had to be better than that. And I knew it had to happen while we were all together. It was the only way I could see us moving forward.

But what the hell was last night about?

The morning was beautiful. It gave me hope. The sun was already extending its fingers, offering the healing of a new day and I willed this to be true. I had not slept much the night before, and I wondered if Mum had. It's funny how a day can bring so much joy, then in one turn of events, it all comes crashing down.

I hadn't felt this level of anxiety for weeks and certainly hadn't missed the physical effects it brought with it. I hoped spending some time together today would help. Maybe the history of our beautiful surroundings would encourage Mum to talk to me and open up.

'Let's go for a walk, Mum. I'm sure Rex would like that.'

'Good idea, Grace, he always did love a bushwalk. I need some fresh air to clear my head a bit after the long trip.'

I know that's a lie, Mum.

The night before had been tense. I'd fallen asleep reading through my notebook when the voices woke me. They were relatively quiet at first but soon became insistent. When I woke, I thought perhaps I was having a dream, but not so. Rex whined beside me, looking towards the door. The voices were very familiar, those of Misha and Negeenah. Their fight was also very real, and their seething tones were both as harsh as one another.

'Stay here, Rex, you'll give me away if you come. No offence, boy, but you are pretty loud and clumsy sometimes.'

I decided to sneak down the hallway to eavesdrop. Closing my bedroom door carefully behind me, Rex stayed put on the bed. From the shadows, I could see Mum and Gran. They stood only inches away from one another in the front sitting room, their body language speaking volumes. I was relieved the lights were dim. Still, I would need to be careful not to be discovered.

'I will not discuss it further, Misha. It was a mistake. Look what he has done.'

'It was his duty, Mum. You know about that. He *had* to cut us off for our own safety. I agreed with him. This will be okay. I'm fed up, I don't want to risk our lives anymore. I am so sick of looking over my shoulder. I'm tired of it, Mum.'

Both women were fuming, refusing to back down, fuelled by years of suppression. I got the feeling the emotion was stemming from far more than just this one incident, whatever that was.

'What if his actions have destroyed her chances of having a

normal, successful life? Did you think about that? What about her scholarship… Well?'

Misha turned away, then abruptly faced Negeenah again, walking closer to her still.

'You of all people. What a joke. How can you sit there and say that about him? The famous Negeenah. Your actions changed all our lives. The whole family. Did you ever think about that?'

'Every day of my life, I pay for my choices, Misha. Don't ever think I could forget.'

I shuffled back. My body seemed to be making a choice of its own to get me out of there. It was wrong to be prying. I felt a little ashamed and scrambled silently back to the quiet of my room.

Leaning up against the closed door, I slid to the ground, desperate to make sense of what I'd just heard. Rex came to my side, licking my face.

Were they talking about me?

And who is 'he'?

Could we really be in danger?

What has Negeenah done that affected us all?

Sleep hadn't come easily that night.

As I expected, Mum seemed preoccupied as we walked out the front door this morning. Rex greeted us eagerly, he never tired from the thrill of a walk. Animals, I was coming to learn, understood how to just be in a moment, and enjoy simple pleasures. I wondered if that was the key to a calm mind.

I wish it could be that easy.

Looking up at the vibrant blue sky, I could already feel the sting of the sun's rays. It was going to be another scorcher. We were both wearing sun hats, insisting Mum grab one on our way out. I'd learned their necessity in less than a week of being here, courtesy of my peeling red nose from sunburn.

'The hot days are so much better out here, don't you think, Mum?'

She laughed.

'Well, that's something I didn't think I would ever hear you say, Gracie.'

'I mean the air, it's so beautiful and calm. I suppose now that I'm looking at things a little differently, I can appreciate it.'

My heartfelt words felt foreign even to me.

'Who are you, and what have you done with my daughter?'

Misha chuckled again, at least I was helping to alleviate the tension. The night before had taken its toll. Mum squeezed my hand.

'It's so nice to hear you talk like this, Gracie. It seems like you are feeling a little better about life, hey? You look so good, refreshed and alive.'

I stopped, facing her. Her simple white dress was light on her brown skin. Her beauty seemed magnified by our surroundings. It felt good to be in Mums presence. I needed her, I knew that now. I loved her so much.

Do I dare tell her?

She didn't look like the city lawyer that raised me. This was a different Misha.

We hadn't gotten far, standing in the middle of the driveway, almost trance-like in the magic of the early morning. A slight breeze, carrying the sweet scent of wisteria, ruffled through my new orange sundress. Mum had brought this with her as a gift.

'Yeh I'm getting there, Mum. I've discovered a lot about myself that's for sure. However, we have a bit to work out... you and me, I mean. If you want to... if it's not too late. I'm hoping we can be honest with each other from here on out.'

For the first time in my life, I felt like an equal in our relationship.

'I'm here, Gracie. Nothing you could do could keep me from loving you. I know we can get through this. I've made some big mistakes, and you are the last person I'd ever want to hurt.'

Misha dropped her head, sighing heavily. Looking at her, I saw her through a completely different lens. Gran was right; education did bring the most powerful form of change. I understood so much more. Now I saw a woman who had been through so much. I saw deeper than her beauty. Her own mask appeared cracked, the burden on her face now evident. She had held too many secrets.

I saw the loneliness and isolation the past had forced upon her. She had asked for none of it. I had never considered her a victim of her past, not that she had ever acted like one. She was not the enemy I'd created in my mind.

'Come on then, Grace, let's just enjoy our walk and see where the wind takes us.'

Mum's smile was veiled. She was buying time, the caution in her eyes was obvious.

I couldn't help myself. Leading us toward one of my favourite tracks, I knew exactly the destination. It was time.

First, I'd take her to the small cemetery, then the cottage. It was a brave move, but I needed to see her reaction. Surely, she'd open up. Rex led the way, bounding ahead. I branched off toward the cemetery path.

Trying to appear relaxed and casual, internally my body was quivering. My anxious heartbeat seemed even louder than the bracken snapping under our boots and the babbling creek up ahead. I dared not look back. I didn't want to see her reaction. Not yet.

'Where are we heading, Gracie?'

I could hear the strain in her voice. I took a very deep breath to ground myself but dared not turn around.

'I think you know, Mum.'

I continued my steady pace, wanting to avoid hearing Mum say, we should turn around. To my surprise, she didn't. Instead, she silently followed behind. We soon arrived at the small clearing enveloping the gravesites. Fresh flowers had been placed under both the headstones. Negeenah had been here again recently. She had always kept her promise to Azyan, it seemed, to look after his family.

The day became still around us, the air noticeably cooler by the creek. Mum moved silently up beside me, neither of us feeling the need to utter a word. Even the birds had ceased their chatter.

Time stood still.

'It's okay, Mum. I know all about the family who used to live here with Gran. Our family. I saw them in my dreams, and Gran told me the rest. Well, I'm assuming I know most of it. But who really knows with the secrets you've both kept for so long.'

Stop, Grace. Don't.

I regretted my words the instant they left my mouth. It must have been a lot to cope with for Mum right now. I didn't mean to sound so harsh. My anger just kept resurfacing, always when I least expected it.

'Please don't start on me, Grace, not now. Just give me a moment.'

I watched as Mum moved forward and fell to her knees in front of the graves. Her eyes fixed on the bright flowers, she reached out and gently touched them. She looked up, staring deeply into the headstones, seemingly frozen in a moment that was all too real. I knelt beside her. There we remained together for a long time.

Mum broke the silence, her voice was quiet, almost distant.

'After all that happened in Afghanistan, this was to be our fresh start. Australia was full of wonder. Promises of freedom, family, and peace. Our beautiful country, it was being devastated.'

She paused, obviously reflecting.

'But the deaths of these beautiful people, our precious family, it was the final blow. It has been hard to take. First the girls, then Azyan. It all could have been so different. It should have been different, they deserved much, much more. I loved them deeply. So did you, Gracie. I wanted more than anything for you to grow up with them.'

Azyan?

I realised that up until now, I'd assumed Azyan was still living and working in Afghanistan. Gran had never indicated anything different. Not a hint.

'Azyan died, too? Gran never told me.'

'She was trying to protect you, Grace. Azyan was killed because of her. And he was not the first to have suffered this fate. Negeenah is a wanted woman, still to this day.'

What the hell?

I stared at this apparent stranger before me, my mum, who I had known all my life.

But had I really?

Speechless, I felt a coldness expand into my core.

Now my mum felt more like an intruder than ever. Obviously there was so much more I didn't know. What did she mean Negeenah was a wanted woman?

Surely, this can't be real.

Mum had given up her huge revelations in such a calm and non-emotive way. Her tone in itself had shocked me. Monotone. Like she was disconnected from the situation. Maybe that is how she had learned to cope.

Never once growing up had I felt any threat to my life, to our lives. I simply had had no idea. Misha had worn the brunt of it all.

'I met Bluey, Mum. He said I knew them, Azyan, Asadi and Kinaaz. He said he remembered us playing together very clearly.'

'Yes.'

'Then why… why can't I remember?'

Mum reached for my hand.

'You were very young, and I made sure we stayed well away from here after their deaths. I couldn't be here anymore, Grace. I needed to be far away. I needed to protect you.'

I pulled my hand back from her, crossing them over my stomach.

'So, I did come here then? We visited them before they died, right? So many of my dreams… were about Kinaaz and me. I saw a photo in a chest in the barn. The image was exactly as I had dreamt it many times. You knew you must have known. Mum, you never helped me understand. Why? You acted like the dreams meant nothing.'

Mum shuffled closer, the colour had drained from her face, and I could see beads of sweat on her forehead. She took her hat off, her hair instantly wild and untamed around her. But it was her eyes. They spoke of terror and tragedy, screaming in silence, remembering what had been.

'I'm sorry Gracie, I knew your dreams were of great importance, but it wasn't the right time. You were not ready to know.'

Why did everyone treat me as if I was an idiot?

I felt like I had been backed into a corner again, always ending up in the same place.

'So instead, you chose to get Samir to do it, right? Just casually let me know he was not my father. Did you think for a minute I'd be cool with that? Could you not see that started my downward spiral?'

Suddenly it was all crystal clear.

Most of my life was fake. The person I thought I was, Mum had just created. It was all a lie

I stood and turned to go. It was always the same story. I was conflicted. I needed her to see my pain, see me, but I knew I needed to shut the hell up.

'I don't want to hurt you further, Mum, but I can't do this anymore. Can't you see…? All this has hurt me, too. And you know what stabs the deepest? That you still remain silent.'

We didn't make it to the cottage that day. I stormed off on the track toward the homestead. Rex didn't follow me.

'Traitor!'

I screamed back at him through the bush.

I was exhausted, racy in my head. The invisible weight pressing me down, making each step harder as the bush became blurry. My anxiety often presented like that. It had started the night Samir left. I had no idea what was happening to me then. In fact, the onset of my first real panic attack was one of the scariest moments of my life. Everything in my body felt very wrong. That night, alone in the dark, I almost called 000. I was sure I was dying. Now I knew. I had done my own research: I suffered severe anxiety and panic. I never told a soul, preferring people to think I was unbreakable.

'Would anyone even care if I did tell them the truth?'

I seethed with anger; my whole body was screaming out.

How is it that no one ever hears me?

Vanished

On my return, Zarnish Estate was eerily quiet, but I was relieved Mum hadn't followed me back. I needed some space. Even though I was pissed off, I could understand why Mum hadn't believed in me, for a long time, I hadn't believed in me either. But things were different now.

The doors and windows which were normally long open come mid-afternoon, to let in the fresh summer breeze, were all closed up. The house smelt musty, the air stale.

Strange. Especially for this time of day.

'Gran, are you here?'

I headed toward the kitchen, hoping there was some bread left, and some strong tea as well. Despite the agitation I felt, a slight smile formed.

Tea? That's hilarious. Not too long ago, I would have wanted alcohol and cigarettes.

The kitchen, too, was deserted. In fact, the whole house was silent. I seemed I really was alone. The homely things I'd come to love were absent. On waking, I always headed to the kitchen relishing the warming aromas, the coffee pot bubbling on the stove, and the remnants of whatever recipe had Negeenah bustling about that particular morning.

But today, all were missing. The room looked untouched from the night before. The unwashed cups and saucepan used for the hot chocolate we had devoured before bed were still on the bench.

Come to think of it, it had been like this when I grabbed an apple before I left. Negeenah was nowhere in sight then either. My mind had been on other things earlier, however, so it's not like I paid it much attention.

Oh well, probably for the best, what was I going to say to her anyway?

Sitting at the kitchen bench, I glanced around in search of answers. My mind was skipping ahead at a million miles an hour. I wondered what on earth to do next. Negeenah, without question, had become a source of comfort for me over the last few weeks, and I needed that now. I needed her. What was confronting, however, was at the same time, my mysterious grandma was the very reason my world was so unstable.

She's probably out with Jinta.

By the time night fell, however, Negeenah had still not returned. Mum had come back with Rex a few hours after me, and things remained tense between us. I needed to escape. Despite the homestead being enormous, it felt tiny right now with the two of us together and awkward. I didn't know what move to make next.

The air felt thick and oppressive.

The same as the night Samir had left.

I'd listened to Mum wandering around the house from the safety of my bedroom, for hours. Rex, too, seemed unsettled with the unease between us. He was sprawled out on my bed as usual, but his ears remained alert. I'd been grateful upon hearing him scratch on my door. I needed his company, and instantly forgave him for not following me back to the house earlier today.

'Grace, can I come in?'

Mum knocked tentatively. Lying on my bed, I felt too tired to argue and too stubborn to admit I was starving, so when Mum opened the door, food tray in hand, I smiled despite myself.

'I made us some macaroni cheese.'

She smiled too, but the sadness in her eyes was still apparent. This comfort food had long since been a peace offering between us. It was always the beginning of the truce, a ritual each time we fought.

'Does Gran often disappear like this, Gracie?'

Mum joined me on the bed, cross-legged. I could see she had been crying. The steaming bowls smelt so good.

'Nope, she's never been away this long, not once since I got here. She takes Jinta out all the time, sometimes alone, sometimes with Bluey or Tracker. But she's always back by dinner. When she goes into town, she always lets me know.'

We began eating in silence. As much as I was enjoying the rich sticky pasta, my gut also churned. We didn't have to say it, we both knew something was wrong.

'You'd know her movements better than me these days, Grace. I hope she's okay, I don't even know who we could call. Maybe we should go and look around the property, she might have had a fall or something. Your Gran and I argued terribly last night. I knew it would be tough returning here... Perhaps that's why I never have.'

Yep, I heard!

Why don't you go and tell me what the fight was all about then, hey, Mum.

Not now Grace.

Just shut the hell up.

Agreeing we needed to head outside and look around, we shovelled in enough pasta to get us through. Our silent truce had been activated once more. But for how long.

The surroundings of Zarnish Estate appeared vastly different at night. It was still mild. Negeenah had often described the nights in the NT as if they were mystical, full of magic. She told me it was joyous when night-scented plants come into their own, releasing sweet fragrances as dusk falls. Tonight, the moon was full and round, beams of light spread across the land, illuminating everything in our path. Gone was the chatter of the birds, replaced by the song of the crickets filling our ears.

Deciding to remain together, we went to the barn first. It was pitch black, but I knew immediately that Jinta was gone. Only Rahman greeted us as we opened the big heavy doors, neighing loudly, stamping his feet. He kicked at the back wall. He hadn't been fed. With trepidation, I threw some feed into his stall, as his large flighty presence still made me nervous.

'So, she's with Jinta somewhere. I've never known her to ride at night before, she's big on safety, always telling me it's a long way to get help should something go wrong. I wish Bluey or Tracker were around; they'd know what to do. Hopefully, if we have no luck tonight, they will turn up early in the morning.'

Misha stared at Rahman over the stall door. Was she even listening to me? He came to her, settling at once, nuzzling her neck like an old friend. Horses never forget Negeenah had once said.

Heading first to the milking sheds, we then searched the paddocks beyond. The cows were intrigued by our presence and followed as we headed toward the old windmill in the far corner of the main paddock. Negeenah had not been in the vegetable patch or gardens close to the house. Nor had she been at the front of the property. Rex trotted by our side, sniffing and enjoying the night's adventure. If he sensed trouble, he certainly wasn't letting on, instead seemed genuinely excited.

'We don't have a choice, Mum, we need to go out to the cottage and gravesite. It's the only other place I can think of where she might have gone.'

Frowning, Mum slipped her hands into her pockets, moving uncomfortably on the spot.

Ask me how I know about the cottage, Mum, I'm ready to tell.

She cleared her throat.

'Okay, Grace, lead the way.'

It was approaching midnight. The air had a slight dampness about it now, but the bracken underfoot remained dry and brittle. The nocturnal animals would have heard us coming long before we arrived. The creek's flowing water seemed louder tonight, its sound was mesmerising.

An owl hooted somewhere in the bush beyond, echoing through the stillness. The moon lit up our track as I led the way. As soon as the cottage came into sight, my heart sank. It was dark inside. Its only company tonight were its memories.

'I don't think she's here, Mum, but I'll go inside and check anyway. You go and check out the back.'

I liked this new version of myself, the confident one. Mum grabbed at my shoulder gently from behind. Her eyes were wary.

'I don't think you should go in there, Gracie, it could be dangerous. It's been locked up for a long time.'

Turning back, I faced her head on. Even in the moonlight, I could see the strain on Mum's face. With her cheeks still wet from tears, she looked almost frightened. My stomach lurched and I felt the familiar spike in adrenaline. But this time, it didn't feel like anxiety was encroaching, instead a strange empowerment.

A shift in our relationship was evolving. Spending time at Zarnish had matured me. I was taking charge like I never had before. For the first time in my life, I could see my mum needed direction, almost as if she needed looking after.

'I've got this Mum. You know me well enough to know... I've visited here before. This cottage is a powerful place, its nothing to fear.'

'You don't understand Grace.'

I stepped up carefully onto the small veranda, aware I needed to avoid falling through the rotten flooring. I pushed on the door with my body, experienced now in turning the old stubborn lock at the same time.

'Come in and see, Mum.'

I turned back to where she'd been standing, but no longer was she at the foot of the stairs.

Just like that, Mum was gone.

𝔉ather

Although my torchlight was almost useless, the moon provided enough light to move around the cottage. Complete silence hemmed me in, it felt warm and grounding.

Where are you, Gran?

I hadn't been all that worried about her absence, but now I was beginning to feel like something was gravely amiss. I checked my phone for messages and to see the time. It was 11.37pm. The hairs lifted on the back of my neck. Not once had Gran gone out at night other than to check on the horses in the barn.

The lapis stone glimmered in the moonlight, seemingly dominating the dimness of the room. I went to it, running my fingers along its soft surface, images of my dreams in the mine flashed through my mind like a silent movie. I picked up the photo in the frame sitting beside it once again. Wandering over to the bed, I sat down, my torchlight shining on his image.

'Bashir, where are you?'

The sudden surrounding chill was overwhelming, causing my teeth to chatter. The dead of night had brought with it freezing conditions. I banged my torch in an attempt to regain its light, it was no use, it was dead. Where had the moonlight gone? Cloud cover, perhaps? This didn't make sense considering the stars were bright and had literally filled the sky when we began searching for

Negeenah. Remembering my phone in my pocket, I fumbled to switch on its light.

I was no longer in the cottage.

But my new surroundings were not totally unfamiliar. I'd been here before in my dreams. Moving my torchlight around, my suspicions were confirmed. I was back in the same little stone dwelling, the hut I'd seen in the village, providing shelter for the lapis miners in Afghanistan. Bashir, I'd discovered, was the name of the man that resided here.

Did he still?

'So why am I back here?'

My voice seemed out of place in the quiet. My breath expelling a fog-like cloud into the stillness. I was all alone this time. The room was exactly as it was before. Dimly lit, with the same stench of damp earth. The rumpled bed on the floor, the small crate table and the wooden stool in the middle of the room. The photograph still had pride of place.

Again, the image sent a shiver down my spine portraying a happy Bashir and Mum. The wooden box Bashir had been carving also remained on the table. Now, however, the box looked complete. I knelt down beside it. Each side had delicate carvings, as did the lid. Picking up the box, I carefully admired each side. I took my time to take in all the little details within the wood. Resting it in the palm of my hand, I opened its lid. A tune began to play, filling the silence.

A dizziness took hold as I stumbled away from the music, pressing my hands against my ears.

It was unmistakable.

The tune I would have known anywhere.

The tiny ballerina inside began to twirl, just like I'd seen her do many times before.

I was overcome with emotion, choking back tears, gasping for breath.

'You are from my dreams. I would know you anywhere.'

My heart pounded, and I forced myself to breathe. Moving forward again with shaking hands, I picked up the precious box again and lowered my trembling body slowly onto the stool.

This little box represented so much.

The lapis stones.

The music.

The little girls.

The bush.

Kinaaz.

Myself.

'Why am I seeing you here? What connection do you have to my dreams? To me?'

I closed the lid carefully, regretting it the moment I did as the music ceased. Looking under the box, I searched for a marking.

WHAT!

A sudden heaviness expanded to my core. Fumbling, my phone dropped onto the floor, I felt desperately around in the darkness. Had I really just seen what I thought I had? My mouth was dry, and I blinked hard, willing my eyes to adapt to the blackness.

What did this mean?

How could it be possible?

Without warning, the door suddenly burst open. Men barged into the room, they appeared frantic. Gripping the box tightly, I backed into a corner of the room.

More men entered, some were injured, blood streaming from their faces and arms. Another had a large cut to his upper leg. He moaned in pain, dropping to the floor.

The dim lighting in the room, and all the injured men covered in dirt and blood, made it difficult to ascertain if Bashir was among them. Was he alright?

The scene was brutal. Another man entered carrying a body. The unconscious man in his arms was unrecognisable. Some lanterns were retrieved from outside, and a large medical box was also carried in. The little space, silent just moments ago, was now chaotic. The smell in the room was a pungent mix of blood, dirt, and explosives.

The men took off some clothing and made a makeshift bed in the middle of the hut. The crate and stool were moved aside, and all eyes were on the man. He was badly injured.

With one hand still clutching the box, the other moved to my mouth. I'd never seen a person so badly injured.

His face was covered in dirt and blood; I could see the ripped flesh. Tiny stones and rubble were embedded in his skin. His whole body was gashed and torn. The men worked at great speed to cover a large hole in his stomach, trying desperately to stop the blood.

There was so much blood.

The man didn't move.

The shock of witnessing this made me nauseous; too much to bear.

As I watched the desperate scene unfolding, I could tell the hope of saving the man was fading. Some men wept openly. Others were on their knees, faces down, praying.

This has to be a mining accident. These men worked in such dangerous conditions. I remember the force of the explosion last time. Dynamite. These poor men. Someone was close to losing a husband, a brother or maybe even a father today. But if truth be told, this sort of thing most likely happened all the time. From what Negeenah told me, it seems like it still does.

The men kept a bedside vigil deep into the night. It reiterated to me how these men bonded like family in the months they endured this hardship. Conditions at the base of the lapis mountains were tough. But these men were tougher. They never gave up. As I watched, I thought, too, of the woman and children left behind in their villages. How hard it must have been for them. Did my mum or Gran go through that? I felt so humbled to be connected. The people of Afghanistan truly are inspiring. I am blessed to be able to witness their strength in adversity.

Despite their own injuries, some of the men were laying hands on the unconscious man. I could hear their prayers, some chanting, others singing soft hymns.

Still, the man did not move.

They checked his breathing regularly, nodding to one another, relieved his weak pulse remained. As the hours passed, I became more and more restless. My body ached, and I was so cold. I wandered around the room. Not once did I let go of the little music box. Inside I had placed the photo of my mum and Bashir. I would return it to him but wanted to keep it safe amid the chaos.

Venturing out the front door, I could see dawn had come. The crisp air felt good after being trapped inside the airless room for so long. The rising sun was bringing a slight warmth to the village. Small fires burnt along the pathway, directly outside the many wooden doors. There was a stillness about the village that was very different to the excitement I had witnessed in the men last time. I walked toward the base of the mountain. Looking up, I stopped mid-stride; a fire was raging in and around the entrance to the mine. How did any of them survive that?

Noise from the camp alerted me that something else was going on. I headed to Bashir's hut. A whisper was travelling through the wind. Men dropped to their knees as the news spread. They began to wail in deep sorrow. Obviously, the poor man must have died despite fighting so hard. My heart was genuinely sad for the men.

Slipping back into the crowded room many remained. Clothing now covered the man's entire body, but his blood had already begun soaking through. The men, all on the ground, looked toward the body on the floor. Some were silent, others chanted.

'Bashir, Bashir, Bashir.'

The sound of the name took the breath from me. I, too, dropped to my knees.

'Bashir... no. Mum had known you, but why? Who were you? I need to understand. Please help me to understand.'

Did my mum know of his death?

Closing my eyes, I felt the mental fog wash over me, I rubbed my chest, willing a deeper breath to come, the tightness overwhelming. I remembered. Had I really seen those words on the bottom of the music box?

'Gracie… are you still in there? Negeenah's obviously not here. Let's go. I need to get out of here.'

Mum?

Her tone was urgent. I opened my eyes and wiped the tears away. I hadn't even noticed them tumbling down my face. The small cottage surrounded me once more. The moonlight streamed in the window. The lapis stone sat on top of the drawer. Everything was the same, yet now, everything was different. Confused, and barely out of my latest dream, I rubbed at my temples.

'I'm in here, Mum. I just need a minute.'

My response sounded as weak as I felt.

Rex nudged his way through the front door of the cottage, followed by the tentative steps of Mum. Misha stopped at the entrance, soaking it all in, much like I'd done on my first visit. Her eyes paused on the small cot. Apart from her head movement, she was as still and silent as a statue.

'Mum?'

As her eyes darted toward me, she appeared startled by my presence.

'Are you okay? You sounded a little off, Gracie. I couldn't see Gran anywhere out there, I really think we should…'

Abruptly her dark eyes widened, fixating on my lap. Mum's mouth remained open, she blinked rapidly.

'Oh, sweet mother of God. Grace, where did you get that?'

She raised her hand, pointing to me as she spoke. Looking down, there in my lap, sat the music box. Until now, I'd been unaware the precious find remained. Flinching, I almost knocked the box onto the floor.

'I can't believe it, Mum. It must have come back with me… I mean, I found this… well, it's hard to explain.'

Misha crossed the room silently and sat close beside me on the bed. She reached for the box, taking it gently from my hands. Just like I had done earlier, Mum traced the edges and carvings with her fingers. She smelt it, hugged it to her chest, and then just stared. I reached over and lifted the lid. The soft music began to play as the tiny dancer twirled within. The photo remained inside, as did the lapis stones.

Tears began streaming down Misha's face, soon she sobbed violently, her whole body shaking as she hugged her arms into her stomach.

'This is too much, it's all just too much. What have you done, Grace? Where did you get this? I... I don't understand.'

I held her until she quietened. I reached for the box after a while. Had I really seen it?

Maybe my mind had made it up.

In the seconds before the men came bursting into the hut, my eyes had fixed on a revelation on the little box. The words, they would change everything... if they were true.

Closing the lid gently, I turned the box upside down. Even in the moonlight, I could clearly see the carved writing underneath.

'My baby Gracie 2000.' I spoke in a whisper.

'That's right, Gracie... he was your father. My beautiful love. Bashir was your Papa.'

Misha crawled further away on the bed, curling up and hugging herself as she sobbed.

I had encountered many shocks and surprises over the past few months. But this, by far, felt the most confusing. I had poured all my energy into finding my real father. In the blink of an eye, it was all taken away from me... again. I'd found him alright, but never had I thought it would be like this. How could I ever explain to Mum that I had just witnessed Bashir's death? Mum had loved this man and then lost him.

This man, a stranger, yet not.

He was a hero.

A brave man.

My father.

To the rational mind, none of this made sense. Regardless, I knew. Our souls had connected somehow in my previous dream when the first mine explosion had taken me by surprise. Bashir had spoken to me. He had placed the unpolished lapis stone in my hand. I still had this carefully tucked under my pillow.

'Remember, I will always love you, Gracie. We did it all for you.'

Those spoken words had new meaning now. He had looked me directly in the eyes, desperately trying to maintain the grip on my hand. I remembered it all so clearly, but how could I ever tell Mum or Gran, for that matter?

Mum rolled over and sat up beside me on the bed once more. She looked pale and beyond exhausted.

'My life was not always easy growing up, Gracie. But this great man, your father, was the absolute love of my life. He made everything all right. Bashir made me believe anything was possible. We met by accident. However, now I can see it was a blessing; it was meant to be. I wanted nothing more than to be with him forever, with you, too. Our precious baby to come.'

Mum had stopped crying and was looking intently at the photo in the box.

'I was nearly seven months pregnant when this was taken. Negeenah took it, actually. We felt so much joy, yet we had to hide it.'

A little wobbly on her feet, my mum walked over to the set of drawers. She picked up the framed photo of Bashir, tracing the outline of the lapis stone beside it with her hand.

'In the end, it was all because of this precious stone. The magic of it brought us together and then… brutally tore us apart.'

I had a lot to process. I wanted to be alone, to fight off my unkind thoughts.

'If he loved us so much, Mum, why did he leave us? Why are we here?'

'He didn't leave us, Gracie.'

She crossed her arms, standing directly across from me.

'He let me believe someone else was my dad.'

'No. No, it wasn't like that.'

I have to get out of here, I can't do this right now.

I stood.

'Sure looks that way to me. As always, there are things I don't understand, right? I've heard it a million times.'

The familiar irrational anger began to rise inside me, its heat penetrating from the ground up. My skin burned from the internal fire. Mum motioned for me to follow as she returned to sit on the bed. I remained on the spot, ready to bail.

'We had it all planned out, Gracie. As you know, it was a turbulent time when the Taliban were in power. When I became pregnant with you, it was forbidden to have a child out of wedlock in Afghanistan. It was considered a 'moral crime' of adultery. Even in the case of rape. Women were sent to jail, and in some cases, it was deemed punishable by death.'

'Then why didn't you marry?'

'We wanted to, but it was not that simple. Bashir's family had organised for him to marry another young girl. It was an arranged marriage. A payment between the families. He knew nothing of this bride to be. Bashir was venomously against his father's choice. We still intended to marry but knew it could not be in Afghanistan. Part of the reason Negeenah and I left was to keep you and me safe.'

I swallowed hard.

'Part of the reason? So why did Bashir not travel with us?'

Mum looked at the ground, breaking eye contact for the first time.

'This is for Negeenah to tell, not me. But I can say, Negeenah had spent much of her life helping other women. However, things went horribly wrong. There was injury and death. Overnight she became a hunted woman. The Taliban authorities wanted her executed. Most likely, they still do. We needed safe passage out of the country, and quickly.'

What the hell.

I sat wide-eyed on the edge of the bed. It was like a movie, but instead, it was my own family she was talking about. What on earth could Negeenah have done?

'Long story short, Bashir and I agreed I would leave the country with Negeenah. She had the right connections to make that happen. It was going to be far safer for you to be born in Australia.'

'But I still don't understand, Mum. Why couldn't Bashir just sneak off with us?'

'We wouldn't have gotten far. Negeenah and I came to Australia on humanitarian refugee working visas. We had arranged to be hired help at Zarnish Estate. Bashir was going to finish up his last six months working in the mines and then follow us here. This little box was to be the gift he gave you, the very first time he laid eyes upon you.'

Mum's lips began to tremble again. She smoothed her hair, taking a big breath.

'That was all he wanted, to be the best father he could be. He loved you before he even knew you. He was so proud of this little music box. He used to write and tell me about the countless hours he would spend in his hut, carving it.'

Misha looked lovingly at the box. It all fell dramatically into place at that moment for me.

'But he was killed in a mine explosion instead, right?'

My words jolted Mum; her eyes reflecting her confusion.

'How did you know that, Gracie. Did Negeenah tell you?'

I shook my head.

I wish I'd never had to see any of it.

'I saw him in my dreams.'

The code

It was in the early hours of the morning before we left the cottage, making our way back along the track. So many questions remained. Like where did Samir fit into all of this? But Mum and I were unanimous about one thing, our immediate priority was finding Negeenah.

Tiredness, both from lack of sleep and emotional overload, was hitting us both. The unease of not knowing Gran's whereabouts was the only motivator keeping us putting one foot in front of the other.

'If Gran has not returned by the time we get back, Gracie, I think the best thing we can do is get some sleep. Fresh eyes and a sharper mind will help us in the morning, I'm sure.'

How could she possibly suggest that?

'I just don't know where else she'd go, Mum. I'm really starting to get a bad feeling about this. What about friends close by? Do you know anyone?'

Misha took her time in responding. Her torchlight guided us, but the moon seemed even brighter than before. The stars sparkled like diamonds. The air was fresh but not cold. Our footsteps were the only sound breaking the quiet. In different circumstances, this would have been the picture of a perfect night.

'No, I don't know who she really befriended out here. My bet, not many.'

Irritability seemed to come from nowhere, I wanted immediate action.

'Oh, yes, that's right... you just left her out here all those years ago. Even though she had just lost her brother. All alone she was. Right, Mum?'

We nearly collided as Mum turned to face me. Her own eyes flashed with anger now, their intense glare made them appear almost electrified.

'Don't you dare judge what you fail to understand, Grace!'

I laughed, but with an edge, stomping around her I took the lead, not caring whether she followed or not.

It wasn't a surprise the house remained just as we'd left it. Sadly, Negeenah had not returned. I tossed and turned in bed. The clock read 3.35am. Moonlight beamed across my room. Rex yawned, looking innocently at me as he stretched out in the rumpled covers. I just couldn't lay there any longer. I had to do something, anything. Closing the door to my room, I left Rex on the bed and crept down the long hallway towards Negeenah's bedroom.

Apart from standing in the doorway a few times, chatting to Negeenah as she put washing away or changed the bedsheets, I'd never been in her bedroom. Flicking on the light, I entered, closing the door quietly behind me. Her big four postered bed was perfectly made, mine had been a crumpled mess since I'd arrived. The quilt on top was thick, handmade from many brightly coloured pieces of material. Books were piled high on the bedside table. A small glass jar contained flowers that reminded me of a rainbow. I could see they were picked from the cottage. A wooden chair was in the corner of the room. It, too, was piled high with books. A heavy wooden dresser was beside the French doors. Like those in my bedroom, the doors opened out onto the wide veranda. A group of photo frames took pride of place on top of the dresser. Pictures of family and friends left behind in her beloved Afghanistan, I suspected. I took my time to look at every one, each with its own story to tell.

My family. I hope I can meet some of you one day. Would they want to meet me?

I felt calm just being there. Perhaps it was the smell of her still lingering in the room. Maybe it was the comfort Negeenah's presence brought. Despite trying to remain distant and detached since arriving, no question things had changed. I had changed. I had come to fiercely love Gran.

I would fight for her, do anything to help her. I couldn't lose her now. I was sure Negeenah would understand my need to be in her room. Surely, I wasn't snooping, right?

I crawled onto the bed, flopping down onto the fluffy pillows. As I rolled to the side, my shoulder hit something hard. Reaching under the pillow, I pulled out a large leather-bound book.

I opened it eagerly, my body tingling with anticipation. Doing a double take I stared at page after page of drawings. Beautiful, incredible images. Some with a handwritten scribble. Most with strange letters that made no sense underneath. Obviously, these belonged to Negeenah, but was she the artist? Was this some sort of code underneath the pictures?

I sat further upright, no longer feeling the weariness the long day had brought, but instead conflicted. Reluctantly, I closed the leather-bound treasure.

If this were mine, I'd want it to remain private. I owe Negeenah that.
Bugger, I hugged the book to my chest.

Were the pictures dated? What was with the encryptions? I never knew she could draw, but I suppose I never thought to ask what her hobbies were.

One thing I did know, even from the brief moments I'd looked at the drawings, they were not simple pictures, quite the opposite, in fact. Her creations were magnificent, so full of emotion, unnervingly sad.

Did they represent her story?
My fingers caressed the soft black leather. It had a sweet smell,

combining the scent of the leather hide and Negeenah's kitchen spices.

I began to negotiate with myself.

On the other hand, maybe it will help me understand if I take another look. Secrets have been kept too long. Surely, I owe it to myself to find out. What if this book helps me discover where Gran is now?

I took a deep breath and stretched my shoulders back, the muscle pain revealing I had been sitting quite tensely. I looked around the room once more, willing my ears to pick up even the slightest sound in the house, Mum would not approve of me going through Negeenah's private stuff.

Convinced I was alone, I began to search the beautiful drawings for clues.

Before long, I was captivated by the raw emotion spilling from the pages, like I was inside Negeenah's mind. It was both beautiful and devastating; all these years, she had told her story through her art.

I need to find out what these letters mean.

I let the book rest in my lap, trying to make sense of everything I was seeing. What a horrible burden to live with. No wonder she has hidden herself out here. However, in more ways than one, she is still trapped. If she has lived with the hardship of being hunted by the Taliban and dread of being caught, then she obviously feared for us, too.

Sleep now would be impossible.

Pushing the French doors open quietly, the coolness of the night danced across my face. The vibrant moon would soon disappear, being replaced by the dawn of a new day.

'Gran, where are you? Please be okay, Gran. I need you. We need you. Maybe you don't think we do, but I'm telling you. I've never known anyone like you... Please come home.'

As I spoke my prayer softly into the light breeze, I hoped my voice would carry it to Negeenah, wherever she was. I felt the weight of fear and longing in my heart. Anxiety, but for an entirely different reason this time. The woman I had fought myself to remain distant from was now someone I could not imagine living without. I felt overwhelmed and exhausted. Desperation was setting in.

Yet rising above all these emotions, I began to feel something else. Purpose. I wanted to carry on this woman's incredible legacy. The thought itself scared me, but it was undeniably strong. Obviously, I had not a clue where to start. But tonight, in this moment, it made my skin tingle even imagining I could make a difference like Negeenah had.

Did she even realise the positive impact she'd had on so many other women? Something told me she didn't; she could only see the hurt she thought she had caused.

Had that prompted her to disappear?

Did the fight with my mum tip her over the edge?

Negeenah was my family.

That mattered to me more than anything now.

Paradox

My thoughts moved to the leather book I'd found in the barn. I still hadn't had an opportunity to look through it. Perhaps it might reveal some information that would lead us to Negeenah. As I quietly shut the French doors, I realised there was a problem. It was in my backpack. In all the craziness, I'd left it back in the cottage.

Idiot, Grace.

I knew I'd never sleep now anyway so I might as well go back and fetch it. My phone and notebook were in there, too. I placed the sketchbook back under Negeenah's pillow and smoothed the bed, satisfied no one would be any the wiser I'd been here. I headed down the hallway, stopping briefly in my room to retrieve two things. I grabbed the pry bar I had stashed secretly under the bed. Then I woke Rex, whispering in his ear.

'Come on, you big lug. I need you to come with me.'

I ruffled his sleepy body. He yawned, and stretched, then seemed instantly alert to the prospect of another night adventure. He was a little too bouncy.

'You need to be quiet, Rex. If Mum wakes, trust me, buddy, we are in big trouble.'

The journey to the cottage was swift, the blue moon proving ample to light our way. Luckily the path was now familiar, as I was a million miles away thinking about Negeenah's drawings. Her life. Her experiences. It was hard to imagine another human enduring what she obviously had. Yet most of it I was still just guessing about. I really hoped one day soon, she would let me in, tell me about her battle scars. Bits and pieces I could piece together, but I got the feeling there was so much more.

And then there were the strange letters in the sketchbook. A code? I knew of various codings used throughout history, designed to keep information from enemies. I wondered if this was what Gran had done. Come to think of it, there was a painting in the entrance hall at Zarnish which had coding underneath. I'd get to that later.

Just as I suspected, my backpack was resting at the front door of the cottage. It had been easy to miss on our way out, especially after the revelations we'd shared. Tonight seemed especially dark in the cottage, I felt a little on edge. The music box was still next to the lapis stone on top of the drawers. Mum had thought it seemed like a good place for it, next to the photo of my father. I wasn't so sure.

Maybe I should take it back with me? I don't want to lose it again.

'Just one more thing I need to do before we go, Rex.'

I crossed the room, kneeling in front of the small chest. He followed closely seeming a little needy tonight.

'See, Rex, it pays to think ahead. I couldn't open this last time, remember? Now I have my pry bar with me.'

Laughing too loudly, emotional overload and exhaustion were making me a little heightened. I often camouflaged anxiety with humour.

The old chest resisted, and Rex was not helping. He sat so close it was hard to get the bar at the right angle with his big body in the way. Ruffling his head I smiled.

'Are you trying to help or hinder me, Rex?'

Perhaps it was sealed tightly for a reason? Maybe it was meant to be that way. Like Bluey had said, best we leave the past in the past.

Yeah, like that's going to happen…

The more the wooden top lid resisted, the more determined I

became. Eventually, the lid gave way. I sat back to get my breath, pleased with my persistence.

A chill ran through my body as I imagined the possibilities. Someone had gone to a lot of trouble to make sure this was sealed tight. But that someone obviously hadn't counted on me. I wiped a slight sweat from my brow. Regathering the loose curls that had fallen over my eyes, I tied my hair into a bun.

The chest itself was very old. Like the bigger chest beside it, its dark wood had been carved in intricate detail. Elaborate patterns and swirls covered the entire box.

'I saw this type of furniture on the computer. I'll bet it's of Middle Eastern origin, Rex. I bet these travelled with Gran or Azyan when they relocated here.'

Rex nudged me affectionately, beginning to whine. Standing over the chest, he pawed and sniffed at the top as if willing me to hurry up. I slowly raised the lid. A pink blanket was folded on top, covering the contents. As I lifted it out carefully, my eyes focused on the delicate embroidery around the edging. Beautiful little flowers. In one corner, words were sewn into the soft material with fine blue cotton.

'Grace. Born March 22nd, 2000... OMG Rex! This was mine! Look at how gorgeous it is. I bet Negeenah made it. She did love me, even all that time ago... maybe she made it and never got to give it to me. That's why it's still here.'

I lifted the blanket, holding it lightly against my face. I could smell the faint, sweet scent of a baby. Looking back into the chest, there was a second pink blanket. It, too, had soft flowers on its edging. A strange hollow feeling formed in my chest.

This one had not belonged to me. This blanket had been made for Kinaaz. I stared at the hand-sewn words.

'Kinaaz. Born March 22nd, 2000... Wait! What! That can't be right! We were born on the same day? What the hell!'

I sat on my knees, trying to process. My eyes stung with tears.

'No wonder she has been in my dreams my whole life. We were kindred spirits. Sadly, she was taken too soon hey.'

Why couldn't I remember.

I leaned into the chest again straining to see the remaining contents in the darkness. Carefully I lifted out some more soft material. Once in the torchlight, I knew instantly what I was looking at. I'd seen them many times, but now, for the first time, I could touch them.

I let out an involuntary cry, my hands trembled.

One was a little yellow dress with tiny blue flowers on the sleeves, neck and hem. The other was a plain white dress. Folded up with the pieces of clothing were a number of soft blue hair ribbons. My mind raced, I needed a logical explanation, but there wasn't one. My head was re playing conversations with Negeenah and Mum, searching aimlessly.

'My dress, my little dress, Rex. And my hair ribbons. Why would my things be here with Kinaaz's? I just don't understand.'

Rex barked, cocking his head at me.

'I knew I felt a connection with this cottage. I absolutely must have spent time here.

But why, if Kinaaz lived in the main house? It would make more sense if we spent time there. Maybe Negeenah did actually live here? I always assumed she lived as she does now at Zarnish.'

Bewildered, I took the items and sat on the bed. I needed to get back, as the sun would be rising soon, but I also felt reluctant to leave. I reached for the photo of my dad, then the music box and lapis stone. Placing them around me on the soft quilt, I compelled my mind to remember anything that would place me back there. Opening the lid to the box, the tiny dancer began her twirl as the soft familiar tune filled the room's silence. I closed my eyes, the sound soothing me instantly.

I felt tired. Confused. Images darted through my mind like someone holding flashcards in front of my eyes, forcing my attention not to wane.

My dad.

The mines.

Afghanistan.

Negeenah.

My mum.

Samir.

But mostly Kinaaz.

As they reeled through my mind like a twisted movie, I became aware the tune from the box had altered. It was the same melody, but it now sounded like someone was humming it softly instead. Opening my eyes, I knew instantly. I was no longer in the cottage. My music box was nowhere to be seen.

I failed to recognise where I was. It was darker than before. In the distance, I spied a dim light. Was I in some sort of building? Or back at the homestead? While trying to adjust my eyes, I strained to listen. Yes, it was humming, I could hear. Not close, but definitely there. I was sure it was the tune from the music box. More prominent to my ears, however, was the unmistakable dawn chorus, the sounds of rural Australia.

The medley ensemble I had come to love. I recalled the mornings that had lulled me over the last few weeks. They were magical at Zarnish Estate. The world came alive, always beginning in the trees, and joined shortly after by the strengthening light as it began spreading its wings of vibrant gold. It made even the tiniest of flowers glisten as the morning dew began to dry. Right now, despite hearing it, darkness still surrounded me.

The space I was in was tight. It was like a hallway, except I could touch the roof when I stood. The walls hemming me in were rough and uneven. My touch revealed a cool and slightly damp surface. The earth, the floor beneath, was dirt and gravel. Similar, yet different to the lapis mines.

Struggling to see, I tentatively began walking toward the light and the sounds of the birds. It had to be an entrance and, therefore, also a way out. The thin tunnel smelt musty, as if water was near. I could see an opening ahead, the entrance braced with large wooden beams. They appeared well-worn and rotten. Beyond this, I could see the outline of thick bush.

Where on earth am I? Obviously not in Afghanistan. I'm still in Australia but in what looks like a mine shaft. But why?

It was near impossible to see in the tunnel without a torch or phone light, but turning back into the cave, I began with trepidation. I headed toward the faint sound. I couldn't just leave it be.

It was haunting but somehow peaceful. Familiar, yet still too foreign to place.

'Hello? Is anyone there? It's Grace...'

The soft, slow melodic humming continued. As I suspected, I could not be seen nor heard.

Feeling my way, I passed a slight bend in the tunnel. A tiny lantern light became visible. It was very faint, placed on the ground in one corner. As I moved closer, I could see a crumpled figure on the floor. It was huddled, knees drawn to the chest. A rug covered the body and the head. The humming broke into familiar song. I drew a sharp breath.

'Negeenah? Is that you? What are you doing! We've been looking for you everywhere!'

Her body was almost impossible to see in the dark. But I didn't need to see it, I just knew it was Gran. We had formed a bond in the last few weeks, and that connection was so very real. The sound of her humming was enough.

I rubbed my sweaty hands down my t-shirt, unsure of what to do next. Up close, she looked terrible. Older. Worn out, like she had given up.

'Hey Gran, it's Grace. Can you hear me? So, this is where you disappeared to,'

As I crouched beside her, a horrible thought dominated my head.

'Surely you haven't come here to die? Why would you do that? I won't let you do it. I need you. I love you. Don't be so selfish.'

My voice was desperate, high pitched.

'I've just found you, I let you in, I trusted you… you are the one who brought me here! What are you doing Gran?'

Beside her were a few books and some old photos. A large lapis stone was resting in the dirt. Photos of family in past times. Photos of another life in Afghanistan.

Was she trying to remember - or to forget?

In her hand, she held her necklace. She never took that off! I spied a more recent photo beside her cheek, of me. I turned my head away for a moment, forcing a slow intake of breath. What was happening?

The photo was taken back when I presented my lapis lazuli assignment at school. Both Mum and I had been so proud that day. Misha must have sent it to Negeenah. I didn't know whether to feel humbled or furious.

'Why would Mum do that yet tell me nothing about you, Gran? We have wasted so much time. I needed you. I have always needed you. How could you not know that.'

I felt desperate, but with no clue as to what to do next. She couldn't hear me obviously.

And even when I awoke from this dream, how would I know where to find her?

'I don't understand. What are you trying to achieve here?'

I wanted to shake her, but did I dare touch her?

'Get up… please… get up, Gran.'

My screams were louder than the dawn birds, but it wasn't enough. I reached out and grabbed her shoulder. Instantly, what felt like an electrical current ran through my body, jolting me back to the rough ground. Negeenah stopped humming. Her eyes flashed open, locking with mine.

Rex prodded me roughly, again and again. Dizzy and disorientated, angry tears spilled from my eyes. I held my hands up to my face, overwhelmed by the scene in front of me, trying to block it out. Rex nudged me again, this time with more force, knocking my body sideways.

Wait, Rex? Where did he come from?

Slowly registering my environment had changed, I sat up, squinting to focus. The light of dawn was edging through the little windows of the cottage. I was once again on the bed. The same morning chorus greeted me, as if oblivious to the pending tragedy. I stood gingerly as this dream had taken its toll.

'I'm okay, sorry boy, I didn't mean to scare you. It was awful. Negeenah is in real trouble I think.'

Rex wagged his tail enthusiastically as I carefully put the items around me in my backpack. I tried to shake off the feeling of dread coursing through my body.

'Let's go, boy. We need to get home.'

I didn't look back as I shut the old door behind me. With the promise of a new day, I willed myself to be positive, drawing on fresh hope of finding Gran. But the memory of her slowly dying, all alone in the cave was too strong.

I thought entering my bedroom directly from the verandah would draw the least attention.

I was wrong. Mum was waiting for me, and clearly wasn't pleased. Her hair was dishevelled, and she was still in her PJs, the bottoms tucked into odd socks. One brown, one blue. She looked so funny. I fought to stifle my smirk, which would only enrage the situation pending. I was in trouble. I'd been in this position many times before.

She had that look.

Shit.

Mum was sitting cross-legged on my bed, the bed that had clearly not been slept in. Her steely glare said it all.

'Where have you been?'

Here we go.

Her tone was harsh and accusing as if she had already made

up her mind I was up to no good. This annoyed me instantly. She always assumed the worst of me these days. I was in no mood for the imminent conversation. Crossing my arms, I held my head high and willed myself to look defiant, but inside, my body was screaming a different reality.

I needed help.

I needed my mum.

All I really wanted was to fold myself into her arms and tell her all about Negeenah's state in my troubling dream.

'Does it really matter, Mum?'

'What do you think, Grace? Is it not enough to have my mother missing. Then I wake from very little sleep, to find you gone, too.'

I let my hair fall back wildly behind me as I laughed, a little too sarcastically.

'Oh, you suddenly care, hey? It didn't matter that I was gone before... in fact, you made me go. Leave my home and everything I loved. All because it suited you. Was I that much of an embarrassment to you? And now you question me and pretend to care?'

It had been a long night. I needed to process everything. I needed space. This wasn't going to end well. Without another word, I walked past my mum. I didn't look at her, I didn't need to. I could feel her hate, it seared into the back of my head.

Nothing new.

Enough

By the following afternoon, with still no sign of Negeenah, things were even tenser. Why was Mum refusing to call the police? That made zero sense!

Typical of the way we generally rolled after an argument, Mum and I had hardly spoken. Cold silence. Perhaps we were both as stubborn as each other, as it was always the same. This went on until one of us could stand it no longer and attempted to mend the rift. Most often, it was my mum. These times made my anxiety soar, but pride always seemed to hold me strong. Even when I wanted to make amends, my stubbornness to prove a point would stop me.

But she just never listened.

Why couldn't she just listen?

I was worth it, surely.

Negeenah had told me not so long ago, that if I dared stop hating myself, then everyone else's opinion wouldn't matter so much.

Mum's did.

On the inside, I knew I'd been out of line this time. Although I wasn't ready to admit it, I felt ashamed. My shame was much bigger than just the previous night's fight.

Is that what caused Negeenah to run away from us? Had her own shame from the guilt of her past actions led to her intended demise? I needed to show her she was wrong.

Despite having searched another full day, we were no closer to finding her. I knew the bush was full of danger, but Negeenah was smart and she knew it well. The heat had been intense. Despite her strength, without food and water and possibly injured, she couldn't last long. Time was running out. I felt sick to my core.

Mum looked terrible. The dark circles around her red-rimmed eyes told it all.

Talk to her Grace. You got this.

Neither Bluey nor Tracker had been around, and we had no idea how to reach them. Where were they? They never stayed away this long. I wondered if Negeenah was even on the farm anymore. What if she had returned to Afghanistan? Was that even possible?

Surely, she wouldn't just up and leave? I couldn't shake the niggling feeling that perhaps Negeenah did not want to be found.

I'd never seen Mum drink so much before. She seemed to have a glass of scotch in her hand whenever I saw her. I dared not ask her for a swig. Tonight, we sat in silence on the veranda, picking at our dinner. I wasn't hungry, and by the looks of it, neither was Mum.

I couldn't take this bullshit between us another second.

'It's time we called the police, Mum, I know I keep saying it, but I need you to listen.'

Mum turned to face me for the first time since we'd sat.

'Yes, I'm listening. Negeenah would not want us to, that much I know. But you're right, I don't think we have much choice now.'

Finally, she's listening.

'I'm worried, Grace, really worried. Why would she do this to me?'

I couldn't believe what I'd just heard. I spat my drink out onto the dirt. At this moment, she disgusted me.

'You really think this is about you, Mum?'

I could hear my sarcasm, but I didn't care. One minute I desperately wanted to be at peace with Mum, then the next, I despised her.

Truth

Returning from the stables later that night, Mum looked as exhausted as I felt. She had gone to feed Rahman, also hoping to see Tracker or Bluey if they were around. I decided to be the grown up, try to make amends between us. We needed all our strength right now.

'How is Rahman, Mum?'

I sat tall, making sure my body language was open.

'Flighty, he's really unsettled. We'll have to put him out into the paddock in the morning if the men don't show up. Do you know the days they come?'

I didn't, I should have but I simply hadn't cared enough. I shrugged my shoulders, sipping my hot chocolate. It was hot tonight, too warm for my drink, but it was more out of comfort that I'd made it. Negeenah always said, 'A soothed soul sleeps deeply.' Hot chocolate was part of her theory.

We were far from soothed souls tonight.

Mum joined me at the table, sitting heavily and bursting into tears. She reached for the whiskey, pouring a generous serve.

'What are we going to do, Grace?'

My mind was already elsewhere.

'Mum, why didn't you ever tell me I was born on the same day as Kinaaz?'

Oh bloody hell, Grace… shut up.

Misha had been focusing on her liquid friend but looked up abruptly into my eyes.

'Well, in my defence, Grace, you knew nothing of her until a few weeks ago.'

'True, but not by choice. You have to admit, it's pretty freaky we were born on the same day. No wonder she has been with me in my dreams.'

Misha moved toward the sink, staring absently at the herb pot which needed some water. She smiled suddenly.

'It sure was busy for Negeenah that day. Luckily for all of us, she had delivered plenty of babies back in Afghanistan. Just another way she would care for women back then. I watched her and even helped with birthing a few times in safe houses. Negeenah was a self-taught nurse you know, Read as much as she could from medical journals. Incredible really.'

Just as quickly her smile faded.

'Do you know that the Taliban soldiers often allowed her into their jails to help women deliver their babies? Negeenah would negotiate all kinds of deals to get inside at a massive risk to her own safety. Just imagine having a baby in those filthy, terrifying conditions. No wonder so many didn't make it. Not that the Taliban cared.'

I thought about this. The more I discovered about Negeenah, the more I admired her. Not many could truly proclaim they had impacted the world as she had. And all the while risking her own life. Would I ever have a purpose as noble?

Then it hit me.

What did Mum just say?

Why would Negeenah have been so busy the day I was born? What did Mum mean by 'all of us.' I opened my mouth to speak, but Mum put her hand up, smiling sheepishly.

'Yes. You were born here, Gracie, in fact in the very cottage you love so much. It's an incredibly special place for me, too, you know.

For a time, I thought we would live here forever. I loved life at Zarnish and couldn't wait for Bashir to join us.'

How the hell did she expect me to respond to that little bombshell?

I wanted to break something.

Yet another lie. And again, I had been stupid enough to believe it. So that was my little crib? This validated the instant connection I'd felt. It was real. Even though I'd been told a different story all of my 15 years, my soul had known.

I felt a tightness in my face, like my skin was contorting into a snarl.

'Bloody hell, Mum... What do you want me to say to that? I don't want to fight anymore, but you make it very hard.'

I got up to go, I'd had enough. My heart pounded.

'Wait, Gracie, can you just hear me out?'

I shot her an intense, fevered stare.

'Why? Does it even matter anymore? And anyway, how do I know it's the truth?'

But I did sit back down, not once releasing her from my glare.

I wanted to know.

I also wanted to see Misha squirm.

Mum sat beside me, surprisingly, replacing her defensive stance from only moments earlier to a look of clear defiance.

'Best not to judge me too harshly, Grace. It's easy to do when you haven't walked in someone's shoes... I think perhaps I'm guilty of that, too. Negeenah deserved more credit and loyalty than I gave her over the years.'

You think?

'It's becoming evident that the women in our family, well... we are all strong and stubborn, too.'

It felt strangely satisfying, that she was comparing my likeness to Negeenah.

Her face softening again, smiling a weary smile she squeezed my hand. I didn't squeeze back, but remained on my chair, that was good enough. I could have already stormed out. Instead, I reached for Rex, resting his head on my lap. He always knew when I needed him.

'As you know, Grace, Australia, and the Northern Territory were to be our new home. We had big plans for Zarnish Estate. All of us, me included. Bashir was to meet me here as soon as possible. But sadly, it did not come to pass. I wanted nothing more than this to be my forever home. Safe, surrounded by family. Some of the things we endured in Afghanistan were more than any human should bear. Unfortunately, I was privy to many examples of torture and tragedy, living as Negeenah's shadow.'

Mum poured more whiskey into her glass as she spoke, twisting her curls around her fingers, her bottom lip quivered slightly. Like an instant obsession, I felt unable to stop staring at her lips. I wanted them to still, it was unnerving.

'It may surprise you that Zarnish, to this day, still runs as a very profitable business, but we'll talk about that at another time. Needless to say, Negeenah has been able to stay on and run the farm without the worry of income. Samir is also a part of this, as was Azyan before his death.'

Okay, you've got my full attention now.

Leaning closer, I nodded slowly. I went to interrupt but the mention of Samir made my mouth ready to fire questions, but Mum put her hand up to stop me.

'The second winter here was brutal. Pneumonia took hold of Asadi and Kinaaz. We did everything we could, but it was not enough to save them. I was so scared you would suffer the same fate. I had already lost my great love, your father. I could not endure anymore. To this day, I still see their faces when I close my eyes at night. They were so cold, so very cold in the end. Kinaaz fought so hard. And then I mourned Bashir; he never did get to hold you, his precious daughter. I always wonder, if I had stayed in Afghanistan, would things have been different for us?'

Misha skulled her drink, tears rolled softly down her face. She didn't try to hide or wipe them away. No question she had been heartbroken, still was. Yet never had I seen this side of my mum. Not a hint. Mind-blowing really. She had been protecting me, obviously.

I'm a horrible daughter. A poor excuse for a human. She has every right to hate me.

I reached for her hand. She grabbed it eagerly.

Maybe it wasn't too late for us.

We sat in silence. I was deep in my own head. Finally, Mum spoke.

'It was very hard on Negeenah. I think she felt responsible somehow for their deaths. But it was no one's fault. Azyan had provided a safe home for us here, she owed him her life. Negeenah knew she could never return to Afghanistan, so she set about making the best life she could for us. You and I stayed in the cottage, Negeenah in the main house. We were going to move into the main house with her, but that never happened.'

Mum went to pour another drink, but I gently took the bottle from her. She sighed, offering no resistance.

'It wasn't long after that that we received the news that Azyan had been killed. The official report said it was a fatal road accident. But when Samir came, he told us the truth. Azyan had been brutally murdered. It was a message from the Taliban. A way to repay Negeenah for her supposed crimes against them. She may have been oceans away from her home, but she was far from free. You have to understand, Grace, I was so scared.'

I could never understand, I knew that now.

'So that's when we left? You took us all the way down to Melbourne? It's so far away. She must have been devastated to see us go.'

'Negeenah understood my decision in the end. I'm not saying it didn't bring unease and disappointment. But she knew I could finish my law degree in Melbourne. When the Taliban came to power, as you know, I was unable to finish my studies. But it was more than that. As much as I love your Gran, I am ashamed to say I also felt we were not safe being near her. She had the Taliban looking for her. Maybe, had it been just me, I would have stayed at Zarnish. But not with you, Grace. I'd already lost so much. From the moment you were born, you became my number one priority. All I wanted, was to make the best life I could for you. Protect you from a life of fear. A life on the run. I wanted us to have a fresh start. I knew Bashir would have wanted that, too.'

I stared at my mum, trying desperately to imagine what she had gone through.

How could I? How could anyone?

'Please, try to see, Grace. I know you feel like I have betrayed you. But I promise, I just wanted more for you.'

'But Negeenah would have needed you, too, and me for that matter.'

'Yes, and I am not proud I left her here all alone. I imagine it only got tougher after you and I left. But part of me was bitter. Bitter that she had put me at risk during the rise of the Taliban. I realise now that those were selfish thoughts. She was so young herself, desperately trying to help the beautiful, oppressed Afghan women. I was thinking with a clouded mind back then, dense with the fog that grief and sorrow brings. I was overwhelmed. Alone.'

I shifted uneasily in my seat. Biting my lip, I fumbled with my leftover apple pieces.

'It just seems like such an extreme move, Mum.'

She shrugged, staring at the table.

'Yes, I suppose it was, but I had help. Samir organised everything. He set us up for our new life. He has been very kind to us. Done more than he needed to. But there were many times I almost gave up and returned here to Zarnish. It was a lonely road.'

Never once, in all our years, had she let on. I thought we were close.

I sat up in my chair, stretching, A heavy stiffness had set in, as had the headache from hell. There was one thing that continued to haunt me... why exactly was Samir involved?

Cleopatra

Exhaustion was the only reason I slept that night. The sounds that usually lulled me only proved to be a distraction. Rex seemed unsettled, too. He disappeared at some point in the early hours, and I found him the next morning lying on the mat beside Gran's bed.

How was it that roosters never missed their morning call? Finally, I'd been in a deep sleep when woken at dawn.

I'd hoped, by some miracle, on entering the kitchen, I would see Negeenah here, but it was merely wishful thinking. The warm kitchen smells, the morning coffee pot, and the baking mess were all absent. I wondered if Mum had woken yet. I willed myself to be positive, find a way to turn things around. But the heaviness in my heart remained.

We need help with this, and we needed it today.

Returning to my room with my coffee and burnt toast, I was eager to pull out Negeenah's leather pouch to see if that could help in any way. Despite it being shoved into a box in the barn, disregarded, I could only hope it had some value now. Some contacts in there would be good, maybe even the mobile phone numbers for Bluey or Tracker. If they even had a phone. I stared outside my window.

It simply didn't make sense that Bluey and Tracker weren't here.

Were they with Negeenah?

Everything was still in my backpack. I carefully took out my precious music box, the framed photo of my dad and lapis stone, rearranging them on the table next to my bed. No matter where I ended up from here, I wanted them close. They were the link to the real me, and I wanted to know who the hell that was. I paused to listen again to the sweet melody, lifting the lid on the music box; the tiny dancer twirled around and around.

With its beautiful dark leather, the old pouch looked like something Gran would have cherished. I imagined her travelling with it tucked under her arm, hidden by her burka. I wondered how often she had made her way to the safe houses or jails to be with the Afghan women.

Had she ever been caught? How would she explain herself?

I began to unravel the thin leather straps which were meticulously wound, and tied by a precise knot, ensuring it remained tight. I felt restless, desperate for the contents to reveal some solutions.

Inside were pages of notes and official papers, most in Afghan dialect. I pushed them to one side. Grabbing my attention, however, were the unopened envelopes, tucked into the back, tied together with string.

Had they been hand-delivered at some point? There were no postage stamps or markings.

The envelopes were all addressed to the same person.

Cleopatra!

Just one simple word. Was this a joke?

'What's this about Rex? Who is Cleopatra? I mean, I know who she is, but why on earth are these letters addressed to her?'

Seemingly disinterested and flat in his demeanour, Rex was no help at all. It made me sad to think he was affected too. I jumped off the bed and gave him a reassuring pat.

'I'm going to find her, Rexy. You have my word, everything will be alright.'

His eyes looked so sad. Clearly, animals felt emotion as we did. How did I once believe this was not possible? For all Rex knew, his master had left him. Truth be told, it looks like she did.

I just wish I knew why?

Cleopatra.

Suddenly I remembered, I'd seen that name before since arriving at Zarnish. I racked my brain, closing my eyes to focus.

Yes!

I jumped up, grabbed the letters and headed to the study. It was the title of a folder on the computer. Time I cracked her password and discovered exactly what Negeenah was hiding. Weeks ago, I'd seen the folder tucked carefully inside another file, titled 'Farm'. Despite thinking it strange at the time, I wasn't interested in anything Negeenah had to offer, so I didn't pursue it. Now everything was different.

I pinched my lips together. As focused as I was and despite many attempts, I just couldn't guess the password. I had no clue.

'Maybe this is a waste of time anyway, Rex. But something tells me it's not. She is clever; we know this. I've tried all the animal's names, property, family… what else could it be?'

I stood, needing a distraction for a minute. I once again picked up the letters; maybe they could tell me something.

Why hadn't Gran opened these?

I stared at the bundle for only moments before making my decision to undo the string holding them together. No dates, no names, nothing was evident on the outside. It was impossible to tell how old they were. I reached for the letter opener on the desk, sliding it carefully along the edge of the first envelope. It was handwritten, scrawled in black cursive writing.

February 2000

Dear Cleopatra,

Since your departure, we have missed you dearly. We are so grateful to hear of your safe passage. We long for your leadership, your passion and your encouragement. Despite things remaining difficult, we have continued on with your work. You have given me the courage and the skills I need to help others. You made many sacrifices for me, and I will be forever grateful. Please always remember how important you are. You saved my life. I wish you well. As you always taught us, I will endeavour to Breathe Grace on our people.

B.

My mind raced, I had to see more.

Cleopatra was Negeenah.

I was committed to this invasion of privacy now, so if I was going to get in trouble for snooping, I might as well make it worth my while. But why the fake name? And why hadn't she opened a single one?

March 2000

Dear Cleopatra,

I pray daily you are safe. The Taliban continue to search for you. They are merciless. They ask many questions, eager to know your whereabouts. Never will we tell. Not that we know. Thank you, the words are not enough, I know. But your time, educating and building the safe houses for so many of us will never be forgotten. I could never repay your kindness, but I will serve you by repeating your actions and educating women.

Forever grateful,

Breathe Grace.
L.

May 2000

Dear Cleopatra,

I write to tell you of the great impact you continue to have here. Our people will forever reap the rewards of your hard work. Thank you for teaching us the invaluable literacy skills that will ensure we have opportunities that previously would have been but a dream. Your instructions and patience will never be forgotten. You have inspired so many of us to continue to rise, even if, for now, it is in secret. You have saved my life. I can never repay you, so I pray for your happiness and peace. Stay safe.

Breathe Grace.
A.

June 2000

Dear Cleopatra,

Finally, I have been released from jail. The women have provided for my safety. You are the reason I am alive, as is my precious child. He is one now. I pray for you and your safety. We honour your legacy, your bravery and your courage. I bow down in thanks. You saved my life.

Breathe Grace, as you always said.

G.

July 2000

Dear Cleopatra,

I can only hope you received the safe passage you deserve. I am so grateful for the safety you provided me and my children. We owe you our lives. I pray you can forgive yourself. You had no choice. The Taliban continue to offer a reward for your capture. We will never tell. Please know you are loved, and hundreds of women continue to be secretly educated because of the safe houses you set up.

Many blessings,
Breathe Grace,
S.

September 2000

Dear Cleopatra,

I needed to let you know how grateful I am to you. I didn't get to tell you in person, but I was so pleased to hear you got out safely. It was the right thing to do for your family. Had it not been for you, I would be dead. I remain in jail but am provided with education. Secretly, of course, but I wanted you to know that many continue your work. We are determined to rise despite being hidden. Your selfless sacrifices will never be forgotten. Many speak, in but a whisper, of course, of your courage and determination to educate and provide shelter for us.

Thank you.

We continue your work to Breathe Grace on the women of Afghanistan.

T.

I'm such a stupid, dumb, selfish excuse for a human.

These beautiful letters. The thickness in my throat built as I held the remaining bundle, running my fingers over them. All of these women had risked their own safety to get these to Gran. But who had brought them here?

I knew nothing of the real world.

Negeenah was so much more than I'd given her credit for. Only weeks ago, I believed I was such a good judge of character. I shuddered now, thinking of the bitch I was to her when I first arrived. Despite every bit of attitude and rudeness I'd thrown her way, she never gave up on me. In fact, it was at her insistence I'd come here at all.

And now, she was gone.

I'll never forgive myself if something bad has happened to her.

She deserves to know we love her.

The leather chair beneath me felt cold and hard, the air in the study stale. The grandfather clock in the hall seemed extra loud. I flinched each time it chimed.

Negeenah was a hero, but clearly, she couldn't see it. Since the invasion of the Taliban, she had worked tirelessly for women's safety and education, despite it being illegal and a risk to her own life. Something really bad must have happened to make her flee.

I stared at the computer screen. Almost without conscious thought, I knew. I sat upright and began typing the password. In an instant, I was in, with access to Negeenah's private folder.

Breathe, Grace.

Two simple words that seemed to mean so much to so many.

I gulped some cold coffee, almost nervously, as I stared at my success. Within the folder were a number of personal documents: Negeenah's birth certificate, scanned passport and bank details. Also, a folder titled 'Zarnish Estate Business Portfolio'. I'd look at that later. This had to be what Mum had talked about earlier. Briefly I wondered what type of business or businesses she could be running from here and with whom.

Then I scanned a folder containing many emails. It wasn't a surprise to see her alias name was Cleopatra. I smiled as she always managed to link her precious lapis stones into her story. What better way! Cleopatra was a very powerful, influential woman of her time.

Clever Gran, I like it.

Turns out Negeenah had regular correspondence with a large number of people. All foreign to me, except two. Samir and Mum. Apparently, both had maintained regular email contact with Gran for years.

Typical, again I'm the last to know.

I began to scan them. Each contained dates, numbers and names, locations, and drop off points. What on earth did all this mean?

Samir

'Grace… Grace, are you here?'

Shit.

I snapped back into the present moment. realising I'd been staring at the computer screen so intently, my eyes blurred moving them away. Damn, I still needed more time. My headache was back, and so was Mum. They were one in the same, really.

Her normally nimble step was replaced with stomping down the hallway. I could hear her pausing at each room, checking to see where I was. I hurriedly stashed the opened letters into Negeenah's folder and threw it under her desk.

'Grace!'

Her call was louder this time, almost urgent. Rex sat up and barked from beside my chair.

'I'm in here, Mum, just checking the computer to see if I can find any contacts.'

I was sweating bullets and although it wasn't a complete lie, I felt a tad guilty.

Misha was already dressed for the day in jean shorts, boots and a white shirt. How did she always manage to look so elegant? The only indication she'd been outside was the slight sweat on her skin. I'd not even managed to get out of my PJ's.

'Can you get dressed? I need you outside, Grace. We must make some big decisions today. This has gone on long enough. I have contacted the local police, and they're coming out later to meet with us. And there are jobs that need to be done around here.'

Someone was in a mood.

I'd seen her like this many times. This is what I liked to call her 'robot mode'. It was her way of coping when she was stressed. Funny how we all have our little habits. Normally she annoyed me in this state. But today, I felt sad for her. She needed me, and I knew I had to try not to let her down. Again.

'I'll meet you in the stables in ten minutes Grace. We'll move Rahman into the paddock. I've fed him. I can't believe Bluey or Tracker still haven't shown up.'

I jumped up and followed her out, talking to her back as she marched ahead.

'It's strange the men haven't been here for days. In the past few weeks, they seemed to have been around more often than not.'

Rather than poke the bear, I got ready at lightning speed. As I approached, Rahman was carrying on in the stables. I hoped Mum didn't expect me to lead him out. I had the feeling he didn't like me very much.

I could hear familiar voices. Instantly I felt lighter, as an unexpected release of tension kicked in. The men were back. Surely, they would know something. They'd find Negeenah. I picked up my pace, almost skipping.

The glare of the sun was intense, blinding me momentarily until I escaped it inside the darkened barn. As my eyes adjusted to the figures further down, I caught my breath, grabbing at the wall to steady me. The heat rose from my feet, my breath became short and fast.

No. It can't be.

Samir?

All eyes were on me.

'Hello, Gracie.'

How did he really expect me to respond?

'What are you doing here, Samir?'

I planted my legs wide apart, crossing my arms, making sure my tone was forceful and deliberate. I didn't want to give him a hint of the weakness and confusion I felt inside.

'I'm here to help, Grace. Misha asked me to come. I've only just returned to Australia on business. You all must be so very worried. Come here and hug me my girl.'

Hug him?

Was he kidding?

I wanted to spit on him.

To tell him to piss off and leave us alone.

He had no business being here. This was not his family. He chose to leave us.

Again, the dreaded emotions of the last few months flooded back. I didn't feel right. I felt like I was going to throw up. I stumbled over to a hay bale near the door and sat. Putting my hands on my head, I willed calm to take over.

Not now, please not now. Breathe, Grace.

I just needed a minute.

I had not expected this, ever.

Samir came over and sat beside me. Mum hovered in the background. She looked uncomfortable, like she didn't know what to do or say. His steady hand on my back calmed me. But I didn't want him to have that effect so angrily I shook him away.

'Grace, please. Let me help you.'

At this I shot off the hay bale, spinning around to face him.

'I needed your help long before now. But where were you? You chose to walk away. You're a traitor, a liar. A fake.'

I nearly spat the words at him.

'You have every right to hate me, Grace. I understand. But please, will you let me explain?'

My laughter had an edge.

'Well, I wish someone would have the balls to tell me the truth. You guys owe me at least that.'

Mum looked away; Samir held my glare.

'But no bullshit. Just tell me what the hell this all is about. I might just surprise you with what I already know.'

'Fair enough Gracie. Come and sit back down please.'

Reluctantly I sat, ready to exit the second I felt the need. Misha sat by my feet, resting her hand on my knees. Rex ambled over and leaned up against her. Rahman continued to kick and neigh in his stall.

I hadn't even noticed I was crying. I brushed the tears away indignantly. Staring at Samir he seemed rattled as he looked back into my eyes. Maybe they really did have the fire I felt in them. He moved uncomfortably before breaking my glare and looking at the ground. Misha focused on Rex, stroking his head.

'I understand you have been investigating things, Grace; I admire you for that. It doesn't surprise me one bit. You are the third generation in a family of very strong women. As you now know, for many years before you were born, things were extremely tense in Afghanistan. The Taliban had seized power, and life, as we knew, it abruptly ended. Everything was taken away from us. It was far worse for women.'

Samir continued to stare at the dirt, speaking quietly.

'We love our country and the beautiful people that reside there. Together with Misha and Negeenah, we decided to do what we could to help free Afghanistan from persecution. We did not know how long the Taliban would be in power or how, in fact, it would all end. We felt an obligation to our people to do something.'

Keep talking, I need more.

'Negeenah saw she could help women by educating them in secrecy. She was passionate about this and driven from the start. She began setting up safe houses all over Kabul, even in the surrounding villages. It was a huge risk. But she knew the only way to create change was to educate. As you are aware, women were banned from gaining any formal learning, working, or even leaving home. But with

Negeenah's encouragement and careful planning, she managed her way around this. Your mum was a huge part of it, too. You should be very proud of the woman she is, Grace. Misha is responsible for saving many lives.'

I frowned, my tone sharper than it needed to be.

'Of course I'm proud of them. But all the lies, Samir. And there's still heaps you guys are not telling me, I know it.'

He nodded, looking over at me for the first time.

'I know. Right or wrong, we have tried to protect you from this truth your whole life. But there is more, you are correct. To this day, we still are in business together. I mean, your mum, Negeenah and I. One part of that business operates here, on the farm. We will get to that. The other involves providing safe passage for families, mostly women in danger, out of Afghanistan. We smuggle them across the border and set up new lives for them.'

What the hell!

I stood, backing away slightly, needing to create a little space to process this heavy revelation.

So, my own family were responsible at this very minute for smuggling humans to safety.

'I'm guessing that's dangerous, right? But unquestionably noble.'

My voice was more subdued. It was a lot to take in. I looked at Mum for confirmation. She smiled weakly at me, reaching up for my hand. I took it, returning to sit beside Samir.

For a while we remained in silence, my unease brewing within.

'So, I was just part of your smuggling business really then, Samir…? What I still don't understand is why you guys made me believe we were a family. That I was your daughter.'

Samir slumped forward, covering his face and began to cry. Soon big tears spilled down Mum's face too. I didn't know what to think. Clearing his throat, Samir took my hand and kissed it gently.

'My beautiful, Grace. I always thought of you as my daughter, and I always will; I promise you that. I will honour you until the day I die. I am so very sorry for the mistakes I have made. Never did I want this hurt for you. Bashir would have wanted me to look over you always. His greatest wish was to join you and Misha in Australia to meet his precious baby girl. He dreamt of being the best father and husband he could be. He was such a fine man.'

I forced a deep breath, confused at what I was feeling.

'When Negeenah and Misha needed safe passage from Afghanistan, your mum was heavily pregnant. A crime that was punishable by death under Sharia law considering she was unmarried. There was no way they could have gotten through the border on their own. Women were only permitted to travel with a chaperone, preferably their husband, with no exceptions. Misha would have needed proof of marriage in her obvious pregnant state.'

Mum piped in.

'Gracie, Samir risked his own life to save us. He knew there was a price on Negeenah's head. That meant us, too, and it wouldn't have taken long before the Taliban found us. We literally had to leave within 24 hours of the incident. Bashir agreed to falsify documents, claiming we were married. Samir travelled with us all the way. He'd never done this for anyone. I will be forever grateful, Grace, and in time, I hope you will see the truth, too.'

I squeezed my eyes shut, hugging my arms across my stomach.

So, he did care about me. They both did. That's not an action you take on lightly... wait...

The incident? What incident?

I had to move. Rahman was getting flightier at being holed up inside his stable, acting out exactly as I felt. I stood, breaking the intense grip both my mum and Samir had on my shoulders. Without a word, and feeling their stares, I walked over to the unsettled beast.

I reached for Rahman, attempting to calm him. He responded for the first time since my arrival, nuzzling my underarm. Perhaps it was the numbness that dulled my fear of him, or maybe I just didn't care if I got hurt anymore. Without thinking, just like I had watched

Gran do, I reached for his halter and began leading him out toward the paddock. Gran would want him to feel happy.

He deserved to be free.

We all did.

Once the gate was opened, Rahman burst into a canter and then ran. Wild and fast, erratic yet necessarily controlled in his movements. He stopped abruptly, just once, looking back at me for acknowledgement. Raising his head, he neighed loudly as if to show me his gratitude for his newfound freedom. I stood in awe of his powerful presence, the sun calming some of my angst. I felt proud I'd achieved this, and I felt sure Gran would have been proud of me, too. Once I'd not cared an ounce what she thought of me. Nor did I care if she admired who I was. Truthfully, I hated me. Often still do.

But now, I wanted nothing more than to stand beside Negeenah. She was a hero, an amazing example of what an educated woman could be and do. I wanted to be just like her. To make a mark, to make a difference with my time on this earth. I wanted Negeenah to look at me with pride.

Did Negeenah understand her impact? Or did she just see the bad stuff? Why hadn't she read the Cleopatra letters? It was Negeenah who had told me; shame and guilt were powerful emotions. They often speak so loudly to our souls that truth is drowned out.

They cloud our judgment with their poison. Shame and guilt whisper lies into our minds. Gran was right.

The hand on my shoulder startled me. I'd thought I was alone in the paddock. That's the way I wanted it. Leaping forward, I spun around to face my intruder.

'Whoa, steady on there, lass. You were a million miles away. Shaking like a leaf, ya were. Don't let old Rahman ruffle ya skirt; he's all talk.'

He smiled broadly.

'Bluey! Oh, thank God.'

'I, I didn't hear you coming... I, we...'

Bluey's smile faded, his face clouded with confusion. I began to cry, sob, in fact. I felt such intense relief that he was back, and I wanted to hug him. Instead, I fell to my knees in the dirt. The ground was cool and soothing. I didn't attempt to swat the flies sticking to my face. Curling up, I wanted to just disappear.

This was all too hard.

'Lass, what the heck is the matter?'

Bluey knelt down beside me, then pulled at my arm, forcing me to sit up. At some point, Rex had joined us, too. He licked the salty tears from my cheek.

'Everything is wrong… Where have you been… We needed you!'

It wasn't his fault; I had no right to be angry with him. Obviously, I was making him uncomfortable, but the tears wouldn't stop.

'What ya talking about, girl? What ya saying, everything is wrong? Negeenah gave us the week off. Said there was a ton of work coming up with the harvest and all, so we should head north for a bit. She ain't never said we could do this before. Tracker and I have been fishin' one of our favourite billabongs. Bloody peaceful out there, except for his ramblin'. Bloody hell, he never shuts up with his Dreamtime stories.'

I stood, pacing, grabbing at my hair.

OMG! She had planned it all!

Gran's intention was to go off and die. By removing the men, she knew she had a better chance of not being found. That pissed me off. My dream flashed through my mind. It all made sense. It was real, so very real.

But why? Why would she do this?

What harvest was Bluey talking about?

Was it too late to save Gran?

It had already been days.

Ahhh. Get your shit together, Grace!

'Bluey, Negeenah is missing. The police are coming this afternoon. It's been three days already, and we haven't seen nor heard from her.

Jinta is gone, too. Gran had a fight with Mum one night, and the next morning she was just gone. I dreamt about her. She's in trouble; I know it. But I just don't know how to find her. We have searched everywhere.'

Bluey was already walking back toward the barn. Fighting the dizziness and willing my brain to clear its fog, I followed.

'That bloody stubborn old woman. We're here now, lass. Don't give up just yet. She is a tough old bird, that one. And they don't call him Tracker for nothing.'

Tracker

Many decisions were made at the kitchen table that morning. All grievances were put aside. Our priority was Gran. Strong black tea and fruit cake were placed in the middle of the table, not that anyone indulged much.

My thoughts jumped from memory to memory, what signs had I not picked up in Negeenah. I looked from person to person. What a mix we were. Tracker and Bluey were old and worn. I'm pretty sure they still wore the clothes I had spied them in on the very first day. Right now, however, I was so grateful for their return. They were as much a part of Zarnish Estate as Negeenah. The anguish on their faces was real.

Mum sat next to Samir. I had never seen her looking this wild, and earthy, like she was very much part of this place, too. It suited her. She looked real and powerful, despite the desperation in her eyes. And Samir, clearly knew his way around Zarnish. Why would I expect any less, I suppose. He spoke to Bluey and Tracker in a familiar tone, like they had been friends for a very long time. Perhaps they had. And then there was me.

I was a part of Zarnish Estate, whether I liked it or not. A month ago, I would not have thought it possible to have fond and protective feelings toward this place and its people... but now I knew... they were *my* people.

The only precious piece missing was Negeenah.

I reached over and removed the untouched teapot and cake to clear more space. Samir spread out a large map on a table before us. It showed the property boundary and surrounding land. Some 220 acres was the extent of Zarnish Estate. I knew it was huge, but never could I have fathomed it was that big. I could see the house and expanse of its surrounding bush I had explored so often. The cottage and graveyard were in there somewhere. The map showed the creek running through it, winding back around behind the paddocks. I realised I had never been that far, assuming the land beyond the windmill belonged to someone else. In the distance, I saw there was dense bush, and the terrain became rocky and undulating.

'Today, we search this area.'

Bluey seemed confident, and I for one was happy for him to take charge. His old leathery hands pointed at the map. He stood over it as he spoke.

'I know she rides beyond the poppy fields. She likes the billabong way out there; she told me once it's a bit like home. Never asked her why.'

Poppy fields? What was he talking about?

We could hardly argue, none of us had any better leads or ideas. But I had to speak up.

'I still think we should talk to the police this afternoon. They could do an air search or send tracker dogs or something. We're running out of time.'

'Not yet, Grace. Negeenah would never want the police involved. It is a great risk to her to be exposed.'

Samir seemed very certain, and Bluey and Tracker were nodding, but it just didn't make sense to me. Mum touched me on the shoulder, and I flinched.

'I don't really care. Gran's safety comes first. It's been three days! How do you not all get that? Look around you, this land is harsh, unforgiving… and what's more, I think she intended not to be found.'

Instantly, all eyes were on me. My mounting frustration evident as I was done with not being heard or being involved, for that matter.

'What do you mean, Grace? Why would you think she intended not to be found?'

Mum looked at me intently.

'If you know something… please, share it. Did you have a dream?'

'Course she had a dream.'

Tracker smiled, patting my hand as he spoke.

'Yer been haven' them yer whole life, right? Ya birth here was not a mistake, Grace, I knew it from the first moment I saw yer chubby little face. Wriggling around in yer mum's arms. Lass, yer connected to this land.'

I stood, needing a little space, heading to the sink for some water.

How could he possibly know that about me?

How could Tracker know about my dreams?

I gulped down some water, buying time. Would they think I was crazy if I told them what I'd seen? On the other hand, what if I was right? My gut told me I was.

Negeenah's scrapbook came to my mind. Without a word I headed to retrieve it. There was one image I just could not forget.

Heard

The kitchen fell silent as I returned with Negeenah's precious sketch book in hand. I looked at Tracker for reassurance; he winked and nodded in encouragement. Opening the book, I placed it carefully on top of the map, with movements short and jerky.

'I think she is here.'

'What is this, Grace?'

Samir looked intently at the charcoal drawing. It was beautiful, a foreign place, yet somehow eerily familiar.

'This is one of Negeenah's drawings. She is very talented. There is some writing and some sort of strange code throughout the book. I'm not getting into how I found it. The point is, that this picture represents an image I saw in my dream. Negeenah was there, and I am pretty sure she has gone there to die.'

All eyes studied the drawing, no one moved.

'Grace, look at me.'

Mum's tone was serious. It was accusing yet desperate.

'Are you sure? We don't have time to waste on hunches.'

Take a breath, Grace, ignore her.

Tracker put his hand on my shoulder.

'Let her talk, Misha. Explain yourself, girly. Go on, what ya got to say is important.'

I'd underestimated this man.

He had a lot of confidence in me. Why? It was like he understood the part of me that no one else did. This was not the time to let my anxiety win. Gran would tell me to be brave and, speak my truth, stand up for what I believed in. And this was for her.

Taking a deep breath, and deliberately not looking at Mum, I relayed my dream. I expressed every detail, telling of the cave, the way Negeenah was surrounded in photographs. The dim lantern, the bush beyond the opening of the cave. The sounds of the birds. Her humming.

When I finished, I pointed to the sketch on the table. Its detailed markings showed the entrance to an old cave, with bushland surrounding the rocky opening.

'You see, this is exactly as I had described it. I don't get how, but I just know this has to be where she is. Are there caves around here?'

Misha and Samir looked at each other. Mum was crying. Samir's eyes brimmed with tears, threatening to spill over at any minute, too. Bluey and Tracker stood, nodding and leaning back over the map.

'Well done, lass. You might have just saved the old bird's life, yer know. There are plenty of caves in them hills beyond the paddocks. We've just got to find the right one.'

Bluey agreed with Tracker.

'Best we get to it then, hey. There's a hell of a lot of these bloody caves all around Zarnish. Let's pray we find the right one.'

Much to my disgust, I was told to stay at the house, just in case she returned. It was decided Bluey and Tracker would head out east beyond the paddocks. Rahman took the lead as Tracker followed on a horse he had borrowed from a neighbouring property. Samir and my mum headed west on the farm bikes.

What the hell! Give me a break! After revealing where Negeenah might be, I was supposed to stay behind like a good little girl and wait for news from the cavalry?

I watched as the trail of dust behind the search parties heading in opposite directions eventually faded.

Please find her.

Restless, I wandered through the house, Rex pattering along behind. I opened the windows and doors to encourage the fresh air inside. The flowers Negeenah had placed around the house were fading fast. I thought maybe I should pick some more… Gran would really like that on her return.

It wouldn't take me long to get to the cottage and back…

'Come on Rex, I say we go.'

I was pleased to see flowers still in full bloom, making the cottage appear vibrant and full of life. I wasted no time picking and placing a colourful array into my basket. Their smell was so strong, sweet and rich: nature at its finest. These would be the perfect welcome home for Gran. Maybe I should do the grave flowers, too?

What had my life been like as a baby here?

I stood in the open doorway, visualising my mum rocking me in the wooden chair and sleeping in the little cot? I tried to imagine her giving birth to me on the bed, with Negeenah running from one new mother to another as Kinaaz also entered the world. Mum must have been scared, surely? I closed my eyes and stood, taking in the beautiful sounds around me. It must have been hard for her to leave.

I didn't linger too long. I couldn't. I had promised to remain at the main house, after all. There was plenty of time for visits, and I didn't intend on returning to the city just yet.

Shit, did I really feel that?

How was it possible in such a short time that I'd become so attached? I never thought I could be swayed from Melbourne. Grappled with my mixed emotions, without warning, Rex collided with me suddenly from behind.

'Rex! Slow down there boy. I was just thinking… it wouldn't be so bad if I stayed out here at Zarnish a little longer, would it? Would you like that, mate?'

Rex jumped up, placing his paws in my hands and doing his best to reach up, trying to lick my face. It felt so nice to be wanted.

Fleetingly I felt as free as a child again. For a moment at least, I forgot the oppression of our present reality, and the darkness it brought.

The headstone

If I just kept busy, I could keep my anxiety at bay. Keep the toxic thoughts from penetrating the armour I had built up around me over my 15 years.

Was Negeenah dead?

What would happen to Zarnish Estate if she were?

NO!

I had to block it out. Stop the voices in my head. I had to believe she was alive. Bluey said not to give up. He seemed like someone I could trust, and at this moment, I didn't have much of a choice.

Why was I so mean when I first came here?

STOP!

I grabbed at my head.

'Leave me alone, anxiety. I hate you! I am stronger than the lies you tell me.'

Screaming at myself in the mirror, I pinched my cheeks.

'Get out of my head!'

Was this insanity?

I stood idle in the hallway for some time, the day seemingly dragging on and on. It was so hot, even inside the house, whose thick walls usually provided solace from the furnace outside. The cicadas had already begun serenading the garden earlier than most afternoons.

Leaning against the wall I stared at what had become my

favourite painting. I'd looked at it a million times, but today it seemed different. A deep oak coloured frame surrounded the picture. A bold image of a valley. Vivid green strokes of paint dominated the sides, depicting tall, lush green trees, almost like a pine plantation. In the middle of the picture, a wide river, ashen in colour, wound its way between the trees like a snake. The river edges were heavily pebbled in browns and limestone colours. The vast, seemingly rapid moving water led my eyes towards the blue, mauve mountains beyond. They were the most beautiful mountains I had ever seen. Tipped with snow, mist enveloped the peaks, making them appear surreal, almost magical.

Where was this?

Maybe one of the gorges in the Northern Territory? But from what I knew, there were no big mountains like this around here, especially snow topped.

A flush of adrenaline surged. How had I missed this? Leaning in, I could see, just like Negeenah's sketch book, the painting also had a jumble of letters, small but legible in the bottom right corner, just on the edge of the frame. Would it be too far-fetched to think this was some sort of code? Where did I start?

I wondered, if Negeenah did paint it, and create the sketches she had secreted, and used indecipherable codes. What was she hiding or afraid of?

The only logical thing to do was look at the sketchbook again. There was no one here to stop me anyway, and I knew Rex would agree. After all, he wanted her back as much as anyone.

Making myself comfortable amongst the pillows on Negeenah's bed, I got to work. I took a moment to gather myself. I hugged her precious book tightly to my chest. Closing my eyes, I inhaled her smell.

Images of Negeenah in the cave flashed through my mind like a leaf being thrown about by the wind. She looked so weak, lying in the dirt, shivering from the cold. I forced my eyes open and took a deep breath, trying to forget. I needed to focus. I couldn't change the past, but maybe, just maybe, I could the future.

Page after page of Negeenah's art portrayed her pain and sadness. The sketches appeared mostly to be memories and reflections of Afghanistan. I couldn't be certain, of course, but it seemed there was more than enough evidence in front of me to suggest that to be the case. I stared at one tormenting picture of a woman. She was wearing a blue burka and was amongst many other women, all covered in cloth from head to toe. I could see her beautiful dark eyes. They shone powerfully through the darkened slits. One arm was raised high, with the book in her hand.

Was this in defiance? Negeenah had been a passionate educator; this had to be a depiction of her. I got goosebumps just looking at it. Another image showed some sort of safe house or a secret classroom. The room was bustling with women. My mind returned to my dream portraying the silence and fear in the room that day when the surprise knock on the door came. I'd never forget the raw terror.

The adoration the women had shown for Negeenah, and their determination to learn despite the repercussions that would have come if they were caught, was impossible to forget. Again, her drawing depicted the women shrouded in burkas, all dark except for her. Like in the other pictures, she wore blue. Was that her way of representing the lapis stone? Or perhaps it was her way of remaining in the light as darkness had enveloped her world.

My phone beeped in my shorts; it was a text from Mum. Deflated, I read and reread the brief message. They hadn't found Gran. They would continue searching until sunset. No news from Tracker or Bluey, either.

My eyes grew wet and my vision blurry. I felt as though I was shrinking.

Surely today we would find her. This was all my fault.

I headed for the kitchen for some water. I searched for chocolate, too, my comfort food. More than anything, I needed this to end. I could only pray that it would, and well. Did I even have the right to ask for my prayers to be answered? After all, I had done some pretty shitty things in my time at Zarnish Estate and the months before.

Negeenah would reprimand me for thinking this way. 'God's mercy and grace start afresh for us every day, lass.' If I had heard her say it once, I'd heard her say it a thousand times.

What I wouldn't give to hear her sweet voice right now.

Climbing back onto the bed, racking my brains, I was desperate to know about the code and what the muddle of letters meant. Nerdy me had briefly studied their use during WW2, but nothing specific came to mind now. I continued to flick through Gran's sketch book.

Time slowed as I blinked rapidly trying to process the image staring back at me. As intense as it was beautiful, a close-up image of a young woman radiated from the page.

My rational brain refused to believe.

She had strong dark eyes, portraying courage and life. Her long dark hair glistened in the sunlight, and a knowing smile on her lips radiated wisdom. She wore a flowing dress, and her lapis necklace rested on her neck as she looked out across the land at Zarnish Estate. Scribed in the bottom corner was her name.

Grace.

What the hell?

I stared back at myself.

Negeenah had drawn this image of me, but not as I was now. This clearly was her vision of the future me.

I don't understand. When had Gran drawn this? More to the point… why?

'This is too weird.'

I stared for the longest time, before continuing to flick through the book. Rex half looked in my direction and, after a lazy yawn, settled back to sleep on the rug. I was almost at the end of the sketch book. The final page and its drawing seemed to be stuck to the back cover. I carefully pulled the paper free.

Depicted was the grave site. Negeenah had drawn the graves of Azyan and Kinaaz. They were beautifully detailed, all grey charcoal except for the splashes of colour from the base of the flowers. It took me a moment to register, however, that something was different about the scene.

The image didn't only show their graves. There was a third grave alongside them now. A simple rounded headstone. This, too, had flowers placed at its foot. Carved into the headstone was just one word. A name.

NEGEENAH

'No. No. NO!'

I wished I could return to a state of ignorance. My eyes burned. I drew a sharp breath, hurting my chest as I did. Underneath, there was a coded message. I slammed the sketch book shut and threw it across the room. I wanted to undo what I had seen. Erase it. I began to sweat.

I'm going to throw up. I'm not okay.

Blindly walking toward the French doors, pulling them open in desperation, I tried to gulp in some fresh air. I fell to my knees, and tears spilled onto the bluestone flooring. I stared at the glistening blue colour my tears created on the dusty stone before jamming my eyes shut again.

'NO!'

I pounded my fists onto the ground.

'I won't let you do this, Gran. Do you hear me?!'

Jinta

It was late afternoon as I sat in the study, staring blankly at the computer screen. Where to begin.

Think, Grace.

I willed my mind to focus. I needed to be smart. Obviously, Negeenah didn't want anyone to know the translation of words under the images. Another way she felt she had to protect herself, or us, I guessed.

I picked at my nails, quite enjoying the sharp pain. Another anxious habit I was trying to stop. Agitated, I stood and paced the room.

But, on the other hand, codes were meant to be solved, right? Had she known this moment would come, me being here? Had Tracker? Did the men know about the code?

What had Gran done that still caused her such fear?

Was it really so bad that she was willing to sacrifice her life?

Did she really believe she could be found at Zarnish Estate?

Surely if that was going to happen, it would have.

I was driving myself crazy.

Soon the sun would begin to set. The humidity had been high throughout the day with little breeze. The evening would hopefully bring us some much-needed rest from the heat. It was hard not to succumb to the overwhelming heaviness. Strange how emotion can actually physically hurt, like a force pressing down upon my heart.

Staring at the dinner I'd made everyone earlier, I bit at the inside of my cheek. It was my best attempt at spaghetti; I could only hope it was palatable. If the others were anything like me, most likely, they wouldn't taste the food they were eating anyway. It was hard to feel or taste anything.

Loud barking interrupted my thoughts.

Rex?

I hadn't seen him all afternoon. It was unusual for him not to be by my side and I felt a pang of guilt. Was he alright? The increasingly urgent barking continued as I made my way down the dark hallway to the front door. Normally he just came in, as he knew how to push the fly screen door open with his nose. I hadn't heard him bark like this before. It was high pitched and insistent.

Was there someone unwanted on the property?

'Hey mate, what's wrong?'

Rex went nuts when he saw me. I opened the screen door and bent down to greet him. But he wasn't interested in my attention. Instantly, he turned and raced off toward the stables.

'Hey, Rex, come back here, boy. What's going on?'

Strange.

The cockatoos screeched in the gum trees above, piercing the air with their shrill calls. It was hard to hear anything over their banter as I fumbled to slip my boots on.

As I made my way through the leafy trees lining the path to the stables, I froze. Rex, sitting by the big wooden doors, panting in the shade on a lonely patch of grass was looking very pleased with himself. He was not alone. Jinta grazed silently beside him. She looked up at me before neighing loudly and flicking her head. She stamped her feet, flaring her nostrils, clearly agitated.

Omg, Gran's back!

I felt a flood of relief, running toward the stable doors. The tension immediately began releasing from my hunched shoulders. Everything was going to be okay.

I'm never letting Gran out of my sight again.

'Gran? Gran, where are you?'

Jinta was still saddled up, so I figured Gran must be in the stables getting some feed for her. I pushed the wooden doors open. It was dark inside. Still. Empty. And even as the sinking feeling set in, and my gut knew, I refused to acknowledge its reality.

'Gran! Hey, are you alright? We've been so worried.'

Clasping my hands to my chest I searched frantically. She was not here. Maybe I'd missed her, and she had gone inside the house. Doubling back, I retraced my steps, calling out to her. She was not in the house.

What the hell is going on.

I ran back to the stables, falling to my knees beside Rex. Jinta came up behind me, nuzzling my neck and chewing on my hair.

'I don't understand. Where is Negeenah? Where is she?'

Jinta neighed loudly in my ear. I could feel her hot breath on my skin. For the briefest of moments, I had felt elation, such a huge relief. But in an instant, all that was gone again… as was Negeenah.

Get it together Grace. Think.

Jinta had somehow returned to Zarnish alone. Which meant Gran was still out there, maybe injured or dying. I felt numb, like I was falling. Then it struck me… Had she let Jinta go deliberately? Did Negeenah know her horse would make its way home?

She loved that horse dearly, I knew she would never intend her harm. I needed to focus. Poor Jinta, she would be tired and hungry. The least I could do was feed and water her and attempt to take off her saddle. I had little clue how to do that, but I would give it my best shot.

I should have listened when Negeenah had tried to teach me. I shook off the shame, needing to put it aside for now. Again, I heard Negeenah's whisper in my ear. You can't change the past, lass, but you certainly can impact the future greatly if you trust yourself.

I was almost starting to believe you Gran.

Okay, let's do this.

'Good boy, Rex. Thanks for letting me know Jinta was here, mate. We'll find Gran. I haven't given up yet. Don't you either okay.'

Gently grabbing Jinta's bridle, I led her slowly toward the stable. That was a good start. I noted the sweat glistening on her coat; she looked dirty and weary.

'Come on, old girl. Let's get you sorted.'

Rex ambled in beside us, sniffing around as he went. Again, I felt like an imposter, my inner critic screaming.

Belief

Mum and Samir had returned a few hours before Tracker and Bluey. The men had arrived late in the evening. I watched them approach as a dim orange glow was all that remained on the horizon, noting the slight cool breeze finally bringing some respite from the heat of the day.

No one had seen any sign of Negeenah.

The evening was tense, the reality of Jinta coming home without her master only casting a further dark shadow. Despite us all eating together at the kitchen table, little was said. Normally having plenty to say, both Tracker and Bluey remained silent, almost unresponsive. No one, it seemed, appeared certain as to what to do next. That was not a good sign, their indecisiveness causing stabbing pains in my stomach.

The plan was to embark on further searching the next morning. It was agreed that the police would be called in after that, if necessary. Samir had told me that Negeenah had always feared police intervention because of their possible link to the authorities in Afghanistan. But that would need to be put aside now, as we were running out of time.

Mum didn't look good. Her skin was red and blistered from the sun, and she'd rolled her ankle searching the rocky terrain. She was downing one shot after another to dull the pain. Sleep was what we all needed, but no one would find it easy to come by tonight.

Unable to sit still, I headed outside to wander around. The stable lights were still on, maybe that was where Tracker and Bluey were spending the night. I wanted to see how Jinta was doing anyway, and I was sure the men wouldn't mind if I checked in. An owl hooted somewhere in the distance. The stars were vivid in the sky, and the half-moon was an eerie yellow.

'Hey, girly. Come to check up on me, has yer?'

'Hey, Tracker. I couldn't sleep. I can't stand this waiting around. I feel helpless.'

Tracker was brushing Jinta down, checking her over for any injuries. He lifted her hooves, scraping out the dirt compacted in her shoes. I watched intently as he rubbed the dirt between his fingers, smelling it for a while. Was he looking for clues?

'Yer need to sleep, lass. Yer no bloody good to Negeenah or me, tired. I figure our best bet is Jinta. She might just lead us to her tomorrow.'

Leaning against the wooden railings of the stall, I watched his every move. He was so intriguing. The scars on his arms and hands were prominent. How had he got those? Where was his family? Mostly though, I couldn't get past how much he seemed to know about me.

'So, do you want me to come and search with you then tomorrow, Tracker? I don't know if Mum will let me. But I want to go so bad. I nearly went crazy here by myself today. I can't stand it.'

He stopped grooming Jinta and placing both his hands on her back he looked intently at me.

'Settle your spirit, lass. Leave yer mum to me.'

I went to respond but he held a hand up to signal he wasn't done.

'Grace. I want you to think for me. Quiet yer spirit. Look inside ya heart. I know this is bloody hard for you to understand. But I know stuff. Fact is, you know where she is. You girl, you have the answers. It's part of yer destiny here.'

How did I respond to that? Does he think I'm somebody else? I can't. Why is he saying this weird shit to me.

'Tracker… I'm sorry I was so rude to you early on. I didn't realise you were such an important part of Zarnish and to Negeenah. I'm sorry. But I don't think I can help the way you want me too. I have dreams but what if I can't put it all together…'

Again, Tracker held up a hand for me to stop.

'The past is gone, lass and tomorrow is what counts. You, you hold the answers Gracie, its written in the land.'

Perception

Back in my room, I tossed and turned underneath the sheets.

They don't know me.

I'm not made for here.

But at least tonight I'd been given a chance.

What if I let everyone down?

I ruminated on my conversation with Tracker.

Why was he so sure I could find Negeenah?

Sleep, I needed to sleep. Tomorrow will be a big one. Tracker assured me I would accompany him on the search, and that no one would argue with his decision. I was to ride Jinta no less. With my inexperience, I hoped I could even stay on her, to begin with, let alone be an asset. Tracker had convinced me Jinta was a gentle giant.

Jamming my eyes shut, I willed my mind to calm. Rex rested peacefully beside me; his breathing sounded methodical, almost reassuring somehow. I listened to each breath, and slowly its rhythm became my own.

Frantic screams woke me. I fell back, hitting my head on the stone wall I was leaning against. The light was dim, the air dirty, filled with smoke and dust. Somewhere in the distance, I could hear an explosion, maybe gun fire; I couldn't be sure.

In front of me, in what appeared to be an alleyway, was a woman. She was cowering in the corner, desperately trying to protect herself and her two small children. Her black burka providing little protection from the savage assault. A bag of books and papers lay torn up and scattered on the ground around her. She screamed at the men to stop as her babies cried out in terror.

What was happening?

Trying to get my bearings, my own fear reigned. I was back in Afghanistan, this time witnessing a horrendous act of brutality. Two men with assault rifles continued to beat the woman, screaming at her. This woman would die in front of her children if something wasn't done.

I stood, willing my courage to urge me forward, numbed from fear. I'd never been witness to anything like this. Beyond the dark and stench of the alley, I could see the bustle of a busy street.

Could no one hear this attack?

Or did people simply need to turn a blind eye in order to protect themselves?

I began yelling frantically for the men to stop. But like every other time, I could not be heard.

The woman was beginning to fight with less vigour, her strength wavering. She crouched in a fetal position. The men, Taliban soldiers, I could only assume, were relentless. They kicked her with their boots, stomped on her body and spat on her head. Her burka was half torn from her face, revealing her bloodied and swollen skin. Her children had crawled a little further down the alley attempting to hide. Tears streamed down their dirty, blood-stained little faces. They clung to each other, wide-eyed and whimpering. I wanted to protect her and help save these vulnerable children.

But how?

I continued to yell and even tried grabbing at the men. But my hand went straight through them like I was a ghost. Suddenly I became aware of two bodies approaching from the busy street, women. They, too, were shrouded in burkas.

One black and one royal blue.

Dropping their parcels and bags, they ran to assist the woman. She lay barely conscious; time was running out. The woman in the blue burka had a metal pole and began beating the men fiercely. She knocked one unconscious before wasting no time attacking the second man. The woman in the black burka went to the children, huddling them closely as she swiftly ushered them to the safety of the busy street.

I backed away, cold fear suppressing me as I pushed my body up against the wall. Despite willing the attack to end, I was left with little choice but to watch it unfold. The woman continued to fight. She had managed to knock the man's gun from his hand and was swinging the pole wildly in the hope it would connect. Her strength and resilience matched her courage.

I looked at the man on the ground. He had landed heavily on broken bricks, and his head bled profusely onto the stone.

He did not move. Was he dead?

Screeching, the woman was pulled back as the soldier grabbed at her head. He had ripped her burka off, and her long black hair was wrapped tightly around his hand. He pushed her to the ground and kicked her hard in her stomach.

The sound of her cry was almost more than I could bear.

I could do nothing but stare, helpless to save the woman. I forced myself to turn away as the man ripped her headpiece off, pressing his gun into her cheek. I couldn't be there; I wanted out. This was all too much.

I covered my ears, remaining pinned to the wall. I'd never seen someone die before, and I didn't want to now.

BANG!

A single shot pierced the chaos, echoing through the small alleyway.

To my absolute shock, the woman in the blue burka stood, breathing heavily, covered in blood. The soldier lay motionless on the ground, his gun still in his hands. Somehow, she had managed to survive. Her back was to me, but I could see she was sobbing and shaking. She crouched by the man, checking to see if he was alive. When she turned her head in my direction, for the first time, I could see her face. Her dark eyes were *wild with terror, yet strong and formidable. They locked with mine. She reached her shaking and bloodied hand toward me.*

'Forgive me, Grace.'

It was Negeenah.

Suddenly, I was running. Confusion reigned. I hadn't been aware I was moving until I'd felt the stinging cuts on my arms and legs. The sword grass was lethal in the bushland.

Bush land?

I was back, somewhere around Zarnish Estate. The sounds of the birds were familiar, as was the draining humid heat. The glare of the day was almost blinding, and I was sweating profusely.

Like a lightning bolt, the image of the alleyway in Afghanistan just moments earlier rocked me. I dry retched crouching down on all fours. Why was I here now?

Where was Negeenah?

The bush surrounding me was thick with tall trees and dense scrub hemming me in. Why had I been running? I didn't recognise where I was, or if I was running from someone.

I forced myself to catch my breath. Just breathe and listen. I needed to be smart and figure out where I was. Behind me, I could see undulating paddocks covered in colourful flowers. I'd never seen anything like that surrounding Zarnish Estate. But I also hadn't been beyond the first lot of paddocks in which the cows grazed.

Why would there be so many red flowers?

I'd seen them before, on Remembrance Day. This was a poppy field.

Just beyond the splashes of colour, I was sure I could see the top of the windmill. Yes, it was definitely there, on the land behind. The terrain was rocky and quite steep. Huge red and brown boulders and jagged rock formations dominated the land, scattered amongst tall grey gums. They looked almost prehistoric. A small billabong was nestled amongst the boulders, almost hidden by tall grasses. I was drawn to it immediately.

The climb in the heat was slow, the dry rocks slippery underfoot. As I made my way through the valley, I could hear the noisy territorial calls of the kookaburra's. Stopping to catch my breath, I could see what appeared to be a cave. It was surrounded by a huge, cavernous rock formation. My pulse quickened as I picked up the pace, slipping and cutting my knee. I barely felt it, all I could think of was one thing.

Negeenah.

Old wooden beams held together with rusted bolts surrounded the entrance. It looked like it might collapse at any second.

'Negeenah! Gran! Are you in there?'

I listened, straining to see into the darkness beyond.

Nothing.

I walked hesitantly into the cave, wishing I had a torch or phone light. Instead, I used my hands to guide me along the cold and rough stone wall.

'Gran, are you in here? It's Grace! Please be here.'

I heard it again. The faintest of humming. The sound was weak, but it was there, somewhere deep within the cave.

'Gran! I'm here, I'm coming. It's going to be alright.'

I tried to move forward, but without warning, I couldn't. I was becoming disoriented in the darkness. As much as I willed my body, my limbs wouldn't budge. Even my mouth wouldn't open to yell out.

Heaviness took hold as I fell…

'Grace? Hey… It's okay. It's me.'

My eyes flashed open. Disorientated, I sat up, a little light-headed from the fast movement.

'Are you okay? That must have been some dream you were having. You were as stiff as a board when I found you. You looked terrified.'

Mum gripped my hands. She was in her PJs, her hair cascaded over her shoulders. She smiled at me, cupping my chin. I was back in my bed.

'Was it a nightmare Gracie? You're safe now. I'm here.'

I reached over and hugged her. I needed her. She hugged me back.

'Rex woke me and dragged me in here. Seems you have a guardian angel.'

I pulled away a little from her embrace.

'It… it wasn't a nightmare. Well, it was, but… it was more than that.'

Would she believe me?

I thought back to the alleyway. Negeenah had saved that woman's life. Just like the letter said.

'Mum, I know about Negeenah. I know she killed some soldiers. But it was in self-defence, and that poor lady and her children… they would have been killed had she not been there. I saw it all in my dream just now.'

The colour drained from Mum's face.

'Oh, Grace. That's something I never, ever wanted you to see.'

Mum hugged me again. She was shaking. I pulled away from her tight grip, looking at her intently.

'And you were there. It was you who helped the children get away, right?'

Mum took a while to answer.

'Yes. To this day, I feel guilty that I left Negeenah there. But she begged me to get the children to safety. Negeenah nearly died that day. They injured her horribly and it's taken her a lifetime to attempt recovery. Truthfully, I doubt she ever will.'

I understood, finally.

I wished I didn't.

Reprieve

Tracker woke me at the crack of dawn as promised. He even beat Stanley with his famous morning alarm call. How early was it? Had I even slept?

'Make sure ya cover yer skin with a shirt and jeans. Got me? We don't need no third-degree sunburn today. I've got everything else we need. See ya in the barn in a few shakes.'

I nodded, rubbing my eyes and still too sleepy to talk. An intense flush of heat rose from my toes as the images from my dream, Negeenah in the cave, came flooding back.

Tracker's prediction had been right. I know where she is.

All we had to do now was find the specific place.

Despite my nerves, I settled into the saddle without much hassle.

I can do this.

Jinta was calm as Tracker had promised. After briefing me on the basics of horse riding, we slowly headed out beyond the paddocks. The cows eyed us suspiciously as we passed, before returning to their morning feed. Bluey had already given them hay. He was heading out with Samir on the farm bikes. Mum was staying at the house, as her ankle was still swollen and painful. I could tell she was annoyed. Rex would stay with her.

'Now, girly, ya need to listen to me. Got that? You fall or get lost, and we are in trouble. It will take us about an hour to travel where we need to go. We will take a break by the river for smoko. You just holla if yer need to stop. I know yer headstrong just like ya mum, but we need to do this right.'

I smiled at him and his stern face. I felt confident I could do this.

'Yep, Tracker, you're the boss. I will follow your lead, I promise.'

If Dad could see me now, would he be proud? Was he looking down on me? I hope he is.

Beyond the paddocks, we kept a steady pace winding up a dirt track on a grassy hill. I was keen to see what it looked like on the other side. The track looked well used, wide enough for a truck or tractor. Tracker arrived at the top first, turning and nodding when he saw I was close behind.

Jinta stopped beside Rahman, lowering her head to munch on a patch of fresh grass. I followed Tracker's gaze across the land, taking in the breeze. Doing a double take, my mouth fell open.

'Beautiful, hey girly? These are our poppy fields. Quite a lucrative business the old bird runs out here.'

'Poppies? How the heck? I don't get it?'

'You will, lass. But all that's for another time. All this is rightfully yours… Anyways, I need to keep me big mouth shut about that hey. Come on girl.'

With that, he pointed Rahman down the hill. Startled, Jinta immediately followed.

I guess we're moving on. But, what the hell had he meant… rightfully mine?

Clearly, our conversation was over. As Jinta carefully led the way toward the vast expanse of red.

Oh! Look at that!

The poppies moved gently in the wind, giving them life; it felt surreal to see them there. Literally this property was in the middle of nowhere. Beyond was a dense tree line and the rocky mountain terrain. I knew instantly.

'Tracker!'

He turned, a knowing smile on his face.

'I saw this in my dreams.'
'I know, girly… I know.'

Spirits

Climbing down tentatively, Jinta neighed and snorted at the sight of the flowing water, eager to quench her thirst. The river was beautiful. Huge gums provided much-needed shade. I waded into the softly flowing water to cool my body. Tracker was already in, fully clothed, his dark skin glistening in the golden liquid.

Back on the bank, I hungrily devoured the bread and cheese Tracker had packed. Such simple food had never tasted so good, despite the flies doing their best to ruin the moment.

'How do you know there are not crocodiles in the water, Tracker?'

He belly laughed so hard that his whole body shook.'

'Who says there ain't girly.'

Was he serious?

A flock of black cockatoos flew low overhead, settling in the trees. Their call was almost mournful.

'Yer know, it's not a good sign that them birds are here. The elders used to tell me they're guides and guardians. They lead the spirits of loved ones on their journey to rest amongst the ancestors.'

What was he saying? That we were too late? That Gran was already dead?

No way.

I stood, my sandwich sticking in my throat as I attempted to swallow.

'She's still alive, Tracker, I know it. I heard her humming, it was weak, but I know it was her. I dreamt of her. I was running toward the cave opening, but I couldn't get to her.'

Tracker stood beside me, starting up at the cockatoos.

'I believe yer lass, but I can also feel in me spirit... we are running out of time. We gotta find her today'

Turning to face me, he placed his hand on my shoulder, his skin was cold.

'Ya need to think girl... try to remember the landmarks you saw.'

I knew I would know the place, given the chance. The image of it was vividly sketched in my mind.

'The cave... it's got a small opening, and wooden beams surrounding it, like an old gold mine. A valley of large boulders lines the path up towards it. I was walking in between them. It was quite steep and dry. I was slipping. Oh, and I saw a billabong close by, on the left of the cave. And heaps of tall trees, some lush, some speckled grey gums.'

Tracker stared at me for some time. He silently finished his food and took a swig from his canister, then cracked a huge smile as he wiped the sweat from his brow.

'You have done well, Grace. Ya might just have saved yer Gran's life. And I reckon I know the place. It's further west than Bluey and I searched yesterday. Not too far from here, though. Silly old buggers used to swear them caves had gold. Travellers would bloody come in from Darwin, cop a squat, in the hope of makin' themselves a fortune. Bloody idiots.'

Tracker was packing up as he spoke, I took his lead. For the first time, I felt real hope.

I closed my eyes for a moment, daring to imagine we'd find Negeenah within a matter of hours. Bring her home to Zarnish, where she belonged.

Please God. I know I've done some shitty things, but do it for her, not me.

As we rode, the air felt alive with promise. We moved ahead in silence, intrinsically knowing we were close. Tracker led the way, his body language portraying newfound hope, and his pace faster. I struggled to keep up as the terrain was becoming steep, and my newly acquired balance on Jinta was wavering. But I was determined. Never had I wanted anything more.

Tracker stopped at the foot of a gully, watching as I gingerly approached.

'We need to let Jinta take the lead from here, Grace. If I'm right, Negeenah is just ahead.'

Clearing my throat, nausea set in. I was second guessing myself.

'We will wind our way up and through there, and this here horse will show us the way, for sure.'

I followed his eye-line as he nodded and pointed ahead at the track through the boulders and trees.

Was this it? This landscape all looks the same. God, I hope so.

Tracker lightly tapped Jinta on the rump and she began the slow, steep climb. I could feel her feet slipping beneath me, making me super anxious we would fall. I gripped on as tightly as I could.

'It's okay, lass, she knows her limits.'

Tracker followed closely behind us. Rahman neighed as if impatient for Jinta to move faster. Then, as we rounded some huge red boulders, we came to a halt in a small clearing.

I almost jumped from my saddle, instantly filled with adrenaline, tears welled in my eyes.

'This is it. This is really it. She's here! I saw it, Tracker. I saw it! There's the billabong, just like I told you.'

My brain was moving even faster than my rambling words. Dismounting eagerly, my foot caught in the stirrup, nearly causing me to face-plant on the rocky ground.

'Steady up, girly. Just get yer bearings for a sec. Yer need to listen to me from here.'

Listen! I led us here!

Breathe, Grace. You got this.

I wanted to run like I had in my dreams. Only this time, I'd get to Negeenah, and everything would be alright again.'

Tracker dismounted and grabbed my arm firmly. The shock of his solid grip stilled me momentarily.

'Listen. Stop, Grace. Yer no good to no one if yer head ain't thinkin'.'

'But she's up there, waiting. You said yourself, time is running out!'

He let me go, then went and tied both horses to a nearby tree. Neighing loudly, they seemed to welcome the shade and the fresh grass to nibble on.

'I know this is the spot, girl. I can tell Jinta has been here before. Look, see the trodden grass and horse shit? Jinta must have waited for her mistress for a day or two before returning.'

Tracker was grabbing at his saddlebag. He passed me a woollen blanket and his canister of water. He then took a long rope and torch, tucking them under his arm.

'You got yer phone? We may need to contact yer mum if Negeenah needs medical help, so there's a doctor waiting. And girl…'

Tracker put his free hand under my chin. He pulled my face away from the cave entrance I was fixated on, forcing me to look at him. I nodded, blinking rapidly, wiping away fresh tears.

'You need to be prepared. I'm just sayin', we may be too late. If that's the case, it ain't goin' to be pretty.'

I immediately dismissed the thought in my head. Never was I going to believe that.

Stepping out of the sunlight into the cave, instant relief was felt from the scorching day. I couldn't quite place the smell, and my eyes strained to adjust. Tracker switched his torch on, and I used my phone light. We moved slowly, cautiously forward despite me wanting to move at lightning speed. This was dangerous ground.

I could feel my fast-beating pulse surging through my veins. All of my senses were on high alert, my anxiety peeking. I strained to hear even the slightest sound, somewhere beyond water dripped. There was a slight bend in the cave wall and a narrowing path ahead. Bending to avoid hitting our heads, we began to trek deeper into the void.

Why can't I hear her humming? I don't see the lantern light from my dream. Something is seriously wrong.

Tracker raised his hand gesturing for me to stop. We had come to a fork, separated by an ominous rock wall. Left, right: the two options of where to go next looked almost identical.

'Close yer eyes, lass. Be still. See her in yer mind's eye, then tell me... which way will lead us to her?'

Was he serious?

Tracker nodded.

'Listen...'

I stood, willing my mind, my heart, to give me the answer. If I was wrong, I would waste precious time. Time, we didn't have. As if sensing my doubt, Tracker reached out his hand and placed it on my clammy forehead. He whispered words I didn't understand. I felt a calm wash over me and closed my eyes.

Leave me, my child. You must continue life without me. Gracie, you are destined for greatness. To Breathe Grace on our people. You must do this for me, for our family. Please, my precious granddaughter. Promise me, you will continue my work, continue to fulfil the purpose of Zarnish.

My eyes flew open; Negeenah's voice had been so clear. Did Tracker hear her, too? I was breathing rapidly. Needing to brace myself, I put my hands to my knees.

'No way, Gran. We will do it together, or not at all. You are coming home with us today!'

I stood... and pointed to the left tunnel. Tracker moved instantly, his faith in me obvious.

'I knew yer could do it, lass. Let's go.'

The lantern ahead was visible now, but only just. Just metres away now, was a small, crumpled frame laying still on the ground, exactly as my dream had shown. The air was thick and stale. My mind travelled to the worst-case scenario. I wanted desperately to call out to Negeenah.

But what if she didn't reply? Or even worse, what if she didn't want us there?

I shook it off.

NO.

It wouldn't matter how she reacted, as long as she did. We were taking her out of there.

Please be alive, Gran.

Tracker stood behind me as I knelt beside her frail frame. The old blanket I'd seen her covered in was crumpled at her feet; she wasn't wearing shoes. I froze, unable to find the courage to touch her. Gran had lost so much weight. Even in the dim light of my torch, her skin looked white and drawn, paper-thin. Her hair was a tasselled mess, limp and lifeless. Yet, despite this, she looked so peaceful.

As it was in my dream, Negeenah had surrounded herself with photos. The photo of me rested in her hands, placed on her chest. Gran didn't move. Frantically I searched for evidence of a pulse, of a breath, of life, but there was nothing. What if the coldness of her skin revealed a truth I didn't want to face? Tracker knelt beside me.

'Talk to her, Grace.'

He placed his hand on my shoulder, encouraging me to make a move. Again, he began whispering, chanting. Was this some sort of prayer?

I picked Negeenah's lapis stone necklace up from the ground and strung it around my neck together with my own. Swallowing hard. It was now or never.

'Gran, can you hear me? Please wake up. It's Grace. We've come to take you home.'

There was no movement. Tracker bent closer to Negeenah's face, checking for a pulse. Desperately I trying to read his face, stealing for bad news.

'She's still with us, but she's very weak, Grace. Keep talking to her. I'm going to get ready to carry her out.'

Pressing my palms to my eyes, I felt a sudden lightness, reaching for her hand.

'Gran, I'm here. Can you hear me? Please, it's time to take you home. I am so sorry, Gran. I was so awful to you. But I love you, I love you so much. You have changed my life. Please, Gran, don't leave me now...'

Without realising, I was shaking her, and my sobs were getting louder. I couldn't help it, it was like a volcano of pent-up emotion finally erupting. I held her hands in mine. They were so cold, so lifeless. I curled her fingers in mine and kissed them. Pressing my body close to hers, I willed any energy I had remaining to pass through to her. I stroked the hair from her face. Still, her eyes remained shut.

'Gran, I know you can hear me. I have so much to tell you. So much you need to know. Please, Gran, I'm sorry. Mum is so sorry, too.'

And just like that, in a barely audible tone, came a reply. Her voice seemed distant, like she was already far away.

'Hush, Gracie, stop with all that fuss. What is done is done. Leave me now. Go. This is where I leave you for another place.'

Disclosure

Negeenah never made it to that other place.

The week following her return was one of mixed emotions and revelations. So near death, it took a long while for her to regain her strength and, in fact, to want to talk to us at all. I was confused by her anger and, even worse, by her silence.

Still, I had faith that given time, she would be grateful to have been found. Mum struggled to get her to eat, and never did she leave her room. The district nurse was coming daily to assist with recovery, but so far, Negeenah had not uttered a word to her either.

We worked as a team to keep Zarnish Estate running. Coming together each evening for a meal with Mum, Tracker and Bluey, for the first time in my life, felt like a real family. Next week was harvest time for the poppies. I was keen to see how it all worked. Mum had taken extra leave from her job. There had been no talk of us returning to the city. That suited me just fine. I felt relief knowing we would stay a little longer. I couldn't leave Negeenah now, not like this. Whether she liked it or not, there was stuff I intended to talk to her about.

The nights were the worst. Sleep was hard to come by. I would wander silently to Gran's closed door, pressing my ear against the hard wood, desperate to hear any sound of life. So many things continued to race through my brain. What if we hadn't found her? Why was she willing to leave us? Wasn't that a selfish way out? Why had she bothered to bring me out here just to go and do that? Surely, she knew it would hurt us. Hadn't we all been through enough? Then my own shame would set in. I was being so selfish, dwelling in my own stupid problems. I knew so little of her hardship, but even the small amount I'd witnessed left me guilt-ridden for making it about me.

It was 1am. Restlessness once again brought its familiar unease. Rex was in with Gran, so I didn't even have him for comfort. I felt so alone. Maybe I could sneak into bed with my mum.

Was that weird?

I still had Negeenah's sketchbook. I'd taken it with me the last time I'd looked at it, leaving it safely hidden under my bed. I couldn't return it even if I wanted to. How would I explain that to her? She was already angry enough that I'd dared to foil her plans to die.

Pulling my hair back into a messy bun, I splashed some water over my face to relieve a little of the oppressive heat. Looking into the bathroom mirror, tonight my reflection was not just my own. I saw Negeenah, and I could see my mum as well. We were one.

My features were maturing, and despite the turmoil of the last few months, I felt a sense of peace and purpose, it was becoming more deep seeded each day. Not that I'd told a soul. Speaking my plans aloud was a whole different thing. I was turning 16 in a week, and for the first time in a long time, I knew what I wanted to do with my life. I needed to talk to Negeenah.

Now I just needed to get her to listen.

Flicking on the study light, I opened the large window and welcomed the gentle evening breeze. I knew I should sleep, but I loved the stillness and magic of Zarnish Estate at night, with the comfort of the musical sounds of the busy insect and animal nightlife. The moon and stars beguiled me, and the darkened air whispered to my soul.

I was determined to discover the strange code Negeenah had used. Maybe then, I'd understand all this a little more.

Yes!

It didn't take me long. Silently fist pumping above me, I felt like my insides were vibrating.

Where would the world be without the Internet?

Completely energized and awake now, I headed to the hallway, scribbling down the jumbled letters underneath the painted landscape. I stopped again to admire the beauty of the valley, the winding river and the prominent snow-topped mountains beyond that Negeenah had portrayed.

If I was right, Negeenah had used a historical code Julius Caesar had designed to effectively hide messages from Rome's enemies. All I had to do was shift each letter three spaces to give me a legible word. This would be a long night, but coffee, chocolate and the adrenaline surging through me would get me there.

The code under the painting was painfully long. At first glance, it was confusing. Then, carefully, painstakingly, I began decoding, grinning from ear to ear.

Ilvxi F objxfk ql jv cxjfiv. Lro Hlqzex Sxiibv. Lro Ixmfp pqlkbp. Kbsbo tfii tb cxii ql bsfi. Lro efaabk pqobkdqe dfsbp rp mltbo.

Loyal I remain to my family. Our Kocha Valley. Our Lapis stones. We will never fall to evil. Our hidden strength gives us power.

Standing in front of the painting again, this time with the decoded message, it took on a deeper meaning. I imagined life in the village Negeenah had described. Laughing and squealing in fun with her brother as they played outside. Her bare legs and arms under her blue cotton dress, browning in the sun with not a care in the world.

Her family, the men travelling for months in search of their precious lapis stones. It had all been taken from her at such a young age. When she had spoken of her family, I knew it was with a heavy heart.

Had she wanted the painting displayed as a reminder of her childhood?

Was the code her way of protecting them should she ever be found?

Racing back to the study, I flicked open Gran's sketch book. This was my chance to decode and hopefully understand Negeenah's drawings. One had stood out. I didn't need the picture to see the image. It would haunt me for the rest of my life.

What did you do Gran?

Fk molqbzqfkd qeb fkklzbkq F hfiiba qeb bsfi. Pexjb F exsb yolrdeq ql jv cxjfiv, vbq obdobq F exsb klkb.

In protecting the innocent, I killed the evil. Shame I have brought to my family, yet regret I have none.

The sketch showed a single black cross, placed under a tree. It was a fresh burial site. No flowers or fanfare, just the head scarves of the dead wrapped around the bottom of the cross. Women gathered around, some on their knees, as if paying their respect. All wore burkas. Despite the misty morning, their faces were clearly drawn to reflect frightened and tortured souls. One face stood out.

Negeenah.

She had portrayed her own eyes as distant, broken and shameful. Yet she had still drawn herself in vivid blue. To me this reflected a defiant sign of strength. Gran's fists were clenched, tears streaming down her face. Her lapis necklace was dangling from her hand, sparkling in the first rays of light.

Had Negeenah sketched as her way of confessing?

No wonder she'd used a code. Should it get into the wrong hands, it could see Negeenah killed for murder in Afghanistan, even to this day. Breathing deeply, trying to process everything, I flicked to the image of Azyan and Kinaaz's grave. The sketch once again sent shivers up my spine in its depiction of a third grave.

Who actually draws their own grave?

I felt a tightness in my eyes as my body tensed. She'd written her name clearly on the rounded grey headstone but coded the rest.

Unbelievable Gran. You just have no idea how important you are to us.

F pxzofcfzb jv ifcb clo jv cxjfjfbp cobalj.
Ofpb Xcdexkfpqxk mblmib.
Objbjybo tel vlr xob.

I sacrifice my life for my family's freedom.
Rise Afghanistan people.
Remember who you are.

The words became blurry as my eyes stung and tears escaped once more. Exhaustion and sadness were taking their toll. Gran was an absolute lionheart, yet she saw herself as a burden, the very reason we could not be free. I hastily wiped my tears away, suddenly keen to get out of this room.

Surely, we're not still in danger?

That was so long ago. A different time, a different place. The Taliban no longer ruled as they did then. But something nagged deep inside me, picking away at my insides.

There were so many secrets here.

My family had gone to desperate lengths to protect themselves. To shield me from any knowledge of their past or perceived threat. There had to be a reason for all of that. And still, they had so many links to Afghanistan, including aiding women to escape. That had to have repercussions should they be discovered. Were the poppies also connected?

Should I actually be afraid?

Trust

I worked all night on decoding Gran's sketches. I had to. I wanted to. Mum woke me the next morning, slumped awkwardly over the study desk. My body was aching, my neck stiff. Rex had joined me at some point. He licked my hand as my mum tousled my hair. As I sat up, rubbing my eyes, I could feel the sticky chocolate crumbs stuck to my cheek. My fuel from last night.

'Couldn't sleep, hey Gracie?'

Mum smoothed my hair from behind and began platting it into a braid. I closed my eyes, relishing her soothing touch. I remembered all those times growing up when we would style our hair together. Laugh ourselves silly at the often outrageous result.

'Your Gran will come around, hun. She's dealing with her demons right now. You know it's not your fault, right?'

I knew that deep down, but it didn't make the situation any easier. Mum hugged me from behind.

'Is that Negeenah's sketch book?'

'Yep. And bloody hell, Mum, it was so revealing… Hey can I ask you something?'

I felt her stiffen.

'Are we in danger?'

Oh Gracie, that's a bit dramatic before I've even had my morning coffee, don't you think?'

I swivelled around to face her.

'Well… are we?'

Mum pulled up a chair and sat heavily.

'What makes you think that, Grace? Is it these? Show me; I've not had a chance to look.'

Pulling the sketch book closer to her, Mum began flicking through the pages. As she did, I could see the skin tighten around her mouth and the tension return to her eyes. It was impossible not to be affected by the images.

'I remember it all like it was yesterday, Grace. Not that I want to.'

Mum pulled me up from the chair, wrapping me into her arms.

'Come on, let's get some breakfast first, hey? I need to make some for your Gran anyway.'

I followed her without a word, tucking the sketchbook under my arm.

Samir came from the stables to join us in the kitchen. Smiling, he sat beside me, pouring steaming coffee from the pot in the middle of the table.

'Perhaps we could take the horses for a ride today, Grace. They need it, I think.'

'Are we in danger, Samir? I mean, are the Taliban still intent on finding Negeenah?'

Mum and Samir exchanged glances. I could see him take a deep breath, thinking about how to respond.

'Perhaps.'

'What the hell does that mean, Samir?'

I eyeballed him, in no mood for cryptic words or games. Lack of sleep was fuelling my anger.

'As long as Negeenah is alive, she will be wanted by rebel forces. She still has a high price on her head in the homeland. We would be naive to assume we didn't need to be careful and clever in our movements. As you know, she is a murderer in their eyes, as unjust as that is. Unfortunately, others have paid with their lives because they were associated with her. That includes Azyan.'

My focus narrowed in on the threat.

'How could this be possible? This is real life, not a movie. How do you really know?'

Misha sat beside me, placing an appeasing hand on my shoulder.

'That's enough, Gracie, another time, hey?'

I felt the heat rising in my face. There was no way I was going to accept that. Surely, they must have known I wouldn't. I flicked open Negeenah's sketch book again.

'Look, both of you, look at this.'

I pointed at the drawing of the group of women gathered. They held books to the sky, shouting words of rebellion to their enemy.

'I decoded Gran's messages. This one says: 'Together we defeat the Taliban. Educating women will save Afghanistan.'

I flicked the page, not waiting for my mum or Samir to respond. I pointed angrily at the image again, this time showing a single woman's face. Her terrified stare pierced through the page into my soul each time I looked at it. Mum took in a sharp breath.

'I knew her, Gracie. She died. She was beaten like a savage, all because her husband falsely accused her of trying to escape. Her children were sent away. They were just babies.'

I steamed ahead in my mission to make them listen.

'It reads, 'Tormented under the veil' when decoded. And look at this one.'

'No, that's enough now, Grace.'

Mum stood. Ignoring her, I turned the page to the close-up image of my own face.

'This one, look familiar? It says, "Breathe Grace on my people. She will rise". Explain that to me please. I'm leaving here right now if you won't. Don't think I can't. I have every right to know, considering I'm somehow, apparently, a big part of the future of Zarnish and, indeed, Afghanistan.'

Mum crossed her arms, Samir stood too, standing between us.

'Don't threaten me, Grace. Have some bloody respect.'

Mum's glare told me I'd pushed her too far. Good! They needed pushing. Standing abruptly, I accidentally smashed my plate onto the tiled floor. Ignoring it, I grabbed the sketch book and stormed outside. Anger engulfed me, too. I didn't care where I went, anywhere away from them would do.

The poppy field

It was Bluey who found me sound asleep in the loft of the barn. Despite my anger, the loft's solitude had a warm and calming effect and had quickly coerced me into a peaceful sleep.

'There ya are. You hidin' from me, lassie? Been looking for yer. Let's go for a ride. Jinta been missing yer, I reckon, I'll take Rahman. We can give them a swim in the billabong, hey?'

Bluey's rugged head poked through the square hole in the floor. His hat was as stained and sweaty as his face. Grey stubble covered much of it. His toothless grin almost appeared childlike. Even through sleepy eyes, I could see their sparkle. I couldn't help but smile, he was such a kind soul.

'Well? Yer gonna stay up here feelin' sorry for yerself or come see something bloody amazing.'

As I sat up, I could feel the straw tangled in my wild curls. Remembering I hadn't even showered, I felt a little self-conscious.

'Fine. It does sound good, Bluey. I haven't been to the billabong, but Negeenah told me about it. She said we all used to swim there when I was little. Kinaaz used to come, too, apparently. Mum and Asadi would float us around on old tractor tubes. Okay, just let me get changed.'

Bluey was already climbing back down as he next spoke.

I remember like it was yesterday. You used to kick ya little fat legs around under the water. Loved it ya did. Good then, well leave yer dark bloody mood behind. We've got some fun to be had.'

Bluey was right. A change of scene was what I needed. Leaving the tension of the house behind me felt so good. I didn't even bother to find Mum and Samir to let them know where I was going.

Screw them.

It was great being on Jinta again. I was surprised at how my riding confidence had grown in such a short time. I could definitely get used to it. Like Tracker, Bluey handled Rahman with ease, despite him being a bit flighty and agitated. I was grateful not to be on him.

Bluey rode ahead, through the paddocks into the bushland beyond. The valley to the left was clearly our destination. Within 20 minutes, we were approaching the vast billabong. It was so beautiful. I was eager to feel the cool water on my skin, wash away some of the anger and hurt, and calm my anxiety.

The amber-coloured water was clear and sparkled in the sunlight. Green foliage bound its banks, and lilies were dappled across its surface. The surrounding eucalypts provided just the shade we needed. The air was totally still, no breeze, no sounds from the birds.

I waded into the billabong from the muddy bank, still in my jean shorts and shirt. As I'd hoped, the water's coolness appeased my hot skin, causing it to tingle. Within seconds I was waist-deep, Bluey was beside me, fully clothed, and threw his body under the water like an excited kid. He remained under for some time, surfacing a few metres away.

'This here billabong was where Tracker's family camped many moons ago before they went further north and left the poor bugger behind. But it was Tracker's choice in the end. He wanted to stay with Negeenah. She became like family to us, I don't intend goin' nowhere. When ya take over, one day, girl, you will have to bury me out here somewhere, I reckon.'

He ducked under the water again, leaving me to float and ponder what the hell he was talking about.

'It's surprisin' there's so much water here,' he said as he resurfaced.

'Bit unusual for this time of year. Can dry right up to nothing, ya know. Billabongs are mostly a seasonal thing, especially out here.'

'Bluey, can you tell me about the poppies?'

He pondered the question for a moment, washing his face with his hands, grinning over at me.

'I could have put money on it. I knew that was comin'. Suppose there is no harm in me telling yer now, hey? We're gonna need yer for the harvest soon anyway.'

He chuckled loudly. Was he aware he had a way of dropping things into a conversation that confused me no end?

Dripping wet, we sat on the billabong edge.

'Back in the day, from the first moment Azyan showed up, he had a plan. He employed Tracker and me from day one. We'd been working on a neighbouring farm. He was a bloody good man and a generous boss. Treated us right, yer know what I mean. That accent was impossible to understand, but he had a good heart.'

I nodded. I wished I had known him.

'First Afghan I'd ever laid eyes on. His wife was a timid little thing. Always looked sickly to me but happy. She had a kindness about her, so did yer little mate, Kinaaz. Bloody tragedy in the end, bloody tragedy.'

I'd lost him in the past again. Bluey was good at disappearing into his mind, I was discovering.

'But the poppies, Bluey, were they his idea?'

'Yep. Samir and Azyan were poppy farmers back in Afghanistan. Made real good money. They bought this joint outright. Had a plan from the start to farm poppies here. It'd only just been made legal in Australia to harvest, with a licence, of course. They get shipped all over the world now, yer know, once we pick all the little bastards.'

Okay! Wasn't expecting that!

'For what? Why are they such a big deal?'

Bluey smiled.

'I had no idea in the start neither. For medicinal purposes mostly. Bloody pharmaceutical companies can't get enough of 'em.'

I nodded slowly, raising my eyebrows.

'Things were not good in their homeland, so Azyan set up a life for them here in Australia. He ain't never gone into it much, but I got the gist life was very different in Afghanistan. He told me once, not long after yer Gran and yer mum arrived, that this was their fresh start. A place he could keep them all safe.'

Except, things went so terribly wrong.

'Anyways, year after year, we'd bring in pickers and harvest the crops. Trucks were organised to take the poppies away. We got our money and started all over again for next year. It nearly all folded after Azyan left; Negeenah felt it was just too much to manage. But she had made a promise to her brother, and we helped her to honour that. After Azyan was killed in Afghanistan, we thought it might all go belly-up again. But, good old Samir, heart of gold that one, stepped up. He runs the business with Negeenah and yer mum now. Clever, hey? Their partners are all over the world, pretty much. I don't get involved in all that side of it. But it's big money, lass, I know that much. At harvest times, all the cottages around Zarnish fill up with pickers. Negeenah feeds them all. It's a festive time, let me tell yer.'

The sun and humid warm air were drying us as quickly as my mind raced. I needed to hear all that again.'

'Bluey... what do you mean about the other cottages? I've never seen them.'

He chuckled again.

'Just 'cause yer don't see somethin', doesn't mean it ain't there, right? I know yer been pokin' around in the little cottage you were born in. Well, there are others like that, only smaller. They were built around Zarnish in preparation for harvest times. Azyan was clever, as I said. They're dotted along the bush line here. Five of them in all.'

So that was how Negeenah could afford to live in the outback.

Another thing right under my nose I never saw coming. I had to admit, I was totally curious to see the harvest in action. It seemed to me that the paddocks were full of colour and ready to be reaped.

'End of next week, girl, that's when the harvest is planned for. You still going to be around?'

He threw me with his question.

Who the hell knows!

I was just focusing on day to day, waiting for things to return to normal. Did I even know what was normal anymore?

'I think we'll be here. I mean, I hope so. I just want Gran to talk to me again. She is so angry. I don't get it, Bluey. It's been over a week, and she's still holed up in her bedroom.'

Bluey threw his head back, laughing. He leant all the way back, resting his elbows in the dirt, the water softly flowing around his ankles.

'Yep, stubborn old goat, that one. Reminds me of someone I know.'

He smiled at me with a wry grin.

'Runs in the family, I reckon.'

'Maybe.'

I twirled some grass between my fingers.

'Hey, Bluey, why did you tell me all this was mine now, Zarnish Estate. What did you mean by that?'

Bluely shot up like a rocket. Suddenly intent we should leave.

'Ahh, nothing. Just an old man getting his words confused, I reckon. I ain't got no right to talk about that with you. That's a question for Negeenah.'

Repression

Wandering the house late that night, the usual silence I'd come to know at this hour was different. At first, I struggled to work out what exactly it was I could hear.

Humming?

It was coming from Negeenah's room. Silently I pressed my ear against the heavy panelled door. Breathing intensely, I held my breath, worried it would give me away. Rex's bark on the other side of the door startled me. I moved back. How did he know?

'Come in, Grace.'

Just three simple words. I'd waited an eternity to hear them.

Inside her dark bedroom, I immediately noticed the air was stale and uninviting. The curtains were drawn tightly shut. The room felt morbid.

Did Negeenah still want to die?

'Grace, come in. No point loitering out there. And shut the door behind you, please.'

She sounded strong enough, like the no-nonsense Gran I'd come to know and love. Rex wagged his tail excitedly. I bent down and hugged him. I'd missed my companion more than I'd realised, but I was grateful he'd been here with her. Near impossible to see, I edged my way to the bed, hoping not to trip.

'Sit beside me, Grace.'

I could barely make out her silhouette.

'Can I open the curtains slightly Gran? The moon is full. It's a beautiful night out, and I would like to be able to see you, even just a little.'

'Fine child, but only for a while.'

Without waiting for her to change her mind, I pushed the drapes aside and opened the French doors. The fresh sweet night air brought instant relief to the stagnant surroundings. I felt the breeze dance through the room and desperately hoped it would lift Gran's spirits.

Even in the dappled moonlight, Gran looked so much stronger than the last time I'd seen her. Relief swept through me. The torment of that day I will never forget. I'd pulled Negeenah from the brink of death.

Stop it, Grace. Be present.

I sat beside her, completely at a loss as to what to say or do. Negeenah reached for my hand. Instantly tears began rolling down my cheeks, until her sobs were almost uncontrollable. My whole body shuddered. Was it relief? Regret? Until this moment, I'd been in control of these emotions sitting just below the surface of my steely facade.

'I'm so sorry, Gran... I just wanted everything to be alright... I just wanted you back. Do you hate me?'

Negeenah sat up further in her bed.

'Hush, child. It is me who is sorry. I have put you all through such a terrible ordeal. And what I wanted for you all was freedom, not more hardship. I am filled with shame and regret. It is me that needs to ask for forgiveness.'

She gripped my hand tightly as she spoke. Rex whimpered beside me.

'No, there's nothing to forgive. You're here now, that's all that matters to us all. And I never want to be apart from you again.'

I knew at that moment, truer words I had never spoken.

'My life turned out very differently, Gracie, to the one I dreamt of as a girl. No woman should ever have to leave her family so young, especially against her will. Overnight I was forced to be a woman. I was simply bundled into the back of a van with few belongings and sent on my way to an alien world in every sense, away from my beautiful Kocha Valley, with its peace and security. From my family. And little did I know then that it would be many years before I saw them again. I had never known a busy city like Kabul. I travelled alone for two days and nights before arriving. I was so terrified I vomited for much of the way.'

Negeenah's reality was heartbreaking. I thought of the angry stance I'd taken when I was first sent to Zarnish Estate. I was a year older than Gran had been when she was forced to marry. It was so hard to comprehend.

'The house I was taken to was very small, with hardly any windows. It felt stifling compared to my surroundings in Kocha Valley. As I have told you, my new husband lived with his mother. I will be eternally grateful for the kindness they showed to me. Many women did not have that luxury. But we were complete strangers, and from the first night, I was made to share my husband's bed. I must have wept every night for a year. My father had given me this precious lapis necklace. He said they would be praying over it every night, that I was to draw on its strength and wisdom to get me through. Soon I was with child. I had to give birth on the floor of that tiny house. I lost a lot of blood, but there was no medical help. I was a shadow of myself for months. I tell you, Grace, if you can die from loneliness and despair, I would have.'

Squeezing both her hands, all I could do was stare at her.

Why did the world allow women to be treated with such disrespect and cruelty?

'But you loved Mum, right? You didn't begrudge her?'

'Oh never, Grace. From her first breath in this world, she became my passion. Misha would prove to be the reason I existed and remained strong. The reason I strived to be educated and, in turn, risked everything to help the women of Afghanistan do the same.'

My body tingled all over.

'And so, then the Taliban came, right?'

'Yes. No one would have ever dared to imagine the damage they would do, and on so many levels. Unfortunately, my girl, they are guerrilla operators, and still very powerful. I was a teacher at that time, and your mum was at Uni studying law. Literally overnight, everything changed for women. Right or wrong, Gracie, I couldn't just stand by and watch it happen. I had to help my people, the suddenly powerless women and their children.'

'But you risked your own life. How were you brave enough to do that? I don't think I could ever do something that courageous.'

Negeenah looked at me for a while. For the first time, she smiled, and I felt its warmth travel to my heart. Her firm grip was intense. We sat, face to face, so close I could almost feel her breath.

'You are wrong, my child. In time you will see the strength you have. None of us realise just how courageous we are until our backs are against a wall.'

We sat in silence for minutes before she continued.

'I set up safe houses throughout Kabul, educating women where and when I could. We aided many escapes, navigated dangerous situations and tried to negotiate for others in prison. Misha was mostly at my side. Initially, she wanted no part in my quest. Still, she soon changed her mind when she began seeing the true fallout from the ruthless Taliban reign.'

I thought of my dream. The two women clinging together on the couch, surrounded by bombing and gunfire. I'd witnessed Gran and Mum enduring a harsh reality.

'It was during this time we met Samir. He was a business associate of my husband. Samir was kind, and willing to help us from the start. He was one of the very few men who had the courage to stand up for Afghan women after his own mother and two sisters had been killed.

Simar cleverly fought against what was happening and the rules the drastic Sharia law imposed at the time. I will never understand to this day why so many men let their wives be treated far worse than animals. I can only assume they were consumed with fear themselves. Samir is a very good man. I know you are angry at him, and I can understand why, but you should hear him out, Grace.'

Suddenly I felt overheated, consumed by judgement.

'Maybe. It's complicated for me. I was so surprised to see him again, Gran. Mum and Samir told me a few things, finally. I know you are all in business together. They told me all about the service they provide women, aiding their bid for freedom. I also know about your poppy cultivation. I'll admit, you are not the woman I thought you were when I first arrived. It is me who should be ashamed, Gran. I hope you can forgive me.'

Negeenah cupped my face.

'How could you know any different, child. I have spent my life trying to protect you and your mum. I live with the turmoil and torture of knowing others have been killed because of me. That hardens your heart, let me tell you.'

I pushed my shoulders back, feeling my strength return.

'Well, we are all together now. Nothing you could ever do would make me love you any less. I really want us to be a family, and I never ever thought I'd feel that. I'm incredibly proud of what you have done. I want to be like you, Gran. Exactly like you.'

Negeenah gently pushed me away, clearly uncomfortable with where the conversation was heading. Her shift in body language was obvious.

What did I say wrong?

'I need to sleep now, Grace. It was good to see you, to clear the air a bit. But you need to leave me now. But child… you must not aspire to be like me. Promise me that. There are things you don't know, mistakes I've made. At a huge cost.'

But I do know Gran. I know it all.

Death

How could I possibly tell Negeenah? How does one start such a difficult conversation?

Hey, Gran, I had another dream. And guess what, I saw you kill two men. So, your secret is out, okay!

I could never bring myself to do that as she was clearly ashamed enough of her past. I sat pondering it all in front of the computer again. I decided to do some more research to pass the time, might as well educate myself while Negeenah wasn't up to the task.

Bored, I poked through the drawers on the side of the desk. They were basically empty, containing only a few stationery items. Nothing of interest. However, my curiosity was sparked suddenly when I noted the bottom drawer was smaller on the inside compared to the other three I had just rummaged through.

'Strange, Rex, they all look the same from the outside.'

It was so nice to have my canine companion by my side again. Rex was spending his days wandering between Gran and me. She was still rarely leaving her room. Poking around the bottom drawer some more, to my surprise, the wood gave way.

'Shit, Rex… check this out. It's got a false bottom!'

Underneath were two envelopes, the top one addressed to Negeenah. It looked similar to the ones I had read from her adoring fans back in Afghanistan, with no postal markings.

So why was it not with the others? Looking at the second

envelope, my heart skipped a beat. I traced the words scrawled on the front of the plain white envelope with my finger.

For my granddaughter Grace.

For me?

Did I dare open it?

Placing the envelopes side-by-side on top of the old oak desk, I stared for some time, frustrated I couldn't seem to find the courage to open them. My thoughts flittered between trust and worry, creating an ongoing debate in my head as to what to do next.

When had the letter addressed to me been placed here? And why?

The house around me was quiet. Everyone was outside already this morning, except Negeenah, who remained in her room. It was now or never. I had to know.

I began carefully pulling apart the already broken seal on the letter addressed to Gran. Unlike the others I had found in her leather pouch, this one had been previously opened.

Curious.

I pulled out the single folded piece of paper. It was dated 2001. The message had been typed and was not signed.

Negeenah,

> *Congratulations on achieving safe passage out of Afghanistan.*
>
> *We admire your courage and determination. Enjoy your freedom while it lasts, for we promise it will be short-lived. You have committed serious crimes against us. For this you will be severely punished, as will your family. We will not rest until you are found and brought to justice. Your capture and death will serve as a reminder to the people of Afghanistan. A message aimed to instil fear and as a reminder disobedience will not be tolerated.*

Your family will also suffer the same fate as they carry your blood. Blood which we see as evil.

Eventually, someone will reveal your whereabouts, and if not, we will find you ourselves.

You know who we are and what we are capable of.

Till we next meet.

Reeling over, I thought I'd vomit. The sudden onset of nausea all consuming. Confusion and disbelief of the venomous words sent a shock wave through my entire body.

Somehow, I knew… this was a very real threat. A powerful and malicious promise. I screwed up the letter and threw it as far away across the room as I could

Staggering toward the window, I desperately needed air, and fast. I rested my hands on the wooden sill, forcing myself to take deep breaths. My body was shaking profusely. I just hoped my quivering legs would hold me up, as a full panic attack took hold. Completely disoriented, I didn't hear Mum and Samir come in. Tunnel vision dominated my head.

I was barely aware of them pulling me back inside and sitting me on a chair. I was clammy and dizzy. Despite knowing these bodily reactions well, each time a panic attack set in was equally as frightening.

'Grace, honey, can you hear me? You're as white as a ghost. What's happened? Are you sick or is this panic?'

Samir was talking at me so desperately fast and gripping my shoulders way too tightly. I could barely comprehend his voice and tried to push him away.

'Just give her a minute, Samir.'

Mum stroked my back, her touch soothing me, as it always did. She began attempting to rationalise my fright and flight response. With a shaky hand I pointed to the letter lying on the floor. As

Samir began reading the letter silently, I watched the colour drain from his face.

He crouched on the floor as my mum grabbed it from him. The air had become thick and no matter how I tried, I couldn't manage a deep breath. I wanted to run but couldn't move.

Both Mum and Samir sat silently on the floor, their bodies touching. I remained slumped forward in the chair. The letter sat on the floorboards between us.

No words came.

Later that evening, Samir joined me as I sat in the stillness of the porch. I could barely make out the rose garden around me, as the moon was no more than a slit in the sky tonight. The flowers themselves made the air smell like honey, and its sweetness calmed my nerves.

The stars were vivid as always, and the plethora of sounds from the insects on night patrol made it impossible for me to be captured by my thoughts.

Perfect. I don't want to think anymore.

I was exhausted. The other side of panic always brought incredible fatigue.

'Hey, Gracie, you feel better now, sweetheart? I'm sorry to bother you, but I just need to know… where did you get that letter?'

I continued to stare ahead.

'It was in the bottom drawer in the study.'

I decided not to mention the letter addressed to me. I wanted to read it for myself and then decide if I wanted to share it with anyone. I'd managed to conceal it inside my t-shirt earlier, hiding it carefully in my room until I felt ready.

Samir looked old tonight. Almost defeated.

'We have to assume Negeenah has read the letter, Grace. The question is, when? It would have terrified her; I'm devastated she never showed me. My concern now is that she clearly believes if she is out of the picture, we will all be safe.'

He covered his face with his hands before running them through his hair.

'I fear it is my fault, Grace. Two years ago, on one of my visits out here, I gave her a pile of letters I'd collected in Afghanistan. They were given to me by a group of women wanting to express their gratitude to her. We had a system in place. We knew being hand-delivered, using her code name was the safest option. Somehow, the threat note must have gotten mixed up with them. Had I known…'

His voice trailed off to nothing. Strangely I felt unmoved, just angry.

'Cleopatra, yes. I found the other letters, Samir, and read them. They are all beautiful expressions of thanks. Unfortunately, though, it seems she has only read the threatening one. My bet, after that she was too frightened to read any more. I would have reacted the same way.'

Without another word I left Samir deep in thought in the darkness.

I knew what I needed to do.

Discernment

Hoping Gran was still awake, I knocked gently and listened for any movement behind her bedroom door. Turning the handle silently, I peeked through the crack. Rex was sniffing at me from the other side, wagging his tail with genuine excitement.

It gave me the encouragement I needed to open the door further. Negeenah's lamp was on, her bed unmade, but she was nowhere in sight. A flush of fear swept through me.

No Gran.

Moving quickly into the room I almost bucked at the knees upon seeing her. The French doors were open, and there she was, sitting in her favourite wicker chair on the veranda. She too was taking in the stillness of night, just as I had earlier.

'Come, Grace, join me, lass.'

She made no attempt to turn toward me as she spoke. It made me smile. How did she know it was me? Clever old duck, as Bluey would say. Negeenah's leather pouch was tucked awkwardly under my arm.

I hope this is the right decision.

Negeenah smiled up at me as I pulled my chair closer to hers. She looked peaceful and serene.

Am I about to wreck that?

'Can I talk to you about something, Gran?'

'You can always talk to me about anything, my child. You are filled with more wisdom than you know. The time is coming, child. Soon, you will see. You turn 16 next week, and a revelation is coming.'

Huh?

Had she lost her mind?

She sounded crazy.

I took the plunge, setting the pouch on my lap. Negeenah stared at it, her expression hard to read.

She is totally going to tell me to get lost. I shouldn't have brought these.

Breathe, Grace. Too late now… speak.

'Gran, please don't be mad at me. I understand if you are. I mean, I probably would be if someone got into my private stuff… but I think I can help you.'

She laughed out loud, instantly easing some of my tension.

'Out with it, girl. You're rambling like a lunatic.'

Okay, green light.

'I need to read you some letters.'

She gestured for me to begin, then closed her eyes resting her hands on her chest. Taking a deep breath, I began. I didn't stop once, not even daring to look up until every one of the heartfelt messages had been expressed.

Phew. Done.

When I finally did glance up, I noticed the silent tears running freely down Negeenah's face. When she opened her eyes, she stared blankly into the night. I waited silently beside her, praying I had done the right thing.

'Are they authentic, Grace?'

'Yep, they're real alright. I found them in the barn, right where you had put them in a box. Remember? I never understood why you didn't read them… until yesterday, that is.'

She closed her eyes again, this time covering her face.

I reached for her hands pulling them away and holding them in mine. She didn't resist.

'Do you understand, Gran? I don't think you really do. Surely you must know the incredible impact you've had, and continue to have.'

Looking almost startled, her eyes flew open again.

'Countless women have been saved, educated, and protected, all because of your courage. You did that.'

I wanted my words to be profound, to sink into her heart. She looked at me briefly before pulling her hands away.

'Thank you for sharing these, Grace. Could you leave them with me, perhaps we can talk again tomorrow? I feel very weary all of a sudden. My life has caught up with me, I think.'

Nodding, I left. She smiled weakly. Rex followed me out.

Man, I hope I haven't stuffed this up again.

Truth be told, I was exhausted myself and grateful to crash out in bed. The lapis stone I'd brought back from the cottage remained on my bedside table, leaning against it, the photo of Bashir.

'Thank you for being my father, thank you for my music box. It doesn't even make sense, but I feel you in my heart... Dad. One day, I'll know you, I hope.'

Lifting the lid to my precious box, my mind rehearsed the tune even before it started.

Bashir must have loved this tune too.

The thought helped me find some peace. I draped my arm over Rex. He was deep in his own dreams amongst the covers. Soon, I hoped, his breathing would lull me into sleep too.

Laughter and chatter filled the kitchen and adjoining dining room, both were bustling with action. The kitchen? How had I ended up there? As my sleep fog lifted, and I adjusted to my surroundings, I knew instantly that I was present in another dream.

Zarnish Estate was alive and vibrant. The long rectangular table was filled with books and stationery. Women sat around the table: Afghan women. They were beautiful, many very young, and all seemed relaxed and confident. It was a world away from what I had seen or read about their living conditions and stifled existences in Afghanistan.

Why were they at Zarnish Estate?

Never had Negeenah mentioned bringing anyone out to Zarnish to house or educate. Two women hurried past me from the kitchen, carrying trays of freshly baked cakes and biscuits. Following closely behind, two excited children were balancing jugs of iced tea. Every woman wore exquisite traditional dresses, free-flowing and colourful. I smiled, realising there was not a burka in sight.

What year was it?

I walked amongst the women listening to their chatter but unable to understand their language. Laughing was universal, however, and I had no trouble interpreting how free these women clearly felt being at Zarnish. As usual, I could not be seen nor heard.

I studied the big whiteboards that were in each corner of the room. OMG these women were being educated!

Suddenly, a hush came over the room as Negeenah entered. Straight away I could see she was a much older version of the woman I knew, but clearly in good health. She looked as strong and confident in herself as ever. So, this was the future?

A second lady came in behind her. Could I trust my own eyes? I dared not blink or move a muscle, fearing the unfolding scene would vanish. I stared, she met my eyes, nodding and smiling ever so slightly before moving on around the room.

She was me.

Only just like Negeenah's sketch, a much older version.

This just got next level weird. I watched as I swanned around the room, holding as much presence as Gran. I laughed and joked with the other women, pointing out things with their writing or reading. The dress I was wearing was so beautiful, long and flowing. It reminded me of the blue and yellow butterfly I had seen so often since arriving at Zarnish. My hair was out, dark curls cascading down my back. Like Negeenah I still wore my lapis necklace.

What did this mean?

Would I really return to Zarnish in the future?

Was I actually going to become an educator?

Or an ambassador for women's rights?

Was Zarnish a safe house?

This scene was so alive and vibrant, making me feel like I never wanted to leave. I'd spent so long hating who I was, yet the person I was fixated on right now, was nothing short of amazing. Could I really become someone who could make such a difference?

The tune from the music box broke my dream. I sat bolt upright, almost knocking Rex off the bed as the vision disappeared from my mind. The little ballerina danced in her circle on the table beside me. As I lay back on the soft pillows, I was captivated by what could be. Nothing about my future made sense, yet, for the first time, I knew.

I want to be the Grace I'd seen in the dream.

And I know exactly how I'm going to do it.

Premonition

Mum and I rode the horses a few times in the days leading up to the summer harvest. Riding Jinta was becoming addictive: the smell of her coat, the power of her frame beneath me, the feeling of the leather reins between my fingers.

But it was more than that. I felt like I belonged on her, belonged at Zarnish. The feeling was so strong now that it seemed pointless trying to reject it any longer. The sensation was empowering, all-consuming, despite it making little sense.

Relishing the time with my mum was somehow healing. I hadn't told her my future plans, the ones my latest dream had awakened. But I was becoming more and more certain they were my true destiny. Never had I felt such a strong pull towards anything. Perhaps, I thought, I had finally found my true purpose. All I had to do was convince my mum that my plan was the right one.

I was excited at the prospect of seeing the upcoming picking day, and it just happened to coincide with my 16th birthday. It would be a double celebration, according to Tracker and Bluey. I hoped so. The plan was to bring everyone together in the evening for a feast. The itinerant workers had started arriving, moving into the cottages for their temporary stay. I'd never seen Zarnish Estate so alive.

Swinging on an old rope tied to the rafters in the barn, I listened as Tracker and Bluey prattled on about Harvest Day. My job, so I was told, was to man the back of the tractor. The best bit was that Negeenah was going to drive it. This had become a tradition, so I had learned.

'Bluey, what exactly do I do while I sit there?'

'Well, yer keep the old bird company, make sure she stays awake for one.'

His laughter bounced off the barn walls, I couldn't help but chuckle, simply because he thought himself so funny. No wonder he didn't seem to need many friends.

'In truth, Gracie, yer job is pretty important. Ya fix yer eyes on all them pickers and commotion going on, make sure it keeps running smoothly. Ya let the team know when it's time for smoko, stuff like that. Also, if someone slices their hand off instead of them poppy stems, yer got to sound the alarm.'

Again, he broke into a cackle of laughter. Tracker was belly laughing, too.

Man, I hope that didn't really happen.

'So where do the workers come from then, Bluey. Can anyone be a picker?'

'Oh, shit no, it's all regulations and contracts and bloody rules these days, to even think about growing a poppy. Negeenah has a contract with a licensed processing company. She would be breaking the law if she grew 'em without a licence herself. The company hire the pickers, and we agree to house and feed them over the duration. Mostly it's the same folk turn up each year. But we sort the blow in cowboy's quick smart. Some make the mistake of trying to tell us how it's done.'

Wow there's more to this than I realised.

'So, how do the pickers actually get the poppies?'

Bluey threw another bale of hay onto the tractor, puffing and panting as he went.

'So many questions today, lass. Well, it's a pretty delicate process Gracie.'

Tracker piped up, which he often did when he'd heard enough from Bluey.

'Yer, the pickers slice the stems off, just below the bulb. Both bits are used to get all the important stuff out. Trick is, putting them carefully into baskets because if the bulb bursts, ya lose the seeds. Get it?'

I nodded, keen to learn as fast as I could.

'Yep, so then the company takes them all away for processing, right?'

'Yer a quick learner girly. Same every year for us, except this year… this one will be one like none other.'

Oh here we go… another cryptic Tracker comment is coming… I can feel it.

He dusted off his hands, looking me square in the face.

'It will be the day yer discover yer true destiny, lass, I feel it in me waters. What do yer reckon, Grace? Yer ready for it?'

I brought the swing to a halt.

'Ready for what exactly Tracker?'

'Yer birthday, silly… the day it was always goin' to happen.'

Frowning, I placed my hands on my hips.

'Stop with the bloody nonsense, Tracker. Leave the girl alone. You don't know it for sure,' Bluey barked at him.

'Yep, too right I do. She already saw a bit of it in her dream. And me, I dreamt the rest. Right, Gracie?'

What the hell was he talking about?

I looked from one man to the other, I felt exposed. I'd told no one about my dream.

'I don't understand, Tracker. What exactly is going to happen to me?'

'Leave her be now Tracker, come on, we got plenty of work to do and the day is a wasting.'

The men headed out of the barn, like nothing much had been said at all. My gaze clouded as I replayed the scene over and over in my mind, trying unsuccessfully to piece together Tracker's riddle.

Damaged

The day before the harvest, I found Negeenah in the kitchen. The sight of her busily making scones and sponge cakes filled my heart as I watched on from the doorway. I laughed at the mess on the bench. Flour, eggs, milk, and vanilla were strewn everywhere, and in amongst it all was Rex. His nose was white, covered in flour.

Gran's face was flushed from the heat in the kitchen, a slight sweat beaded on her brow. The best bit was her humming, a light-hearted tune this time. Without hesitation, my offer of help was gratefully received, and, before long, I was elbow-deep in food preparations.

I felt kind of nervous, wanting to keep the conversation light. Last thing I wanted to do was upset her. But today seemed like the perfect opportunity to bring up the letters again. I had to make sure she understood.

'I re-read them, Gracie. I will admit I'm grateful to have seen them, thank you. It was a very brave gesture to show me. I know that can't have been easy. You have shown great courage and resilience over the last few months. Remember that. And try not to be so hard on yourself. Truth be told, I could do with a dose of the same. I am making an effort to change my mindset, Gracie; I'm trying to believe in the impact I've had on those women's lives.'

Yes, this was progress.

'It's not just in the past, Gran. Think about all the good you're still doing. I know all about it. You still work with Mum and Samir as an advocate for refugees. That's an incredible thing.'

'It's my calling Grace but thank you. I had thought… well, that the letters were something else entirely. That's why I buried them in the box in the barn, unopened. I needed them to be away from me.'

Time to steer this conversation.

Leaning in, I closed the distance between us.

'I found the letter in the study, Gran. I figure you thought the other letters were the same?'

Negeenah froze, within seconds her face drained of colour. She turned away, reaching for her lapis stone.

'You had no right reading that, Grace.'

Her voice was distant, stone cold, completely different from the Gran chatting openly only a few minutes earlier.

Shit. Why did I always go and mess things up?

If I'd just kept my big mouth shut.

The mood in the kitchen turned icy. We continued without a word for some time.

Stuff this… it needed to be said.

'Gran, I found them by accident, honestly. One letter addressed to you and one to me, under the false bottom of the desk. I haven't read mine yet. I'd already read the other letters from the barn and honestly assumed that one would be the same. I know I was wrong… but Gran, as horrendous as it was, I'm glad I know. It's helped me understand your pain and fear so much more.'

Negeenah turned to me, her eyes flashed something I'd not seen in them before.

'You will never understand, Grace, and you are naive to assume you ever could. All I have ever wanted was to protect you from the exposure of such truths. This is not a game. Did you show anyone else?'

Might as well keep going now…

'Yes… Mum and Samir.'

She pounded her hands down on the table.

'Grace, you had no right!'

Her voice was urgent, a deeper tone than I'd heard before.

'Please, leave me now, Grace. I must work out a way to sort this out. And I have to finish the cooking. What a mess.'

I knew better than to hang around a second longer. When a woman as stoic as Negeenah showed that much emotion, it was time to bail. I crept away, mortified that I'd hurt her further.

Surely, she knows that was not my intention.

The harvest

On harvest morning, my birthday, we all woke at dawn. Stanley was extra loud in his morning call, keen to mark the special occasion, it seemed. The day was going to be a scorcher, so the aim was to get the seeds picked and stored as quickly as possible.

So, this was 16. Was it sweet?

Negeenah had barely spoken to me. Not that I blamed her. I was relieved as Bluey and Tracker climbed onto the old truck, buffering the awkward silence between us. As we travelled toward the poppy fields, Bluey was grinning from ear to ear.

'Yep, looks bloody perfect, hey girl. And on yer birthday, too. Seems like yer bringin' us the luck Tracker said, wouldn't yer say?'

Doesn't feel like that to me right now.

'I'll tell ya somethin' for nothin' girl, last harvest Tracker told me yer would be here this year. He told me the day would be one we would never forget because more would be revealed than just the harvest. I just told him he was a crazy old bastard and to shut the hell up.'

Tracker winked and smiled at me. Negeenah didn't flinch staring forward.

Bloody hell, I was kind of getting tired of this shit. I'm not biting.

'What happened to all the red flowers?'

All I could see were hundreds of brown pods. They seemed like the perfect way to change the topic. Gone was the vibrant red carpet, replaced with just brown stems.

'Are we too late? They look dead.'

'That's where yer wrong, lass,' corrected Tracker. 'We pick 'em so we can harvest the seeds inside the pods. That's the gold everyone's after, 'specially them pharmaceutical wankers. Once they brown off like they have, we've got to get 'em in before they crack open, and we lose the valuable little buggers inside. Those tiny black seeds are what we are after. That's the gold!'

Impressive.

Samir and Bluey jumped off the tractor as we continued to move slowly ahead of the group. The pickers were swift and skilful. Mum and Samir were together in the field, clearly, they'd done this before. Just another thing I had not a clue about Mum. I admired her right now though, that was for sure. Beside me, was Negeenah. She kept her eyes forward, only turning occasionally to scan the fields behind us.

Should I make small talk with her? She's acting like a child.

Her mood was annoying me. After all, what had I really done that was so bad? I was only trying to help! I had the right to know the truth anyway. She was being selfish, not even wishing me a happy birthday. That stung.

Stop ruminating Grace, be present.

Negeenah cleared her throat, breaking the silent stand-off between us. I braced for war, ready for battle.

'Grace, I owe you an apology. You must understand that I never wanted any of you to feel threatened or in danger because of me and my actions. Receiving that letter rocked me, I won't lie. I spent so many nights praying it was all behind us. The letter became a driving force behind the thought you'd all be better off without me. But you have exposed many truths and helped me to see there is more to my story. I was wrong.'

I stared at her, not knowing what to say.

'I made a mistake, and I'm asking for forgiveness Gracie. I let fear cloud my judgement. I know now I matter to you all. You say you need me. Well, I need you right back, child, in many more ways than you could ever know. Happy birthday my dear.'

Tears spilled down my cheeks, mixing with the dust and sweat. I reached for Gran. Our eyes met, and she squeezed my hand. No words were needed as generations again collided. Our bond had just grown even stronger.

Truce

The day proved to be tiring but successful. We finally retreated from the now barren fields and headed home. A late afternoon wind caused the dust to swirl, stinging my eyes and parching my throat. The plan was to shower and dress up for the feast and traditional celebration the night would bring. Sounded good to me.

The smell of the meat rotating on the huge spit outside the kitchen made my mouth water with anticipation. Foiled potatoes were roasting in the fire pit below. Even the courtyard looked festive. A long table was laced with beautiful flowers placed down its centre, balloons and fairy lights hung from the trees.

An array of salads was already prepared in the kitchen, and homemade lemonade was chilling in ice buckets. Fresh bread, still warm, was waiting on the bench. Mum had left the fields earlier in the day. Now I could see why. It was shaping up to be the best birthday I'd ever had. Who would have thought?

As I walked from the barn, Samir joined me and casually placed his arm over my shoulder. This time, I didn't flinch but instead felt the ease between us.

'Well done today, Gracie. You should be proud of the job you did.'

'Thanks! I had heaps of fun. I hope I can do it again.'

I really did mean that.

I thought again about my change of mindset since arriving.

Smirking and cringing simultaneously remembering the angry little bitch I'd been. Now at least I had the clarity to see other truths. Negeenah had been right when she said never to judge until you had walked in someone else's shoes. Yep, I'd been self-absorbed, pissed off at the world. Man, I'd hated Mum, Gran and most definitely the man walking beside me now. Go back a couple of months, and I would have spat on him had he dared come this close.

It was time to clear the air between us.

'Samir, I know you're a good man. I was just so confused and angry when you told me you were not my dad... I'm sorry I gave you such a hard time.'

He pulled me a little closer as we walked.

'Ahhh, Gracie, no need to apologise, honey. We should have handled it better, and for that I'm sorry. I know I hurt you deeply. You see, I had just been threatened myself. My identity and business were very close to being exposed by rebel forces. So, we felt it was best I be removed from your life to keep you safe.'

Whoa, that's massive.

'But yet, here you are?'

'Yes. Be that right or wrong, Negeenah and your mum, they needed me, and I'd hoped maybe part of you did too. We all need each other, truth be told. The only way forward is to stick together, be smart and remind each other we should not be ruled by fear. That's no way to live, Gracie. You are all my family. Things will change from this point on, I vow that to you. Together we will plan our futures carefully and live like Azyan, Asadi, and Kinaaz would have wanted us to. Everything will be okay, Grace. I just know it.'

I felt the rush of validation, and the strange warmth of being accepted. I believed him, we were a family, and that's what mattered. For the first time in a long time, I let my hand slip into his as we walked.

Happy Birthday

Sitting on my bed, complete weariness washed over me. I needed to shower the dirt and dust away, but first I just had to chill for a second. Closing my eyes, I stretched out my body. Strangely, the exhaustion felt good. It brought with it a calming, contented feeling. Unlike most times, it was not driven by the familiar anxieties plaguing my mind.

As I lay back on my pillow, the crunch of paper under my head instantly reminded me.

The letter! How had I forgotten!

Pulling it from its hiding place, once again I traced my name with my fingertip. Negeenah had made no comment about it the other day. Maybe it was nothing, of little importance. Well, if I didn't read it, I'd never know right. I smiled, not surprised to find a coded message on the paper before me.

My weariness was superseded by curiosity. Adrenaline pumped through my veins. Negeenah had gone to the trouble to code it. This letter was important. Grabbing my pen from the bedside table, I began working on the jumble of letters. Within minutes I stared at the decoded message I'd scribbled on the thin paper before me.

In the place you first came, you will find your destiny.
Under where you lay, the promised land awaits.

All you need to do is believe you have the strength to follow on.

Breathe Grace on our people.

I read and re-read. My hands trembled. What did it mean?

And how the hell did Gran know I'd find it?

Think, Grace, think.

I willed my brain to process. If Negeenah had believed from the start I'd be smart enough to figure it out, why not just tell me?

'In the place you first came.'

The cottage! I was born there. That had to be it!

'You will find your destiny.'

Did she mean something else is hidden there?

Not wasting another second, I packed my backpack. So, what if I was a little late for dinner. I had to know. I'm sure they would understand. Actually, I really didn't care. Slipping silently out into the early evening, I carefully ensured no one saw me go.

As dusk approached, the bush was alive with the sounds and sights of the pending night. I moved quickly, looking behind me more than once making sure I'd not been followed. The cottage was still and silent. The door opened easily. Dust streamed through the air as the movement interrupted the still space. The final streams of dull light from the day pushed their way through the small windows.

'Under where you lay…'

The bed?

I moved across the room, quickly crouching on all fours to search. Then it dawned on me. The cot! That was where I had slept. That had to be it!

'Under where you lay, the promised land awaits.'

What do you mean, Gran?

A wobbly floorboard underneath caught my attention as it was not nailed securely like the others. I forced my fingers under its edging, ecstatic it lifted quite easily.

Sliding further under the cot, I reached into the dark space. At first, all I felt was dirt and dampness. The chill weirdly refreshing in the heat of the evening. Then my hand touched something solid. My pulse quickened. Wasting no time, I pulled it from its hiding place into the room. My whole body tingled.

'The promised land awaits, you say?'

It was a small wooden box, about the size of a shoebox, beautifully carved, just like my music box had been. I instantly thought of Bashir as I brushed away the dirt.

Was it from him?

My breaths were quick and my movements jerky as I listened intently for even the slightest of sounds, desperate not to be interrupted. Lifting the lid, I paused to examine a folded wad of paper, slightly curled at the edges. Holding the cream paper together was a thin blue ribbon, the same ribbon I had worn each day as a child.

The little girls in my dreams.

Secured in the soft blue bow, marking the top of the package was a ring. It was delicately designed. Made from thick silver, the metal seemed to swirl around a bright oval-shaped lapis stone dominating its centre.

Incredible. But who belongs to it?

I had come for a reason, so why did I feel so nervous. Was I doing the right thing? Should I take it back to Mum or Gran? What if it revealed something further that I didn't want to learn?

Surely there could not be any worse secrets to come in my family.

Oh, for God's sake Grace, the letter and the clues were addressed to me. Open the bloody thing. Don't be a coward.

The first thing I saw amongst the official-looking paperwork was the letter. It sat on top, separate from the rest. This too was addressed to me. The handwriting was different to Negeenah's, bigger and more block-like.

Curious.

I slipped the ring onto my finger, admiring its beauty for a few fleeting seconds. I intended to find its owner but would keep it safe with me for now. Hopping off the floor, I sat on the bed near the window. It wouldn't be long before the moon would be my only light source. Litle did I know, my tiny world would never again be the same.

Dear Grace,

Your destiny awaits. Today, on your 16th birthday, your true purpose and direction will be presented to you. We hope and pray you will see this opportunity as a blessing.

It was with a broken heart I said goodbye to my beautiful Asadi and Kinaaz. They were more precious to me than life itself; I will forever mourn them. Zarnish Estate was created with a purpose. To give them, my family and our people, the chance for a better life. Unfortunately, if you are reading this today, without my presence, I have also fallen victim to evil forces.

Your grandmother, my beautiful sister, has worked tirelessly her whole life to be an ambassador, an educator and an inspiration for the people of Afghanistan. It is our wish, you will carry on her work, our work. You were born from adversity. Through God's grace, you escaped a war unharmed. I believe, as does Negeenah, you were sent here for a reason. You are the chosen one. You were born to Breathe Grace onto our people, to make their lives better, safer, more peaceful and powerful. You are to educate and aid their survival and, in fact, their revival. They are your people, Grace. I believe by now, you will understand this.

It is with those wishes in mind that I leave the title, and all monies and business claims related to Zarnish Estate to you, Grace. Should you choose to accept the terms and conditions set out in the paperwork provided, you will become the sole owner.

After my girls passed, Negeenah, Misha, Samir, and I met and discussed this proposal. It was unanimous. You were chosen to lead our future, Grace. We all agreed to work beside you always, into the future.

So, my dearest Grace, although I did not have the pleasure of watching you grow, I know without question you have the power within to continue to lead our people. Your strong spirit was evident from the moment you were born. My Kinaaz loved you like a sister. We all saw it. We could see you had a gift others did not. One of those being your visions and dreams. Embrace these dear child, and do not fear. They were sent to teach you and guide you in your ways.

Enclosed are two very special gifts. One is the deed to Zarnish Estate and its business portfolio. The second is the lapis ring I wished to present to my own daughter on her 16th birthday. It was her mother's and, before that, her grandmother's. It was, in fact, handmade by your great grandfather. Wear it with pride, Grace. Always remember who you are and the power you have to Breathe Grace over the precious people of Afghanistan and the people of the world.

Yours in faith, love and hope,
Azyan.

I hugged the letter to my chest, staring at the ring on my finger. It soon became blurred through teary eyes. Lightheaded, I forced a deep breath. This was a lot to take in.

What if Azan is wrong about me?

Am I enough to take on this responsibility?

But as quickly as the fear took hold, it seemed to disperse, replaced by an overwhelming sense of calm and purpose. The room stopped spinning and clarity came.

Then and there, I vowed never to take my new ring off again until sometime in the distant future when it would become my turn to hand it on.

Azyan had said, my dreams were a gift and there to teach me. No question, deep down, I knew. As confronting as it was, I'd already seen a snippet of my future.

What if I failed?

I couldn't bear to let her and my family down like that.

I shook my head.

No.

My family believed in me. It was time I did, too.

Serendipity

With each step I took toward home, guided by the moonlight, I became more certain. It was a knowing deep within like I had never felt before. Tucked under my arm was the carved box containing the map of my future, on my finger our family ring.

Yes, I knew, nothing much made sense that was for sure. But this was far bigger than me, and in that, I choose to trust.

The festivities in the courtyard echoed out into the darkness. The shrill of the cicadas filling the air were no match for the music blasting toward me as a greeting, infusing me with its warmth. I felt energized, and for the first time in a long time, completely at peace.

Startled from my moment, a figure approached from the darkness, grabbing my arm from out of the shadows.

'Grace, thank goodness. Where have you been? I was starting to get really worried.'

Mum's tone was bordering on anger and I fought not to get my back up.

'Sorry, Mum, I lost track of time... I... well I found this at the cottage.'

The moonlight reflected her confusion.

Oh man, what do I do now? How do I say this? Or does she already know what's coming?

Pushing the carved box toward her and showing her my ring all at the same time, I held my breath. Mum stood, statue-like at first, taking it all in, then, she simply smiled, embracing me tightly.

'And? How do you feel about it all?'

I raised my chin, feeling the expansion in my chest, willing to commit, even without all the details.

'Obviously it's huge, but somehow… I feel like I'm ready. I want this for my future. Our future. But I don't know how? I mean, what happens next?'

Mum took the box from me, holding my hand.

'Grace… all that will come. I've been thinking lots about it all, waiting until we could share this moment. I think the first thing we will do is return to Melbourne, and finish your studies, so you are qualified and capable of educating and providing for refugees. It may take some time, but before you know it, you'll be back here. In the meantime, all of us will ensure all runs smoothly out here.'

She's been thinking about it too?

'I saw myself, Mum. In a dream, and it was in the future. I saw Gran, too. Will you be here, Mum? I… well I need you to be.'

'Yes, my love, of course, I'll be here. That's all part of the plan. Trust me, a lawyer will come in handy from time to time.'

I breathed a sigh of relief. I was not alone, not by a long shot. She laughed and hugged me again. I melted into the strength of her embrace.

'Now come, let's begin our real celebration. Your family awaits. Happy birthday, my dear Grace.'

I stood momentarily behind her, my legs wobbly as I looked heavenward.

Was this moment real?

I'd longed to feel loved, to have a true purpose and to know exactly where I belonged.

And finally, it seemed as though I did. It was time I saw myself through my family's eyes. I would not let them down.

Panic

The night had been long, surreal, one that would stay forever in my heart. Rex and I climbed into bed just after 2am. There had been so many conversations, congratulations and words of encouragement. I'd been the last to know again, but I could see why. I'd needed to take this journey myself. I felt content and grateful, I'd been granted the opportunity to make a difference. Reaching for my music box, I let the familiar melody fill my ears and senses. The soft tune quickly lulled my exhausted body into the deep slumber it needed.

Something I couldn't place woke me abruptly. My body was heavy and unresponsive.

'Grace, are you in there? Can you come help me with this, please? I need your advice.'

It was Negeenah, she seemed uneasy and very insistent.

Had she been knocking for long?

Rex was nowhere to be seen. Strange, I thought, how did he get out of my room? Perhaps Gran had let him out. Sunlight was streaming through the French doors. It was so bright, clearly it was morning.

Rolling out of bed, pulling my hair back from my face, I headed out, PJs and all. I rushed down the hallway, heeding the urgency in Negeenah's tone. Moving swiftly toward the voices in the dining room, my gut told me something was different. In an instant, I knew.

Once again, I was in the future.

Like before, the room was filled with refugee women. I watched as they worked together, pouring over books and papers. Negeenah was seated at the head of the table. I drew a quick breath, a little shocked by her appearance. She was so much older than in my last dream, and beside her was a walking stick. Yet her smile was as strong as always, the great purpose still clearly driving her. Rex was nowhere to be seen. I hugged my arms around my chest, feeling my body run cold. He would have sadly passed by now.

Was I even still at Zarnish in this period of time? Were Bluey or Tracker still kicking?

They would be very old by now, but no doubt still working.

Walking out through the kitchen, more women were gathered. They were busy cooking. The rich, intense aroma from the bubbling pot had my taste buds and stomach rumbling. Loaves of fresh bread cooled on the bench.

There were more women outside, tending to the thriving vegetable patch. Children ran freely around the garden shrieking with laughter, their fearless innocence filled me with warmth, so different from the little ones I had seen in the alley that day.

An abrupt knock on the front door got my attention.

'I'll get it.'

The voice sounded like it came directly from the study. I smiled, shaking my head at the absurdity of all this, being able to see into the future, hear my own voice in fact. Upon turning the corner, there I was, much older now, a grown woman in fact.

The knocking was becoming more insistent, reflecting the impatience of whoever was outside. But I was instantly drawn to the puppy trotting beside my older self.

The tiny creature, with black curly hair and big brown eyes, stopped, eyeballing me suspiciously. A low growl escaped his cute mouth. It was hard not to laugh, for as ferocious as he attempted to be, he was not in the slightest.

'Hi, little mate, you can see me, can't you.'

I wondered how this crossover happened only sometimes, whereas, in other dreams, I was simply an invisible onlooker. It had happened with Rex, too.

My older self laughed, bending down to ruffle the pup's head.

'Come on, Raff, goodness, you are so tough. It's okay, it must be those supplies I ordered. About time, I say. I needed them last week.'

I smiled down at the little ball of fluff bouncing ahead. Seeing myself like that, defying the very essence of time was really hard to get my head around. How old was I, maybe 30? I wore a long, flowing dress, the colour of rust and gold, its tiny blue flowers shimmering in the speckled light off the hall. I had no shoes but wore anklets that jingled as I walked, and bright red polish painted toes. My hair remained long; half pulled up with a pen tying the bun together. My lapis necklace and my ring remained in place.

I wish my dream could have ended there.

The elation of the moment was to be short-lived.

As my older self opened the door, I watched my smile quickly fade. The colour instantly drained from my face, my stance stiffened. Long rifle barrels came from all directions. Then, I saw the men.

I screamed, but my older self didn't make a sound.

Who were they?

I needed to warn Negeenah.

My throat was so dry, a sudden lump making it hard to even swallow.

What the hell was going on?

On first count, I could see six men, who stood towering over us, ready to strike at any given moment. They reminded me of a gang of bullies at school, about to devour their prey. Dressed in dark clothes, their bearded faces were hardened and angry.

Two of the men stood guarding the door, staring aggressively, their guns resting across their broad chests. I cowered back but older me stood firm, giving nothing away.

The men at the back of the group were clearly agitated and had begun actively casing out the property. They talked in low voices amongst themselves.

I felt an all-consuming sick feeling rising within my veins. Suddenly sure these men were from Afghanistan, and they were not civilians.

Time stood still.

Could it be that moment?

The moment we had all feared.

'Can I help you?'

Older me sounded surprisingly strong. I noted the defiant physical stance I took, crossing my arms over my chest and forcing my chin to rise.

Not once did the older me break their stare.

The men shifted their weapons, moving them a little closer to us, one poking his gun into my chest, pushing older me back slightly. He smirked as he rested it back across his shoulder before spitting into the hallway.

'We have reason to believe Negeenah Karzai resides here. It would be against your better judgement to lie to us. You will take us to her immediately. We have papers allowing us to detain her for crimes she has committed in Afghanistan. We will be returning there with her, where she will face trial and her deserved death. Should you get in our way, we will not hesitate to take action against you, too. You will be charged and committed for aiding and abetting a criminal, the penalty for which is death.'

I watched in absolute horror, as all breath left my lungs. What was my older self feeling right now? I'd barely flinched but could see the muscles tensing in my neck. The pup whined at our feet.

No, this could not be happening. No.

This was not how I saw my future, our future.

What was the point of having involved me, bringing me to Zarnish Estate, if this was how it all ended?

No. I wanted no part in this.

I had to stop it.

But how?

I wanted to run. Hide somewhere.

Time slowed and sound disappeared as sudden movement pushed me back against the wall. Older me had swiftly slammed the door before the men had time to react, bolting it firmly from the inside. I watched as I ran toward the women, yelling warnings as I went. The puppy whimpered. He, too, seemingly just as unsure and confused about what was happening. All I could do was try to reassure him. I locked him safely in the hall cupboard.

The men continued to bang angrily on the door, their animated threats becoming more desperate. Then, BANG.

A single gunshot penetrated the air, shaking the entrance hall. Turning back as I fled, I saw the lock on the door had been blown apart. At the same time, I could hear windows being smashed in other rooms within the house. Terrified screams now replaced the happy laughter and chatter heard just moments earlier.

Where was Negeenah? Where had the older me gone?

Running toward the kitchen, I could see a man outside, pinning a woman to the ground with his heavy boot on her shoulder. She held her child protectively to her chest. His gun was aimed at another group of women nearby. They dropped obediently to the ground as he screamed at them, planting their faces into the dirt.

Where were the other children? Was my mum here somewhere?

Stumbling forward, I swayed, rigid in my movements.

Our beautiful home was being trashed. The dining table had been turned on its side, and two men had lined the women up against the wall. Frantically I searched for Negeenah.

The brutal intruders paced up and down, eyeballing and screaming profanities at the terrified women. A young woman in a yellow dress dared to yell back and within seconds one of the men launched at her small frame, choking and shaking her frail body. He spat in her face and ripped her dress from the neck down before throwing her against the wall.

She fell heavily and lay motionless on the floor.

'Where is Negeenah?'

The men yelled this again and again, moving from one woman to the next, yanking them roughly by the hair. Incredibly, the women remained silent despite the onslaught.

Did they even know where Negeenah had gone?

One man drew a knife and began making small cuts on the neck of another young woman. I screamed, but no sound came out. Falling to my knees, unable to do anything to stop the torture and abuse.

Maybe Negeenah and my older self had escaped?

But I could not imagine them voluntarily leaving the women to fend for themselves.

Another single gunshot sounded, ringing out from somewhere toward the front of the house. Surely if Bluey or Tracker were on the property, or maybe even Samir, they would hear it and come to help? Struggling to stand, I ran toward the front sitting room, praying my family was safe.

Blood smearing the floor confronted me before I saw the person.

OMG. Someone had been shot and then dragged across the room only metres from where I was standing. I stopped, unsure if I could continue. I was not strong enough to witness someone in my family die. Seeing my father pass had been brutal enough.

Then I heard it… I heard my own moaning.

I forced myself to push on. I was here for a reason and had to trust its purpose.

Reluctantly, I entered the room. My eyes fell on the crumpled figure, still trying to drag herself across the floor. She had made it to the doors leading outside.

My older self cried softly.

Her red and gold dress was stained with blood, so much blood. The tiny blue flowers were stained burgundy. Tears freely flowed down her face, and the terror in my own harrowing scream was unrecognizable.

No.

Was I witnessing my own death?

Please, please make this go away. I can't be here. I can't watch this.

My older self had also suffered a blow to the head, blood trickling down her face. The bruising around her left eye was already restricting sight. I crouched, not sure what to do next. I watched as she slowly lifted her dress, revealing a gunshot wound to her upper leg. Her body shook as she attempted to reach for a throw rug on the couch beside us. Pressing it against the wound, she attempted to stop the blood. The excruciating pain was obvious on her quickly paling face. Despite knowing I couldn't be heard, I pleaded with my older self.

'Please, tell me what to do!'

My voice was barely a whisper, raspy and choked with tears.

'I don't know how to help you. This can't be how it all ends. Please, tell me what to do!'

She reached toward me. I froze. Had she heard me?

Her eyes searched mine in a sudden connection. Her voice was barely audible but insistent.

'Listen to me. You are more courageous than you know. I promise you this. You get to choose how this ends. Don't you see? By knowing this could happen in our future, you can protect us from these men. Go now. Negeenah is being taken to the car they have waiting. You must stop them… Stop them, Grace!'

My older self reached for her lapis stone, then reached to touch mine, before passing out. I dry retched, so dizzy now I could barely stand.

Leaving her, I ran outside toward more screaming. In the driveway, two men dragged Negeenah, now motionless, along the ground by her arms. Her face was covered in blood. The image broke me, morphed me into a version of myself I never knew existed.

My fear turned to rage.

They were attempting to load her into their black van, treating her like a piece of trash. Tracker was lying in the gutter motionless. Bluey was attempting to scare the men off, waving his rifle wildly from one man to the next. But he didn't stand a chance. More men came silently from behind. It was all over in seconds, as he, too, was knocked unconscious. They proceeded to kick him repeatedly as he lay in the dirt, laughing and spitting on him.

These beautiful people were my family.

Everyone, everything I cared about was being destroyed in front of my eyes.

'Stop them, Grace'. That's what she'd said.

I screamed violently, vowing to the universe that never would I let this happen.

NEVER!

If I was the chosen one, then I would write my own story from that day forward... the new story of our family.

Not this version.

Resolution

Somewhere, at some point in the dead of night, clarity came.

I was back in the present, but never would I be the same. Sleep was impossible, my mind replaying the events over and over. Only hours before, I'd been witness to not only an omen, but a raw and revealing insight of my life, as it was to be.

If I allowed it.

I'd been given the opportunity to look into our future and, in turn, the chance to change its direction. Like Samir had said, if we all stuck together, planned carefully and had strategies in place for these exact scenarios, we would survive.

The night was beginning to cast its cloak, and a new dawn was slowly approaching. Soon a golden sun peeked over the horizon, tints of pink and grey mixed with the early mist scattering across the sky. A strong gust of wind lashed at my face as though heralding the change of season. I smiled; this change was significant in more ways than one.

The earth's profound message brought me sudden clarity. Despite the weight of the expectations and burdens cast upon me, I knew I possessed the strength I needed to prevail.

Fear, insecurity and doubt would come, but no longer would they rule me.

Challenges would arise, but I would challenge the world right back.

I was ready.

She discovered who she was, and the game changed.

Author note

When the opportunity was presented to create a second edition of *Breathe Grace*, I instantly embraced the challenge. Originally written and published in 2021, she was my first YA novel. Now in 2024 she enters the world once again, as my 6th publication, new front cover and new title.

Fragmented is not only a fast paced, YA thriller, but a book that will challenge every reader. It is thought provoking, and uplifting, and I have deliberately weaved fact through its fiction to be authentic.

In this new addition, I have refined and improved the content as well as added some exciting new chapters. Although designed for a broad range of readers, I am particularly interested in reaching the YA market worldwide.

Like all my YA novels, I weave elements of Mental Health issues within my character profiles. I do this deliberately to normalise the discussions around Wellbeing and Mental Health, areas which I am also very passionate about.

During the process of researching the original book, I was honoured to have been able to connect with many people in Australia, Nepal, and Afghanistan. Many provided me with their stories which I have used within my novel. I was also able to verify my research and ensure I was being topic sensitive and respectful of all cultures. A huge thank you to all who willingly assisted my journey.

Many thanks again to my original edit team, Darren Lines (@darrenlines11) and Kristie Pate (@KristiePateAuthor) Your experience in the writing and editing fields, and your dedication to helping me achieve my best outcome was very appreciated. And to Darren, once again, your kindness, advice, and belief in me as I navigate the publishing world is so appreciated.

To my wonderfully, supportive family. Thanks for all the chats, encouragement and enabling me to live my best author life. A special thanks once again goes to Jill Wilson. Your discussions, research, and dedication to re-editing this new novel was mind blowing. I am so grateful.

To my team of fabulous beta readers, you forever challenge me to be the best I can be. Your feedback is so important. I love that you keep me real and honest in my writing approach.

To my amazing clan of author friends and colleagues. How precious you are to me. Your encouragement and support while embarking on this rewrite means the world. So many times, I've needed editing, guidance and direction, and much encouragement. You are my people! I'd particularly like to acknowledge and send much gratitude and love to Rachel O'Rourke (@AuthorRachelO'Rourke), Caz Carter (@Author&IllustratorCazCarter) and JoJo Leslie (@ Creative-NessDesigns). A huge shout out and many thanks to Alana Lambert (www.bookburrow.com.au) I was so supported with your editing and layout expertise and assistance with cover design. I look forward to many more collaborations.

Thank you to all the people who continue to use my services at *Wings for Grace Educational Consulting*. I love workshopping, teaching, and presenting all things writing & books. Meeting and collaborating with such a diverse range of humans energises my soul.

Thanks to Lamont Books for supporting my author career. I love every event you book me for. How lucky I am to share and workshop my books with the world.

Finally, a big hug and a huge thank you to all my readers. Without you, none of this would be as meaningful. I love receiving your comments, feedback and reviews. I hope I encourage you to be brave and create the best versions of yourselves.

You are worth it.
I hope you enjoyed *Fragmented*.

Love, Kel.
@kelly.wilsonwingsforgrace
www.wingsforgrace.com

Other titles published by Kelly Wilson

Hudson Houdini Escapologist Extraordinaire (Picture Story Book)
Lady Lulu (Picture Story Book)
Breathe Grace (Young Adult Thriller Fiction)
Where the Driftwood meets the Sand (Young Adult Thriller Fiction)
The Shadows in my Mind (Young Adult Thriller Fiction)

www.ingramcontent.com/pod-product-compliance
Lightning Source LLC
Chambersburg PA
CBHW070103120726
47909CB00002B/484